RACHEL DOVE is a writer an̲ ̲
with her husband, their two so̲ ̲ ̲.
In July 2015, she won the *Prima* magazine an̲ ̲ ̲
Flirty Fiction Competition with her entry *The Chic Boutique o̲n̲*
Baker Street, out now in ebook and paperback. *The Flower*
Shop on Foxley Street followed this in 2017 and both books
hit the Amazon top 200. *Chic Boutique* got to #2 in the rural life
humour chart and is regularly in the top 100 of that chart.
Rachel was the winner of the Writers Bureau Writer of the
Year Award 2016 and has had work published in the UK and
overseas in various magazines.

The Long Walk Back came out in January 2018 and she is
currently writing the next book in the Westfield series. She
loves to write romantic fiction, both rom-com and harder-
hitting women's fiction.

In addition to writing, teaching and studying for an MA in
Creative Writing, Rachel also likes to hang out with her
family, read lots of books, and cross-stitch geeky homages
and rude sayings.

Also by Rachel Dove

The Chic Boutique on Baker Street
The Flower Shop on Foxley Street
The Long Walk Back

The Wedding Shop on Wexley Street

RACHEL DOVE

ONE PLACE. MANY STORIES

This novel is entirely a work of fiction. The names, characters
and incidents portrayed in it are the work of the author's
imagination. Any resemblance to actual persons, living or
dead, events or localities is entirely coincidental.

HQ
An imprint of HarperCollins*Publishers* Ltd
1 London Bridge Street
London SE1 9GF

This paperback edition 2018

1

First published in Great Britain by
HQ, an imprint of HarperCollins*Publishers* Ltd 2018

Copyright © Rachel Dove 2018

Rachel Dove asserts the moral right to be
identified as the author of this work.
A catalogue record for this book is
available from the British Library.

ISBN: 9780008310110

MIX
Paper from
responsible sources
FSC™ C007454

This book is produced from independently certified FSC™ paper
to ensure responsible forest management.

For more information visit: www.harpercollins.co.uk/green

Typeset by Palimpsest Book Production Ltd, Falkirk, Stirlingshire
Printed and bound in Great Britain by
CPI Group (UK) Ltd, Melksham, SN12 6TR

All rights reserved. No part of this publication may be reproduced,
stored in a retrieval system, or transmitted, in any form or by any means,
electronic, mechanical, photocopying, recording or otherwise,
without the prior permission of the publishers.

This book is sold subject to the condition that it shall not, by way of trade
or otherwise, be lent, re-sold, hired out or otherwise circulated without
the publisher's prior consent in any form of binding or cover other than
that in which it is published and without a similar condition including this
condition being imposed on the subsequent purchaser.

To my mother, Sandra, who will never read past this page, but cheers me on in everything I do. 2f & 1w forever.

Love Goggle

Chapter 1

August

The heat from the summer sun kissed the tanned and freckled skin of the wedding guests as they walked up the long path to the beautiful Grade II-listed church, the best Harrogate had to offer in terms of the ultimate IT wedding venue. One where God had a front-row seat anyway. Behind an oddly discreet line of police tape, a scoop of journalists jostled against each other, all dressed in their best uncrumpled clothes. All eager to snap the incoming guests, the first glimpse of the happy couple.

Quite the guestlist was walking up this pebbled drive too. The hottest reality TV stars, fresh from the villas and beaches, the latest hot things to rock football shorts on the field, today all suited and booted with the local glitterati, were all here to see the modern love story. Meghan and Harry had nothing on Harrogate's very own playboy and tea baron, Darcy Burgess, who was today set to marry the girl of his dreams or, as the press had come to know her, the elusive girl next door. Uncharacteristically, Darcy had kept his lady out of the spotlight, so today, in the sumptuously beautiful and historic surroundings of St Wilfred's, all eyes would definitely be on the bride.

Past the line of paps, inside the church, the pews were festooned with flowers, laced into intricate ribbons and designs at the end of the aisles. A large, imposing centrepiece full of calla lillies, white roses and the best that taste and money could buy stood on a pedestal near the altar, and the whole church was fragrant with the scent of expensive perfumes and the ambience of flowers. Everything shone and gleamed, from the brass lectern to the cheeky sparkle in the excited guests' eyes.

Today would be talked about for months, a real gem on the Northern social calendar. Taken up by the South, the Burgess wedding was certainly a networking event like no other. No one could wait to finally see the girl who had tamed the great player, Darcy. The girl next door. The young lass from the little village shop. A day of new beginnings, in more unexpected ways than one.

New beginnings came in all shapes and sizes. The day Maria Mallory was due to be married would be the first day of her new life too, but for reasons very different to those the average bride would ever think of. In fact, had she known what was coming, she might have stayed in bed that day, quivering under the duvet and throwing holy water on her wedding gown to expel the demons.

Ask any beaming child in the playground what they wanted to be when they grew up and you would get an enthusiastic answer. Thomas wanted to be an army man, Benjamin a vet just like his dad. Cassie wanted to be a ballet dancer, Alex to help sick people.

Kids wanted to be everything, from astronauts to bakers. But Maria had always been different. She didn't dream of a job. She dreamt of a status, a milestone. Maria Mallory had always wanted to one day be a bride. She'd spent hours at home poring over her parents' wedding albums, legs dangling off the couch as she studied the happy, radiant faces of her mother and late father on their special day. While other kids played video games and rode bikes, Maria made scrapbooks filled with magazine cutouts, scraps of fabric from her mother's workbox, recipe ideas for the wedding breakfast. Elizabeth Mallory worked from home as a seamstress, and her daughter would check her diary fastidiously, looking for bridal appointments. Women would come to their house all the time, requesting custom gowns, having their dresses altered, looking through her mum's designs for the perfect bridesmaid dress to match their perfect white gown. Maria loved every minute, and couldn't wait to get married. When she hit her teens, her determination to be a bride hadn't changed. She helped her mother after school, and eventually took over when her mother got sick, running the business and helping at home while doing her own business degree. Even with the bumps in the road, Maria had never once lost sight of her goal: to get married. To have the life her mother and father once had. In sickness and health, true love, till death do us part. To have the wedding of her dreams.

And what a wedding it was shaping up to be! Every man, woman and dog had been chatting about the nuptials for months, and the moony-eyed public were all rooting for the unlucky lovers to finally say I do, and prove that love really did conquer all. What girl wouldn't want that? Even the tomboys among the fairer sex still had an odd glistening tear at the thought.

But today, as she stood waiting in the wings of the church, missing her parents, sheltered from the view of the baying press outside, with Cassie moaning about her pale peach silk dress beside her, she was... well... disappointed. It seemed everything in her life had been leading to this point, so why didn't it feel that way? Why did it feel like an anticlimax? She told herself it was just down to wishing her parents were there with her. More so than anxiety. She was still having flashbacks to the dream she had had the night before, when she was wheeled out into the church, dressed like a whipped-cream meringue, with make-up

3

Gene Simmons would deem 'troweled on'. She had woken in a deep panic, covered in sweat and in the tight grip of fear. She needn't have worried, though. With her designer gown, make-up artist and professional hairdresser to the stars, all hired by the Burgess family, she looked more than catwalk-ready.

Maria felt like she had reached into the pretty chocolate box and pulled out a disgusting orange cream. She tried to shake off the feeling she was having. It was just nerves, that was all. She had been waiting for this day for ever, since she was old enough to wrap a sheet around her head and marry her teddy bears. Today was the day, and nothing was going to spoil it, least of all her own silly niggles. She felt a prod and looked around, annoyed.

'What?'

Cassie was staring at her, fixing her with a look she had never seen on her best friend's face before, and Maria felt the emotions of foreboding all over again, in stereo.

'Cassie? What... what is it?'

Cassie swallowed hard and, looking around, Maria noticed they were alone. The other bridesmaids, on the side of the groom, were suddenly noticeably absent, and the vicar was standing there, looking very uncomfortable indeed. Maria's heart dropped from her chest, nestling in her sparkly ivory court shoes.

'Cass, what!' She gripped her bouquet tighter in her hand, causing a calla lily to break from its stem. It fell to the floor between them, and Maria's eyes narrowed as she focused on the lone bloom.

'He's not coming, Mar, I'm so sorry.' Cassie's voice was uncharacteristically soft, at odds with her usual ball-busting, divorce-solicitor persona. Maria nodded, and her head kept nodding away.

'Mar, can you hear me?' Cassie stepped forward, taking the bouquet from her and dropping it onto a table nearby. Maria kept nodding, sinking into the chair that appeared like magic from behind her. Turning around, she saw the vicar, his hand on

4

her shoulder, a kindly expression on his face. She could hear the murmurs of the congregation outside, no doubt sensing this wedding wasn't going off without a hitch. In fact, there would be no getting hitched today. Maria's cheeks flamed and tears started to run down her face. She jumped when Cassie slammed her fist down hard on the table, making her bouquet flip on the wooden surface.

'That utter bastard! I swear, I am going to staple his nards to the wall!'

Maria wiped at her tears, frowning when her make-up left a smudge on the pristine, white, long-sleeved glove she was wearing.

'Stay here, okay. I'll see what I can find out.' Cass manhandled the vicar out of the door, muttering things about God and angels and pitchforks to him under her breath. 'Stay put, okay? Don't come out till I know what's what.'

Maria nodded to the already-closed door, feeling like her head was separate from her body. It felt like it was floating somewhere, free, above her head like a balloon. Shock. It must be. Either that or she was about to pass out. A beep shook her from her thoughts. Cass's purse was on the table. *Her mobile phone!* Maria leaned forward and snatched it up, fumbling through the contents to grab the phone and bring up the call display. Before she could talk herself out of it, she dialled Darcy's number and held her breath. *It must be a mistake, Chinese whispers. He was probably stuck in traffic. Last-minute nagging from his mother, perhaps.*

He picked it up on the third ring.

'Hello?' he asked lazily. He sounded a little drunk even. 'Hello, who is this? Hello?'

'Darcy?' It came out as a cracked whisper. 'Where are you? Are you okay?'

A tear ran down her cheek and she went to dab at it, trying not to ruin her expensive face paint.

'Maria.' It came out of his mouth, just like that. Flat, monotone. No excitement, no rushed explanations, no desperate plea for her

5

to wait for him. He said it like he was disappointed it was her, regretted taking the call from a number he didn't recognise. Cass and he had never been that close. 'It's you.'

'Of course it's me! I'm at the church. Are you here yet? The vicar said you're not coming? What's wrong?'

At first, she didn't hear anything, and she thought the call had dropped till she heard the ching of the glass. A sound she recognised. The glass coffee table in their apartment made that noise when she filled his favourite whisky tumbler and set it down next to her glass of wine as they settled down for the evening.

'I'm not coming, Maria. I'm sorry.'

At first Maria couldn't decide whether to cry, wail or laugh. The words sounded so absurd, so silly. She half-expected him to start laughing, that laugh she loved to hear. The one that came from his belly as he celebrated another successful prank.

'Don't be daft, of course you're coming. We're getting married!'

The glass clinked again, hard.

'I can't do it, Maria. I'm sorry. I… Mother… we…'

Maria felt her heart break. 'Darcy, I…'

'I'm sorry. I have to go.'

The line clicked, and he was gone. She went to press the button, to call him back, to shout, to cry, to ask him why he'd said those things. Why her Darcy, the man who should be nervously passing wind at the altar, chewing the fat with his best man to stay calm, was at home, drinking instead. Leaving the woman he loved sat in a dress, in an imposing church setting. Trapped. Stranded in her very own fairy tale. Maria pushed the phone back into Cass's purse, throwing it onto the table as she heard her friend's loud voice coming closer outside.

'Mate, that best man is a total jackass, I tell you. I almost decked the arrogant swine!'

'Cass,' she whispered.

'He won't tell me where Darcy is, or give me his number, and apparently his family didn't even show!'

'Cass,' she tried. Harder this time. Fighting to push the words out of her mouth, amidst the mess of her scrambled thoughts.

Her friend turned and knelt before her again. Maria looked into her eyes and swallowed hard, trying to dislodge the huge lump in her throat. The more she swallowed, the thicker it felt.

'Cass,' she tried again, her voice betraying her. 'Get me out of here, okay?'

Cass nodded. Marching over to the window, she wrenched it open, looking outside. Seemingly satisfied that they had an escape route, she beckoned for her friend.

'I scoped this out too, just in case. Come on, my car's outside.' Maria nodded and five minutes later she was in the passenger seat of her friend's Mercedes, hunched low, being whisked away from her own wedding. For the first time in her life, she was glad her parents weren't there to see how her life was going. Cassie placed a warm hand over hers.

'Stay with me, okay? I'll arrange for your stuff to be collected from Arsy's.'

Maria nodded, too numb to even complain about her friend's nickname for her would-be groom. Darcy Burgess of the Burgess Tea empire, a well-respected Harrogate institution. Currently about to corner the Yorkshire market in herbal teas, they sold everything from ginger snaps to ornamental teapots to go with their amazing tea blends. Beatrice Burgess, the head of the family, was an all-encompassing woman, driven and one hundred per cent committed to making sure her children, Laura and Darcy, didn't do anything to embarrass her beloved empire. She made the Godfather look like small potatoes, and her wrath wasn't something to seek out.

Darcy, who had just jilted her at the altar, in front of their friends. Darcy, who, up until yesterday, she had lived with in his plush apartment in Harrogate. She started to sob quietly. Cassie swore under her breath and turned on the radio, jabbing at the buttons as though they were part of Darcy himself.

'Poncey git. Who wants to marry a Darcy anyway?'

Maria looked across at her in exasperation. 'Millions of women, Cass. Millions. Mr Darcy, Mark Darcy? Come on, I know you have that poster of Colin Firth on your fridge.'

Cass's lips pursed, and she grinned at her mate. 'Okay, okay – but seriously, Mar, you'll be okay. Everything will work out.'

'I called him.'

Cass looked at her, but said nothing, flicking her attention back to zooming through the streets.

'And?'

'He said sorry.'

Cass's lips clamped together, as though trying to ward off something unpleasant from being rammed between them, or trying to escape.

'Oh, he'll be sorry all right.'

Maria nodded, looking down at the engagement ring on her finger. She didn't think for one minute he would be, but what else could she say?

'I'm hungry,' was all she could think of. 'I didn't eat a thing this morning, I didn't want a podge in my dress.'

Her friend smiled. 'I know just the thing to cheer you up.'

Ten minutes later, a very startled food server was taking an order from a weepy bride and a very angry woman in a flouncy peach dress. They took a booth in the back, ignoring the stares of the lunchtime crew and the mothers feeding their children a junk-food treat. Cassie put the tray down in front of them, and Maria sank her teeth into a cheeseburger, a napkin shoved into the front bodice of her couture gown, one Darcy's mother had insisted she wear, rather than one of her own designs. A glob of ketchup dripped from the side of the napkin onto the ivory material, and Maria wiped at it half-heartedly, leaving a small red dot on the fabric. *Oh well*, she thought to herself. *Not like I'll be saving it for my daughter, eh?* She swallowed the last of her burger and looked across at Cassie, who was shovelling fries into her mouth while barking orders into her phone. She reached for hers out of habit, before realising that her bag, containing her keys and phone, was still in the hotel. *In the space of a morning, I have lost my fiancé, my home and my sanity*, she thought to herself glumly. The reality of her situation dawned again, and she felt the threat of her cheeseburger coming back up. Cassie barked out a final command and stashed the phone back inside her tiny peach purse. Her face paled as she looked at the current state of her childhood bestie.

'Maria, you doing okay?'

Maria looked across at her. 'Cass, what the hell am I going to do?'

Cass gripped her hand in both of hers, squeezing it tight. 'Mar, you are going to pick yourself up, get a new place, go back to work, and never speak to Arsy again.'

Maria smiled weakly at her, looking away quickly from the builder who was looking her up and down while devouring a family-sized box of chicken nuggets.

'That easy, eh? Just like that?'

'Yep.' Cass's eyes flashed with determination. 'You can do it. And tonight,' she continued, smiling devilishly, 'we are going to get you very, very drunk.'

Maria rolled her eyes. 'I can't go out tonight. I don't even have anything to wear.' She looked down at her wedding dress, to point out the elephant in the room. Cassie smiled weakly.

'No night out. PJs, boxset, and copious amounts of Chinese food and alcohol.'

Maria nodded. Not quite the night she had planned, but it sounded good right about now.

'Deal,' she said, slurping her vanilla shake. 'But no Colin Firth.'

Chapter 2

One Week Later

'What the hell! You have got to be kidding me!' Maria slammed the local newspaper, the *Westfield Times*, onto her desk and stomped over to the kettle. She stabbed at the button, throwing ingredients into a mug. She reached into the biscuit barrel, shovelling a triple chocolate cookie into her mouth, mumbling as she chewed, before turning to the wall.

'I mean, I am the ONLY wedding planner in Westfield! The only one! How could Agatha Mayweather go elsewhere, when all she does is prattle on about community, and giving back, and fighting big corporations!' She thrust her arms out wildly as she spun around, cookie crumbs flying from her mouth. 'I mean, seriously! I am going to ring that woman up and give her a piece of my mind!'

'Who are you talking to, dear?' a voice at the door asked. Maria whirled around, seeing her part-time assistant, Lynn, standing there, a large flask in hand. Maria flushed and pointed to the wall, where a picture of her mother was framed and hung up.

'Sorry, Lynn, I was talking to Mum. The Baxters got married

again, did you know that? From Love Blooms, the florist? They had a big event on Agatha's estate, and I wasn't even approached to help!'

Lynn smiled kindly, closing the door against the slight breeze of the weather. It was quite autumnal already. She put the flask down on her desk and strode over to the wooden coat rack, taking off her cream faux fur coat.

'I know, dear, they seem so happy now, and about time too. I did worry about them, when they passed the shop to Lily. Idle thumbs and all that.' She waggled her own very busy thumbs in the air.

Maria glared at her. 'And!?'

Lynn sat at her desk, pouring a slurp of tea from the flask into one of the many bone china mugs she kept at work. She sighed and looked at Maria as she stirred, trying to find the words.

'Darling, Agatha didn't want to bother you about planning a wedding when your... er... when you were supposed to be on honeymoon. Your diary was full, so she didn't ask.'

Maria's shoulders slumped as realisation set in. 'She didn't want a wedding planner who got jilted at the altar, did she?' It came out as more of a defeated statement than a question, and Lynn's heart went out to her. She had watched Maria grow from a tiny baby to the beautiful woman standing before her, and whenever she thought of that wretched Darcy fellow, she found herself planning grisly things against his man parts with a crochet needle.

She waved her hand, cutting off Maria's rant. 'No love, not at all. No one thinks that.'

'Oh no?' Maria shouted, dashing over to the appointments diary. 'So how come I have no bookings then, for the rest of the month? Eh?'

Lynn sighed slowly. 'Maria, I know you're upset, but think about it. The diary is empty because you were supposed to be on holiday, that's all.' She took a sip of tea and eyed her furtively, obviously expecting horns to sprout from her head at any moment. Maria sagged over the diary, deflated. 'Oh,' she said softly. 'Of course, yes… sorry, Lynn.'

Lynn raised her hand to wave off her employer's apology. 'Don't give it a thought. Why don't you take the time off anyway – go away somewhere or something? Nice change of scene, eh?'

Maria shook her head. 'I should be in St Lucia now. Somehow a week in some caravan in Skegness on my tod just doesn't sound appealing.' Lynn opened her mouth to speak again, but the phone on her desk started to ring. She smiled kindly at Maria and dealt with the customer. Maria went to the just-boiled kettle, pouring herself a huge mug of steaming hot coffee. As she added more sugar, she had to admit, if only in her own head, that she shouldn't be at work. She felt like the angry wedding performer in that Adam Sandler movie. A movie she loved, and now couldn't watch for fear of murdering someone, or herself, with a noose made from the finest lace she possessed. She should be glad she didn't own a hardware store, the way she was feeling, but Lynn was right: work *was* going to be tricky, to say the least.

She listened to Lynn discussing venues and prices with the person on the phone as she took her coffee into the back, to her office. Once there, she closed the door and sagged to the floor behind it, the steaming beverage clutched in her fingers. She took a gulp and, setting it on the coffee table, crawled across the floor and curled up on the couch in the corner. She covered herself over with a blanket, and promptly fell asleep.

Lynn came in an hour later, tucked her in, and pulled the phone socket from the wall so she wouldn't be disturbed. Maria looked exhausted, even in sleep, and Lynn frowned as she looked down at her. *The poor girl*, she thought as she brushed a strand of blonde hair away from her face. Closing the office door behind her, she went to the diary and looked over the next three months. Christmas was coming, and with it the party season, bringing a very welcome set of clients that had nothing to do with weddings.

Lynn would book the diary up with these, and try to avoid doing any events. The business was doing well – if a little stalled since the wedding as regards the bigger, more lucrative jobs – so a couple of months off the wedding circuit wouldn't do them any harm, and Lynn was determined to protect her employer as much as possible. She bit her lip as she fired up the computer, checking for any incoming enquiry emails that might derail her plan, but it appeared to be blissfully quiet on the nuptials front so far. It was a stroke of luck that Maria had put her own wedding at the end of the main season. Had this happened in spring, it would have been even worse. She just hoped Maria would be feeling better by the time the season was in full swing again. Being a jilted bride, wedding planner and owner of wedding boutique Happy Ever After wouldn't bring Miss Mallory peace any time soon. *Men*, she thought to herself, seething at her feeling of helplessness. *They really did have a lot to answer for sometimes.*

Chapter 3

Maria put her key in the lock of Cassie's cottage, sighing as the heavy, red-painted, wooden door only gave an inch. Pushing and tugging at it, she finally made headway and ended up flat on her face in the hallway, having landed on a pile of post. Tutting loudly, she picked up the huge array of magazines and letters, stacking them as best she could on the hall table. For an organised person like Maria, living with Cassie in her Westfield cottage was quite the change from Darcy's large, sleek, minimalist Harrogate abode. Cassie had bought the place from her parents after university. They had a few rental cottages dotted around the area, and Sanctuary Cottage had always been a favourite of Cassie's. She used to sneak in there with Maria after school to study, away from her bickering mother and father, and Maria loved to spend time with her friend there. Cassie was always so much happier within its walls, so much more relaxed, and Maria loved to see this side of her. After they graduated, Cassie had gone and landed a huge job in a swanky Harrogate firm, and had begged her parents to let her buy the place; they'd ended up giving in just to get some peace.

'Cassie?' she shouted, already guessing her friend was still at work, given that her car wasn't parked on the drive. Locking the front door, she headed for the shower, ignoring the blinking of the answer machine. No one would be ringing her anyway. Other than Cass and Lynn, the only other person in her life was… had been… Darcy. So now she was back to being alone, and it was worse, much worse, now. Because she was all too aware of how it had felt to be in a couple, and how close she had been to having that for ever. After her parents died, she'd got used to being alone – but being plonked back into the status wasn't as easy. It felt like the January slump, dull and rather cruel. Just as you got used to the excitement, the build-up, the change in routine… suddenly, there you were – slap bang back in routine-ville, having to work again, the excitement over, leaving depressed, grey people contemplating major life changes and Googling holiday packages to use as escape pods. An escape pod sounded like a fantastic idea at the moment.

Rinsing off the suds from her hair, she heard a door bang downstairs.

'Cass?' she shouted, squinting at a stray sud that had dripped down into her eye. 'That you?'

She listened but heard nothing. *Cass was never home early; the woman was a machine.* She listened again, but the shower was all she could hear.

The bathroom door burst open and Maria screamed. The other person screamed back just as loudly, and Maria grappled for purchase on the shower curtain while swinging one arm behind her for something to use as a weapon. Her fingers found a shampoo bottle, and she was just about to douse the intruder with Pantene when she heard her name being called. Wiping at her eye frantically, she looked again at the door and saw Cassie standing there, face still frozen mid scream. She put the shampoo bottle down on the side of the bath, willing her frantically beating heart to slow down.

'Cassie! You frightened me to death! Where's the fire?' she laughed, embarrassed at her reaction. Cassie didn't answer at first, looking panicked. Maria turned off the water and grabbed a fluffy bath towel, wrapping herself up. Getting out of the shower, she shivered as her feet hit the cold tiled floor. Cassie was still looking at her funny, and hadn't moved an inch.

'Cass,' Maria said, concerned now. 'What's the matter? Bad day at work?'

Cassie grabbed her arm, pulling her slowly into the guest room. Maria followed, wondering what had happened to make her friend so uncharacteristically anxious. She sat down at the foot of the bed, her pal sitting next to her, putting an arm around her, oblivious to the wet hair that trailed down it.

'I take it you didn't listen to the answerphone message then,' she said softly. Maria shook her head, concern now clouding her own features.

'No, why? Cass, you're seriously worrying me now. Please – just tell me what's wrong!'

Cassie took a breath. 'My secretary was reading one of those celeb mags at work this afternoon, and she came across a piece on Darcy.'

Maria felt suddenly woozy, her breath taken in a sharp gasp. 'Okay,' she said, her voice barely audible. 'Go on.'

Cassie reached into her pocket and pulled out a ripped piece of paper on which Darcy's face could be seen smiling out from above the crease. Maria grabbed it from her, unfolding it. The headline read HARROGATE BACHELOR LICKS HIS WOUNDS IN THE SUN. Underneath were three pictures: one of Darcy in a pair of shorts, looking out to the horizon from a tropical beach, tanned and pensive. Another was of him driving down a beach road in a flash open-top car. His hair was being blown by the wind, making him look sultry, and his lips were contorted in a sad pout. I mean, the man looked depressed, albeit in sunny weather and behind the wheel of a posh car.

The third picture was of him lying on a sunlounger, caught in mid laugh, cocktail in hand. Scanning the pictures, she stopped dead. It wasn't the hand holding the cocktail she was focused on, but the other one. The one held by a slender set of fingers, a woman's, her thumb bearing a fleur-de-lys ring. The person was obscured by a wall of loungers, so only the hand showed, but it was unmistakable. Darcy had gone on honeymoon, *their honeymoon*, and was holding hands with another woman. The article was brief, just a few lines about how Darcy Burgess, heir to the Harrogate tea empire, was 'consoling' himself with an 'unknown female companion' after his aborted wedding to Westfield girl Maria Mallory.

Cassie took the piece of paper back from her. Maria allowed it to slip through her fingers. It felt like it was on fire anyway, her fingertips tingling from the contact.

'How can it say that? It makes it sound as though I left him at the altar. He broke my heart, and he went on holiday! We were supposed to be married now!'

Cassie said nothing, thrusting the article back into her pocket. She strode over to the wardrobe, throwing the doors open, and started thumbing through the hangers. Maria looked across at her.

'What are you doing?'

Cassie grabbed a red dress and thrust it at Maria. 'Put this on.'

Maria looked at the dress, which had been a daring purchase, never worn. The tag scraped at her arm as she laid it on the bed. 'I can't wear that, I should never have bought it!' *Trust Cassie to have rescued that from her old place, Darcy's home. She should have left it there.* She pushed the thought from her head. She shouldn't be ungrateful; after all, she had got all her belongings back without even having to put a toe near Darcy. Which was good, since the toe was attached to her foot, and if she had seen him, she would have used that foot to give him a good kicking. If Cassie hadn't got there first and ripped him limb from limb like she'd threatened to, that was.

Cassie glared at her, oblivious to the violent thoughts swirling round in her friend's head. 'Why buy it then? Come on, get your hair dried. We are going out… NO ARGUMENTS,' she boomed as Maria opened her mouth to protest. Maria felt her foot itch but ignored it. Not tonight, angry toe.

Two hours later, Maria found herself in Harrogate, squeezed into the red dress, shoes pinching her feet, wondering why the hell she wasn't sitting on Cassie's couch eating ice cream, sloshing wine down and crying. She said the same to Cassie as they walked on tottering heels to the nearest trendy bar, Ice, in the wine-bar-and-posh-eatery part of Harrogate's city centre, which, coincidentally, butted up against the legal quarter of Harrogate, and no doubt the two sides kept each other in business quite well too. Walking into Ice with Cassie, it was hard to ignore the stares her friend attracted. Cassie Welburn was, she had to face it, sex on a twenty-nine-year-old stick. She was always tanned thanks to her meticulous salon treatments, plucked and shaped to perfection, and tonight, as usual, she was dressed to kill. Even Maria's daring red slinky number looked tame in light of Cassie's black and silver dress, slashed to the thigh, combined with sparkly silver heels that made her even taller than her just-under-six-foot frame. Maria blushed and nudged Cassie's elbow with her own.

'People are staring, Cass.' Cassie shrugged, propelling them both forward into the bar with a determined swagger.

'Let them stare, girl. Don't worry, I've got your back.' Maria belatedly realised that tonight, thanks to that ridiculous article, the stares might indeed be for her and not her glamorous friend. She cringed inwardly and planted a smile on her face. She took her friend by the arm and, pushing her boobs out and her chin up, headed to the bar. 'Let's get smashed,' she declared.

Four bars later, the two friends were knocking out shapes on a dancefloor. They were now in a place called Fresh! which had a large dancefloor in the back, complete with strobe lighting and a large DJ booth that overlooked the whole area. It was all neon lights, tacky road signs, and club kitsch, but it went well with the

Eighties pop they were currently playing. Maria was laughing at Cassie, who was singing her head off to a Wham! hit while several suitors flanked her, unseen, ready to make their move, like big cats on a gazelle. If only they'd known Cass was the biggest cat of them all. No man could take her down; just ask her clients. Cassie illustrated the point by wiggling gracefully away from a man who dared to wrap his arms around her, shooting him a look that could curdle milk. As the song merged into another, Maria licked at her lips. The remnants of the last shot were sticky on her mouth and she needed something to rehydrate. Motioning to Cass over the loud music that she was heading to get something to drink, Maria took a rare empty stool at the surprisingly quiet bar. It seemed everyone was writhing and thrashing on the dance-floor, all the stools occupied but hers and another next to it. The bartender, a bored-looking youth in a uniform consisting of a black T-shirt and the tightest jeans known to mankind, gave her an enquiring nod as she sat.

'Bottle of water, please, thanks,' she said, getting only an eye roll in return. 'Jesus, who died?' she said under her breath.

'No one yet,' came the answer from her left. She looked across, surprised anyone had heard over the music, and met the brown eyes of a man who made the barman look positively cheerful. He looked wretched; bloodshot eyes under hooded lids, a near-vacant expression, all topped by a head of very unruly brown hair. He had a look of Droopy the cartoon dog. Cute, though – what Maria would call a fixer-upper. Good bones, just needed a bit of renovation. The cut of his rather creased but obviously expensive clothes did him no favours either. He looked like he needed to be steam-cleaned from head to foot.

She shook her head, snapping herself out of work mode. When it came to suits on men, she was always dressing them, rather than undressing. She thought of Darcy's honeymoon suit, the time she'd taken designing it from scratch, making it with her own two hands, just to hang in some wardrobe, untouched and unloved. A bit like her. Unless he had taken it with him, to hang in some foreign wardrobe with another woman's clothes. A traitor suit. One that waggled its sleeves at any bit of clothing going. A slut suit, with no ounce of honour among its fine threading.

'Bad day?' she asked, paying the bartender and taking a refreshing swig from the ice-cold bottle of water. He turned to her again, a half-smile playing on his lips.

'A bad month, to be honest,' he said glumly, throwing back a shot with a flick of his head. Maria nodded in understanding.

'I get that – me too.' He looked across at her, and Maria felt his eyes run over her, scrutinising her from head to foot. She blushed, remembering she looked like a damn Bond girl.

'Ignore the get-up. My mate Cass "dressed me" and dragged me out to cheer me up.'

The man nodded, turning towards the dancefloor, where it seemed everyone but them was. Maria pointed to Cassie, who was currently rubbing body parts suggestively with a man who looked like Channing Tatum's slightly better-looking stunt double. Cassie caught them watching and waved emphatically, tossing her hair into Nearly-Tatum's face, not that he seemed to mind. Maria laughed despite herself. Her friend was mad, but she loved her to bits, despite their normally different views on romance. The man peered back over his shoulder at her, flashing an amused grin. 'So, she's supposedly here to cheer you up, yet you're sitting at the bar alone, drinking water, while she does that?' He pointed again to Cassie, who was now pretty much in danger of being mauled by the males surrounding her. Mauled or peed on territorially. Neither was an appealing prospect. Nearly-Tatum looked all set to beat his chest and run up the speaker tower with her under his arm, taking a few rivals down along the way. Maria sighed and turned back to the bar, hailing the lazy barman, who looked like he was reading a comic book in the corner.

'Two of whatever he's having, please,' she said, motioning to the empty shot glasses.

'Make that two each,' the man added, thrusting a twenty onto the bar. Maria couldn't be bothered to argue, so she grabbed a twenty from her purse and put it on top of his. He smiled.

'In the mood to get drunk?' he asked. 'I'm Mark by the way.'

She looked across at the unkempt but handsome man. Cassie was with her, she was pretty safe where she was, and the thought of getting blasted and having a laugh with a man who wasn't going to jilt her at the altar and take another woman on honeymoon sounded like a pretty welcome way to spend the evening.

'Maria,' she said in reply, as the shots were lined up. 'And you bet your ass I am.'

Chapter 4

Maria was pretty sure her head had been sawn off in the night, jammed with nuts and bolts, and then stapled back on. Even opening her eyes caused her physical pain, but she had a horrible feeling of dread that forced her to push back the pain and peel apart her crusty eyelids. Managing to pull open one eye, she half-sighed in relief as she realised she was lying on her front in Cassie's spare room, her room while she was here. Her relief was short-lived when she saw a piece of paper on her pillow, some unfamiliar writing scrawled across it. Fighting against the wave of nausea that occurred when she moved her arm from her side, she reached for the paper, her fingers barely grasping it. Hungover was not the word. She felt as though she had been dug up. She could still taste the many, many shots she had drunk last night, along with an undertone of chips she didn't remember eating. The paper said:

I had to get to work but thank you for last night. I really needed the company.

Mark Smith

A mobile number was underneath the name, along with a solitary kiss. Maria put the paper over her face, blocking out the sunlight from the window by her bed. A flashback of skin on skin popped into her head, and she grimaced. What the hell had she been thinking? Sleeping with a stranger went against everything she believed. And she did remember sleeping with him, however hazy her memory was. And protection? Oh Lord, she couldn't remember. She rolled out of bed as urgently as she could (which wasn't very urgently at all), crawling to the bathroom as the contents of her stomach warned her they were about to make an appearance. She had just reached the rim, her fingers curling around the cold porcelain, when she spotted something floating on top of the water. A condom. *Thank heaven, the angels, and the makers of rubbers*, she exclaimed in her head. The nausea subsided slightly with the panic, and she rolled onto her back, gripping the base of the toilet like an otter trying to break a clam.

'Cass... i... e... eee,' she called feebly. No reply. She banged her palm down on the tiled floor with a slap-slap sound, as loudly as she could bear with her headache. 'Cass...' *slap* 'iieee...' *slap*. 'Cassie!' she tried again, and heard a shuffling noise in the corridor. Maria was just about to shout again when the door opened and Maria found herself staring at the naked man parts of Nearly-Tatum, and the chips made a surprise reverse appearance after all.

Maria hugged the blanket around her for dear life as she looked at the Saturday morning autumn weather from the cottage window. She was dressed in fresh PJs, post-shower, and was still barely holding it together. Nearly-Tatum, a very friendly Australian otherwise known as Tucker, had made her a coffee and was now making scrambled eggs, in his pants, in the cottage kitchen. Cassie was lying in the armchair next to her, staring pointedly at her.

'Cass, stop!' Maria shuddered as the sound of her own voice rattled the pickled brain in her head. 'I can't talk about it. I can't even drink this coffee.' She put the steaming mug onto the coffee table, alongside a stack of law books and two yoghurt pots, spoons still stuck in. She gagged at the sight. 'Seriously, Cass, I'll clean this place for you, or hire you someone?'

Cassie, legs dangling over the IKEA chair arm, waved her away with her rather feeble fingers. 'I will sort it, chill.'

The radio was on in the kitchen, and Tucker-Tatum was humming along to Bon Jovi as he clanged pans about. Cassie snuck a look at her, grinning devilishly. Even hungover, and with her Little Mermaid PJs on, she was still quite a sight with her perfect, sculpted brows and long, raven-black hair. Maria looked back at her, flicking her eyes to the kitchen. 'So, what's happening today? And what did you get up to last night?'

Cassie raised an eyebrow and shook her head. 'Oh no, missus, you don't get to find out about my night, till you spill about yours!'

Maria groaned. 'Oh, Cass, it was a mistake, obviously. I shouldn't have gone anywhere near a bloke last night. I can't remember most of it, and I seriously think my liver is dying today. Those shots were little cups of poison, I'm sure of it.'

Cassie nodded, wincing herself. The smell of bacon and eggs started permeating the air, and they both licked their lips at the same time. A man, in the kitchen, cooking hangover food. It seemed that Cassie had won the morning after, at least. Not that Tatum-Tucker would be seen again after today. He was already on borrowed time, he just didn't know it yet. It was a miracle he'd even got to stay the whole night. Maria was grateful for the fact that her friend didn't do relationships, given the man had watched her vomit half-naked, held her hair back and picked her up off the bathroom floor. All done with tanned washboard abs and a pair of Captain America pants he had thankfully dashed to put on. Embarrassment was not the word, but he seemed to take it in his stride, calling for Cassie to help while he cleaned up the bathroom and got to making coffee. Now he was feeding them, and she had even seen him heading to the bins, black bag in hand. Cassie was oblivious to it all, having just helped Maria get changed before they plonked down into their respective blanket forts in the living room. It felt weirdly domestic, the longer they sat there, so Cassie turned on the television. Or rather,

24

she jabbed at the remote on the arm of the chair with a shaky, polished finger. It sprang into life, and she dived on it, hitting the volume button with gusto as the sound of the morning news filled the air. 'Arrghh!' they both moaned collectively at the noise.

'Everything all right?' The Australian twang came from the kitchen.

'Yes!' they both shouted, wincing again. 'Yess…' they whispered, shooting each other a sympathetic look as they retreated deeper into their blankets like turtles into their shells.

'And in other local news, Darcy Burgess – is the honeymoon truly over?'

The newscaster couldn't have caused a larger impact if he had parachuted in through the roof. They both jumped off the sofa, commando-crawling across the cream (and slightly stained) carpet towards the dusty TV unit.

'Turn it up, turn it up!' Maria screamed at Cassie, who was pressing the buttons like her life depended on it.

'Just weeks ago, a certain August wedding was heralded as the crown in Harrogate's events calendar, with Darcy Burgess, eligible bachelor and heir to the Burgess Tea Company, set to wed local Westfield entrepreneur and wedding planner Maria Mallory. However, on the day, the wedding didn't go to plan, and pictures emerged from the overseas press of Darcy, looking alone in St Lucia. What happened to the pair? Was Darcy jilted at the altar? The Burgess family have yet…'

'Breakfast, girls!' Tucker said, an apron emblazoned with the chipper slogan 'This came with the kitchen' the only thing covering his half-nakedness.

'Sshh!' They both batted him away. Shrugging, he put their plates down on the coffee table, returning to sit on the couch with one of his own.

'Where did you get that apron?' Cassie asked him, looking at Maria. Maria shook her head, transfixed by the screen.

'It was in the drawer, in a wrapper. You know,' he said, shovelling a piece of bacon into his mouth, 'that kitchen is pretty grim, almost like no one uses it.'

'Sshh!' Maria waved frantically.

'Sshh!' Cassie added, giving him a glare from her mascara-ringed eyes. He snorted, biting off a piece of bacon aggressively at her. She grinned at him before remembering to scowl.

Maria was glued to the screen. 'It says they have yet to release a statement. It's ridiculous, why would they do that?' The look she gave Cassie broke her heart. She wrapped her swaddled arm around her friend.

'Protection, hun – they have a reputation.'

Maria sniffed, wiping away a tear. 'So do I, and a business. I have a living to make, and Westfield is such a small, close-knit place. People talk, and after last night…'

A vision of the events of the evening before swam into focus and Maria burst into tears. Tucker stood and quietly left for the kitchen, sensing the need for privacy. Cassie hugged her tighter.

'We can spin this, you know,' Cassie said, her legal acumen springing into action. 'Why don't we talk to the local paper, see if they'll run your story? At the end of the day, Mar, he went on honeymoon with another woman after jilting you at the altar. He deserves to be run through the press, not you.'

Maria sobbed loudly. 'I can't do that. It's too petty, not to mention embarrassing. How did this happen? Them being so quiet about everything makes me look awful. How can he do this to me, Cass? And Mark last night… I mean, oh God!'

Cassie wrapped her arms around her best friend once more, crushing her under their combined blankets.

'Hey, listen, last night was… well… it was company. You needed comfort, and everyone spins out when they have a break-up. We all do silly things and hurt people. Mark left you his number as well, so it's not all bad. He could be Prince Charming! Darcy arseface could be the frog. This could be a funny story you and Mark tell your grandkids by the fire.'

Maria laughed, prompting a snot bubble to blow out of her left nostril. Cassie visibly shrank away from her, always disgusted by anything gross or remotely like looking after a child. She grabbed the tissue box and threw it to Maria. Maria caught it gratefully and blew her nose.

'That, my friend, is gross. Now, come on, let's eat breakfast before it gets cold. You have to work today, remember?'

Maria groaned. Saturday was the day she worked alone in the shop, luckily. She could get away with drinking vats of coffee in her sweatpants with Lynn not around, and there were no brides booked in, so she could concentrate on doing the alterations at the back of the shop. She made the odd dress or two for the sale racks when she had time, and they sold well to the locals and the tourists, so maybe she could run up a couple of designs to fill the shopfront a little. The display would need changing too, she thought, as she started to eat her cooling breakfast. It would soon be the party season, and the bridal display could be taken down. Thinking of her own gown, wrapped up with the other dresses in the upstairs flat of her shop, her stomach roiled once more. She would return it, she decided, and get rid of it. They'd paid for it anyway. They would just have to get rid of the burger relish stain. Darcy could jolly well spring for a dry cleaner. She needed to try to take back some semblance of control.

It was at that moment that Tucker walked back in sporting his apron and a dish-washing brush. Both having forgotten he was even there, Cassie joined Maria in a loud scream, which sent Tucker diving down the back of the sofa, suds flying, and the girls running to the medicine cabinet for more paracetamol.

'Dude!' Cassie said, ramming a white pill into her desert-dry mouth. 'You need to wear a bell!'

Tucker laughed as he walked into Cassie's room, a tattoo of a kangaroo punching a koala on a surfboard on his sculpted back the last thing they saw before the door closed.

27

Chapter 5

Opening the door to Happy Ever After, Maria heaved a sigh of frustration. Her old Ford car was freezing, the heating having not worked even when it belonged to her mother years ago, but the shop was supposed to be warm, and it was so cold. She always silently thanked Lynn in her head for doing one of the many tiny but wonderful things she did around the business, like setting the heating in autumn and winter. The radiators were cold to the touch this morning, though, no hum of the heating. Wexley Street was a small row of shops linked to pretty cottages at either side, just in the heart of town, near Baker Street and jutting off Foxley Street. Westfield had been home for ever to Maria and her mother and father, and she couldn't imagine living anywhere else. Normally, at this time of year, with the wedding season slowing and the first autumn leaves dropping, Maria would be in her element. Designing fancy-dress costumes for kids that she sold online, catering for the local dances and parties that the festive season brought with it. It was magical.

This time, however, it felt so flat. She was alone. Nothing had changed, it seemed. Nothing at all. The shop was the same, with its slightly wonky walls, peeling paint and old-fashioned features. In its previous life it had been a bookshop, and her father had brought her as a girl to wander among the shelves, delving for literary treasures about pirates and princesses, while he studied one thing or another. It reminded her of the wand shop from *Harry Potter*, complete with dusty shelves and strange owner. Mr Hoffman had died not long after her mum and, with no family to speak of, the business closed. Maria had been dealing with the grief of becoming an orphan, living in an empty house full of memories, and a desire for something new, linked with the familiar. She had sunk all her money from the house into the shop, saving what furniture she could fit in and selling the rest. She had lived upstairs among the stock till Darcy had asked her to move in with him. Now she was back to being here, her safe haven, and she wouldn't let anything or anyone take it from her.

Flicking the trusty kettle on, she shook off her fleecy coat and bobble hat, placing them on the old coat rack. Father's hat still hung there, just as it had at home, perched on top, and she smiled at it fondly. It was on the far wall, near the double-windowed doors of the back room, next to the photo of her mother.

'Morning, Mum,' she said absently. 'You don't have to say a word,' she muttered, opening the back doors to let light into the rooms. It seemed so much darker today. She looked into the back room at her inbox of projects and alterations. Not much there, she mused. Lynn had struck again. She knew her assistant had taken care of everything for her, not wanting her to be stressed with work, but in truth, with the huge blanks in the diary, Maria could have used the distraction. She shook her head to chase away the blues and headed to the counter. Filling her favourite mug with some sweetener, she reached for the kettle and flicked it on again. She mustn't have done it properly the last time, as it was cold. Nothing happened.

Flicking the button impatiently, she waited for the red light to flick on. Nothing. Moving to the light switch, she flicked it on. Still nothing. She sighed and, going into the back room, flicked light switches on and off, tried the sewing machine, the over

29

locker. Nothing, and the phone was off too. Damn it. Heading through to the back, she opened the door to the back pantry and pulled down the cover to the fuse box. Something had tripped, obviously. The electrics had been pretty much untouched since she bought the shop, and probably for years before that. She was amazed they'd passed the survey, looking at them now. She switched one of the switches, which was flipped down, back up, but it tripped again.

She growled and flicked the switch again. The same thing happened. 'What?'

She tried again but got nothing. 'Damn it, I don't need this today. What the hell is going on?'

The shop was due to open soon. She couldn't very well open up with no power! She went to her handbag to get her phone but remembered she had left it at home switched off. Perfect, and the desktop wouldn't work without power. She looked under the wooden countertop, hunting around among catalogues and sample books till her fingers touched what she was looking for.

She used to laugh at her mother and her old-school ways, hoarding things that didn't have a place in the modern world. Now she did it too, and thank God she had. Thumbing through the Westfield phone book, she felt close to her, and her heart squeezed in pain at the fresh wave of loss she felt. Thank goodness for Cassie and Lynn. The thought of being alone was never far from her thoughts these days. She thought of Darcy, what he would think of her if he knew she had spent the night with a stranger. Would he even care? She had studied the pictures from the press so many times now, she felt as if she could draw them from memory.

She was glad her mother wasn't here, in a way. The thought of her sitting in the church watching her only child get jilted was too much to bear. She wondered what kind of person could do that to another person. The Darcy she knew would never have done something so callous. Except he had. He'd done it and never

30

looked back. The photos proved it. She could understand him wanting to get away. God knew she had wanted to escape herself. She could just about forgive him for going on their honeymoon, if she really willed herself to. The honeymoon she had booked, planned and helped pay for, given that he and his family had paid for the wedding. The honeymoon had been her contribution, her small way of exerting her independence. But it was fine. He needed to get away, escape the flak for what he'd done.

Fair enough. She could swallow that, in time. It was the arm in the photo that bothered her. What did it mean? Had he used her ticket to take someone else? Had he met someone there? Was it all for the press? They didn't seem to know who she was, and as it was just an arm, they didn't have much to go on. If it had been staged for the press, wouldn't Darcy have made sure they could actually see her? At least with a face, a body, there would be more context. Maybe she was wearing a resort uniform? Perhaps she was just a member of staff, passing him a cocktail to cheer him up. Maybe she was minging. She could be a moose for all Maria knew. Anyone could have attractive-looking arms. Look at Madonna. Her arms were epic, but looking at them disembodied in a photo, you couldn't tell whether it was the Queen of Pop or Iggy Pop. The crazy thought cheered her no end. The owner of the arm could indeed be no one, just a passing holidaymaker. The thought that Darcy could be that cruel didn't bear thinking about. She'd loved the man he was. It felt like he had died too, in a way. The thought of him being out there, kissing another person with his lips, cradling someone in the arms that used to encircle her, was damn near killing her.

She felt the physical pain of her loss, and took a moment to will her body to breathe again. Grief and a hangover. Never great. She lowered herself to the floor, pulling the phone book onto her lap. Thumbing through, she looked for an electrician who wouldn't charge the earth for a Saturday-morning callout. They didn't have one in Westfield, tending to fix what they could

31

themselves, but this was out of her league. She could call one of the villagers, but given that everyone seemed to be giving her a wide berth, she didn't relish playing the jilted bride *and* damsel in distress. That would be one step too far in terms of feeling pathetic. She needed to prove to everyone, and herself for that matter, that she could still stand on her own two feet. She'd done it before, and she would again. She had to. And it was then that she saw it. The little box advert, staring out at her from the paper. Chance Electrics. Chance. It spoke to her. That's what she needed. Hope. A chance to solve this problem, get her business back up and running and the home lights burning so she could at least keep the wolves from the door while she recovered.

This is it, Maria. She could hear her mother's voice in her head, spurring her on. *You can do this, my girl. You don't need anything else. Use what you already hold.* She nodded at her mother's photo and picked herself up off the floor. Thank goodness there were still phone boxes in the village, she thought to herself as she headed to the nearest one. Pressing in the number, she smiled to herself. No weekend callout fee either. It really was a sign.

Cassie was hiding in her bathroom, pretending to get ready. She had applied her liquid eyeliner three times already. Any more and she was going to end up looking like Marilyn Manson. She could still hear Tucker in the kitchen, humming along to the radio and banging things around. Why was he still here? Robbers made less noise. She half-hoped he was robbing her, because then at least he would go and she could avoid the awkward conversation she knew was coming. This was precisely the reason why she never brought people home. Sanctuary Cottage was just that to her, a sanctuary from her parents at first, and then her job, and now she had a rogue Australian running around, rummaging in her cupboards. She couldn't even ring Maria because her phone was on charge in the living room. She needed to fake a work emergency or something, but what would she say? A carrier pigeon had flown in through the bathroom window? Hogwarts owl? She couldn't hide in here all day, that was certain. She needed to woman up, go out there and face him. Say 'thanks for the hot sex, don't forget to wipe me from your memory on your way out of the door'. What kind of weirdo hung around in the morning anyway, let alone made breakfast? It was definitely bad man code, she was sure of it.

A polite knock came at the door, making her jump.

'Cassie, you okay in there?' His Aussie twang reverberated through the wood.

'Er, yeah, I'm fine. Do you need something?' She tiptoed to the door, listening for sounds of movement.

'Well, I thought we could maybe get lunch, if you like? I don't have to work till later. Do you fancy it?'

'Lunch?' Cassie said, incredulous. 'Why?'

An amused chuckle came back. 'It's what people do, eat at certain times of day. Sometimes they even do it together, have a conversation or two.'

Cassie cringed. She couldn't think of anything more toe curling, aside from turning up to court dressed as a pirate.

What have you come dressed as today, Cass? Professional suicide? Arrgghhhh, me hearties!

'Er, no, sorry, I can't. I have a lot of work coming up, I have to work. All weekend. And next week. The whole month, actually.'

He said nothing, so she put her ear to the door. She couldn't hear anything.

'Okay, so lunch next week then. You eat lunch at work, right? I'll call you…'

Oh God. What was his deal? Did he feel bad? He obviously didn't do this very often.

'Er, yeah?'

'Right, it's a date then. I'm going to go now, let you get on with work and stop listening behind doors.'

33

Cassie sprang back from the entrance, cursing under her breath.

'Nice mouth,' he laughed. 'See you next week! I left you something in the fridge.'

She stared at the door, head cocked to one side till she heard the front door open and close. She came out of the bathroom, heading to her bedroom to look out of the window. Looking out from behind the blinds, she saw him heading down her path. He looked like he was walking down a catwalk. Weird or not, Cassie did have to recognise that the man was an absolute hottie. Shame she wasn't the type to do second dates. Or even first ones. Hell, having breakfast with him had been a first, even with Maria as a buffer. She was just admiring his butt wistfully when he stopped at the gate, turned and looked straight at her.

'Shit!' she said, jumping back behind the curtain. Sneaking a peek, she saw him blow her a kiss before walking off towards Westfield centre. Uber hadn't quite hit the village yet. The villagers were still getting over high-speed internet arriving. Summoning a taxi with the click of a button was more than some of them could take, for now. Hopefully he wouldn't go shooting his mouth off in the village about where he had spent the night. With Maria already in the spotlight, the last thing she needed was for people to think she was hanging around with random men. But as Cassie herself always said, the best way to get over a man was to get under another. It would have done Maria some good, something to take her mind off Arsy Darcy. As long as it wasn't a regular thing. Maria wasn't like that anyway. All she had ever wanted to be was happy and married.

Cassie watched Tucker walk away till he was out of sight, and then headed downstairs. It was like stepping into the twilight zone. It didn't even feel like her house. She looked into the lounge. Same in there. He had cleaned up. Really cleaned. She could smell polish, cleaning sprays. Walking into the kitchen she was hit by a horrible smell. She gagged and headed to the window, throwing

34

it open. What the hell had he done? She looked around and saw the bottle on the side. Bleach. The man was insane. She'd pulled Mr Mop. Every surface had been cleared, wiped clean. She could see her work surfaces for once. It felt like she *had* been robbed. Flicking her foot on the pedal bin, she only saw an empty bin liner. He had even taken the rubbish out. She looked in horror towards the now very shiny fridge freezer. He had even scrubbed the fronts of the damn appliances. Who knew what horrors awaited behind those doors. What would it be? A severed head? A ransom note?

She walked across the gleaming kitchen floor, pinching her nose against the smell of cleanliness around her, and curled her fingers around the metal fridge handle. Taking a deep breath, she opened the door.

Her fridge was mostly empty, aside from a bottle of wine in the cooler. It was always empty, which begged the question of where he had got breakfast from. In her alcohol-pickled stupor this morning, she hadn't even realised that she didn't own a tin of beans, let alone the makings of a full English. Had he been shopping? Oh, dear Lord.

On the bottom shelf was a package wrapped in tinfoil. When she opened it, she saw a ham salad sandwich, cut in half and placed neatly on a plate. On the top was a note, written on a small piece of paper.

Thanks for last night, and since I know you'll probably say no to lunch, I made some for you.
Jesse Tucker

He had left his number, written there underneath his name. A stupid name at that. Who had a last name as a first name, anyway? Another reason never to call him. And she wouldn't be eating his food either. Not a chance in hell. She shut the fridge door again and headed upstairs. She needed to get to the gym, try and get rid of this hangover. Hopefully the stink of her gym bag when she got back would mask the gross smells here. She just hoped Maria wouldn't expect her to keep things like this. It was never going to happen. Who would want to live like this? Life was for living, not cleaning. Cassie headed out, grabbing her phone on the way past. A minute later, she came back and grabbed the sandwich, tucking it into her bag. If she got hungry later, she might as well eat the damn thing. No one would ever know.

Chapter 6

The thing about ice cream that not enough people knew was that it had amazing restorative properties for the body. It soothed the soul, helped some sugar work its way around the sluggish body system when hungover, and cheered up the most melancholy of hearts. Since she no longer needed to fit into a wedding dress, or a honeymoon bikini, she felt that eating the emergency tub of Rocky Road from the icebox was allowed. It was the weekend after all, and it would melt anyway – since the whole shop was still down. It had been two hours, and even though the 'open' sign was flipped, no one had come into the shop. At this rate, next year she wouldn't even have a shop to hide in. She sat on the floor, back against the countertop, legs pulled up to her sides as she balanced the tub on her knees. She could see her mother's picture on the wall, and she looked at it as she did every day. In the years since she had passed, Maria had always missed her. When she'd signed for the shop, the first person she had wanted to call was her mum. When Darcy had proposed, Lynn and she had shed a tear or two about the fact she wouldn't be there.

This time was different. Maria was broken, and she knew it. In her dehydrated, exhausted state, she felt the loss of her mother as though it were yesterday. She shovelled another spoonful of ice cream into her mouth and looked at her mother's smiling face.

'I miss you so much, Mum. I have so much to tell you, and I don't even know what to do anymore.' A sob escaped her lips, and she sucked in a shaky breath. 'Darcy… Darcy left me, and I got drunk… and there was a man… and the business…' She dissolved into sobs, shoving the spoon into the half-empty tub of melting ice cream. 'I miss you so much. I really want to pull it together, but I don't think I can this time.' She heard a noise at the side of her, but ignored it.

'I just need someone to be there for me, Mum, for once. Why does everyone leave?'

'Huh-hum.' There was that noise again. Maria looked to her left and, through tear-stained eyes, saw that the shop door was ajar, and in front of it was a very puzzled-looking man. Quite a good-looking one at that.

'Oh, shit!' She jumped up, throwing the carton to one side and standing up so quickly she got a post-alcohol head rush. 'Oh, ow!' She grabbed her head with both hands, trying to quell the lightning bolt that was striking between her ears. He went to step forward, placing his bag on the floor and closing the shop door. He flicked it to closed, and then just kind of stood there, watching her. Maria was suddenly very aware of the fact that she had been caught mainlining ice cream, looking like a bag lady and talking to a wall. She wiped her eyes ineffectually. Looking down at the floor, she saw that the discarded ice cream tub was now lying on its side, dribbling its contents onto the hardwood floor. It felt like a metaphor for her life, discarded and dribbling away.

She took another stab at wiping her face with sticky fingers.

'I'm really sorry, can I help you?'

The man didn't say anything for a beat. He just looked at her, an odd expression on his face. She looked right back, trying to figure out who this man was and why he was just staring at her.

'I'm the electrician. Are you okay?' He was looking at her as though he was expecting a gust of wind to whip through the shop and blow her away. In turn, seeing him standing there, among the beautiful silks and trains of the front display window, Maria couldn't help thinking how strong he looked. He was dressed in a simple black T-shirt and workers' trousers in a dark gunmetal grey. He had actual guns, big arm muscles she could make out under his short sleeves. It was then she noticed his pockets were filled with assorted tools. He jangled a little as he moved closer, taking one slow step after another towards her.

'I'm James Chance. I believe we spoke on the phone. Maria, is it?'

She nodded mutely, blinking back the tears that kept threatening to erupt. He took another step forward.

'Okay,' he said softly. 'Why don't you point me to the fuse box, and I'll let you freshen up while I get started. That all right?' She noticed his eyes then, blue-green, like beautiful glass marbles, topped off with thick, dark lashes against the darker cropped hair that peeked out from his baseball cap. They were looking at her with concern. It was a look she was all too used to nowadays, and she shrank away from it. The man picked up his toolbox and slowly walked closer to her. She walked zombie-like to the back room and pointed to the fuse box.

'It's there. I'll just… er… go upstairs.' She headed to the back stairs and looked back at him.

'You okay down here?' She realised she was about to leave her business, and her till, unattended, in the presence of a complete stranger.

'I'm fine, don't worry – and listen, I am trustworthy. I have ID, if you want to see it, or I can come back another time?' The thought of him not fixing the electrics was incentive enough to swallow her fears. He didn't look like a serial killer. Although what serial killers looked like was anybody's guess. It wasn't like they had a club badge or bought matching T-shirts.

'No, no!' she squeaked. 'I really can't afford to lose any more business right now. I really need the electrics fixing. I won't be long, please stay.' It didn't escape her attention that she was begging a man not to leave. This was obviously her life now. Trying to hold a man down. Yay. Feminism was alive and kicking in Westfield.

He looked at her kindly. 'I'm not going anywhere, don't worry.' She smiled back, oddly comforted by his words. He turned away, and she headed up the stairs.

Looking in the mirror in the bathroom upstairs, Maria groaned. No wonder the bloke had been looking at her funny, what with talking to the wall. And this. Looking at her reflection was like looking at a poster of Zelda from *Terrorhawks*. Minus the good hair. Hers was stuck up all over, from a mixture of being tousled during stranger sex to leftover hair mousse. Plus what looked and smelt suspiciously like toothpaste. She put the plug in and ran the hot water, nipping to the rail in the other room to see what clothes she had on the hangers. Making her own clothes had its perks.

Heading down the stairs fifteen minutes later, wearing a simple summer dress and tights from her accessories stock box, her hair scraped back into a tidy bun, she could hear the soft bangs of metal on metal, followed by the occasional grunting and muttering.

She stood beside him and he turned at the noise. His gaze flicked over her, his eyes looking her up and down, and she flushed with embarrassment.

'Sorry, I'm having a bit of a day.' She brushed her dress skirt down self-consciously. It was a plain navy blue, brightened up slightly by a thin red belt and sheer tights.

James looked at her and smiled. 'You look nice. Are you okay? It's not my business, but—'

'I'm fine,' Maria said, plastering on a fake smile. It was her stock response nowadays; it didn't even have any meaning anymore. Who was fine these days, really? 'Can you fix my box?'

40

Her eyes widened as her words hit the air. 'I mean, my fuse box, er... my electrics. Can you fix it?'

His lip twitched and he looked like he wanted to say something, but he turned back to the box and pointed. 'This is outdated. To be honest, I'm surprised it's worked as long as it has. The fuse wire was shot, so I've fixed it for now, but you really do need to replace it all, rewire the lot.'

Maria felt like she'd been punched in the gut. 'Is there any way we can avoid that, maybe patch it up?'

James shook his head. 'I can do a temporary fix, but realistically it needs doing now.'

Maria stood there, biting the skin on her thumbnail, shaking her head from side to side rapidly. James stepped down from his small stepladder.

'Listen, you can get a second opinion, but they'll only tell you the same. It needs sorting, the sooner the better. I am quite quiet next week so I can fit you in. I can even start today, if you like – cut down on the days you'd have to close.' He looked around him at the empty shop. 'You're closed today, right? Do you have anywhere to stay?'

'I'm open today, actually, and I don't live here. I'm living with a friend.'

'Because of the power?' James asked. Maria frowned. *Why did he care?*

'Er, no – I don't live here. I lived in Harrogate till recently, but I... now I'm staying with my friend. Cass.'

He said nothing, rubbing his hand down the scruff of his facial hair.

'My friend, Cass, she has a cottage here in Westfield. So it's handy for work.'

He kept looking at her, one brow arched.

'She's a hotshot Harrogate divorce lawyer. She's been really great, actually, putting me up.'

Nothing. He was looking at her like he was trying to work her out. *Why do I feel the need to fill the silences?*

41

'So…' She changed tack. 'When can you start, and do you know how much, roughly?'

She was half-expecting him to start showing his butt crack and sucking the air in between his teeth, but he just shook his head.

'I'll need to get some parts. I'll shop around to see what I can get. With the rewiring, you can redo the sockets and light fittings too. Do you have any ideas?'

I don't even have a clue what I'm doing tomorrow, let alone making decisions like this. 'I don't know, do you need to know today? I don't think I can do that today.'

'You have a little time. Do you want me to come back when I have a few quotes for you?'

Maria found herself nodding along dumbly.

'You sure you're okay? Can I call someone to come?'

'No!' she squeaked, suddenly picturing Lynn and Cassie frantically racing to the shop, having received a mumbling call from a strange, deep voice. 'No.' *Good, that was calmer, Maria. Well done.* 'I'm fine, really, I'm just having a bad day.' *Preceded by a few weeks of total devastation.*

'Yeah,' he said, his head moving from side to side as he openly gawked at her. 'You don't look well. Are you ill?'

Maria went and had a little sit-down on her chair, wrapping her arms around herself.

'I may or may not have had enough alcohol last night to stun an alcoholic rhino.'

He went back to work then, a grin on his face. 'Ah, hangover and a bad day at work. That'll do it. You own the place?'

'Yep,' she nodded, licking her lips to try to get some moisture going in her mouth.

'Just you then?'

She groaned, hitting her head on the desk. 'Yes, just me. A tiny little woman. Don't you read the news? It's old hat now. I'm fine on my own, aside from the binge drinking and awkward sexual encounter. Just fine and dandy. If people can't handle that, it's their tough luck.'

She was staring at the wooden counter, trying to resist the urge to slam her head against it again, when she realised the whole shop was quiet. She sneaked a peek under her arm and looked at him. He was standing halfway up the ladder, looking straight at her.

'I meant in the business. Is it just you in the business?'

Oh, holy mother of hell. He must think I'm barmy.

'Oh!' She laughed awkwardly, a shrill cackle that made her sound like she was auditioning for *Wicked*. 'I thought... well, never mind what I thought. It's fine. No, it's my business but I employ Lynn part-time. She worked with my mother before she passed. I opened this up and she came with me.'

What the hell are you doing! Stop telling him your life story, you bloody demented woman!

He nodded, closing up the fuse box and stepping down the ladder.

'Okay, it's safe now for when you go home, but I really think you need to get it sorted soon. I can come tomorrow if you like. I have a free day.'

I bet you can too, at double the cost.

'I won't charge weekend rates. I'm at a loose end at the moment myself. I have family staying with me and I'd be glad of an excuse to get out of the house to be honest.'

He pulled a face, and she sat up.

'That would be great, thanks. How much do I owe for today?'

He waved her away as he packed up his tools. 'I'll let you have some quotes tonight, and we can sort the bill then.'

She nodded, thinking of her bank account. With the honeymoon costs, and the way business was going, it would be tight. She would be living with Cass for a while at this rate, not that Cass would mind. Her liver might object, though.

He was just finishing up when the phone rang. Thank God

43

she had the power back on at least. She scooped to pick it up and saw Lynn's number on the screen.

'Hey, Lynn, you okay?' She half-watched James pack up as she listened to Lynn chat about her morning.

'Cool, chilled morning then, eh? That's good. No, it's been dead here, and…' She went to tell her about the electrics, but stopped herself. Lynn didn't need to be fretting about that. Hopefully things would be well underway by the time she was in next.

'I'm about to head home myself to be honest. I'm going to take one of the machines to Cass's and work from there. I haven't had a customer all day.'

'Do you think people saw the photos?' Lynn asked tentatively. Well, she obviously had.

'You mean the photos that humiliate me and show I wasted years of my life with a completely selfish arsehole? Probably, yeah. I'm guessing that this is what happened. Like people need another reason to avoid me. I mean, you don't book a wedding planner who can't keep a bloody man, do you?' She spun around with the phone in her hand and saw that James was waiting by the door. He looked as though he was waiting… nay, hoping… for the zombie apocalypse to hit so he could be eaten alive by the undead. Obviously preferable to overhearing her tragic backstory.

'Er, Lynn, a customer just came in. Yeah, I have to go. Speak to you later. Enjoy your weekend.'

'Sorry, I wasn't listening, honest. I just wanted to say goodbye properly. What time do you want to start tomorrow?'

'Whenever, just let me know and I'll be here to let you in.'

He nodded and opened his mouth as though to say something further. He looked like he was struggling to think of something, so she saved him.

'Listen, James, is it?' He smiled, his amused mouth twitching. 'I'm just having a bad day. I promise to rein in the crazy for tomorrow. If you don't want the hassle, I understand.' She plucked a Post-it note off her desk and scribbled down her mobile number.

He took it, opened the door and went to leave. 'See you tomorrow, Maria. I'll contact you later. Stay hydrated.'

She sank back down into her chair, watching him walk off to his van. *Stay hydrated.* She huffed to herself, going to pack up a machine and some work for home.

'As if a glass of water will sort me out, eh, Mum? I need more than that.'

She packed up and, making sure she'd locked up, carried her stuff to her waiting car. Getting in and cursing the crappy heating once more, she continued her conversation with her mother as she pulled away.

'Stay hydrated!' she snorted, shaking her head as she wove through the streets of Westfield. Driving past the vet's, she passed Amanda on her way up to the house, a cat in her arms. She was walking a little strangely and, as she turned, Maria could see why as her little baby bump came into view.

She waved, and Amanda waved back cheerfully. Cow.

'Well, did you see that? Benjamin Evans, going to be a dad. I never thought I'd see the day, did you, Mum?' She drove down the main street, heading towards the cottage. 'She looked well, though, didn't she? Married bliss to the man of your dreams and a baby on the way. Own businesses. Pretty good going, isn't it? At this rate, I shan't even have the shop by Christmas.' She drove the rest of the way in silence till she reached Cassie's home. If her mother had been there, she would have told her to shut up anyway, and get on with it. So that's what she would do. After a spell of vomiting and changing her bedsheets to rid them of the smell of the stranger she had bedded the night before. If she had to caption her life at the moment, #lifegoals #blessed wouldn't be first choice. She would rock #epicfail #passthebarfbag, though.

Chapter 7

Darcy walked off the plane into the tepid Northern weather and shivered. Whether it was the shock of being back in Britain or the dread of things to come he couldn't be sure. He had taken ill on the plane, and not even the complimentary champagne had made him feel any better.

His social media accounts had been deactivated while he was away, and he had left his phone at home, not wanting to be contacted while he went away to escape from his nuptials, as it were. For the first few days it had worked too, once his assistant had informed the hotel that he would in fact be attending alone, and it was no longer a honeymoon. A change of room had saved blushes all round, and a lucky couple newly engaged had been jubilant to score a free upgrade, courtesy of the sad-looking man propping up the bar in a rather tragic-looking gaudy shirt. He had found it in his case when he arrived, a joke present from Maria, he guessed, who had packed his case for him. He had gone to throw it out, but had instead found himself donning it to go down to the evening meal. Penance, perhaps. He tried to think about how Maria was, what she was doing, but he couldn't picture it. He knew she had picked up her things, or someone had. His doorman had called his office to gain permission for them to enter, and his father had told him when he had called to let them know where he was, and his room number, in case any business arose in his absence.

'It's done now, spit spot,' his father had proclaimed down the phone, as though Darcy had just had a boil lanced, or managed to kiss off a bad blind date.

'Hardly, Father,' Darcy tried to counter, but his father was already talking again.

'It would never have worked out and then where would we be, eh? You're bound to find a nice girl when the time comes, a worthy woman, who will want the same things as us.'

Darcy opened his mouth to argue that Maria surely did want the same things as them, for Darcy to be happy, but it was no use. What was the point in arguing now, anyway? The damage was already done. He had chickened out, hotfooting it down the back stairs before the organist had even cracked her fingers.

So now here he was, heading for the arrivals lounge and all that would follow it. He knew he was expected to head straight to the office, but he wasn't in a rush to race back into the cutthroat corporate tea business. His dad had already been spouting about some celebrity ad campaign that their biggest rival, Northern Tea, had produced. Darcy had been spared the onslaught for a few days but he knew his mother, father and younger sister would be ready and waiting to fill him in. It was as though they had just erased Maria from their lives, as easily as deleting a file. Darcy wasn't sure how easy that would come to him, but he supposed he had little choice.

As he went to stand by the carousel with the other dejected-looking holidaymakers, he caught the eye of a woman standing on her own nearby. She was looking tanned from her trip, her hair sporting a threaded braid. She turned and smiled at him.

'Hi, I recognise you, don't I?'

Darcy nodded. 'Probably from the flight.'

She considered this. 'No, I don't think so. Maybe from England?'

She was looking him up and down now, obviously trying to remember. Then he realised.

'It might be my baby pictures.'

The woman looked confused. 'Baby pictures?'

'Yes,' he said, watching the carousel start to turn slowly. 'I was in an ad campaign, for Burgess Teas?'

'Ooool!' she squealed loudly, making half the airport jump. 'You're that guy, the wedding guy!'

She looked around him, looking disappointed. 'Where is she?'

Darcy looked at her in horror as the people around them seemed to come to life, murmuring and pointing. *Oh God*, he thought to himself, seeing his case finally coming down the carousel towards him, like a life raft in a stormy open sea. He pushed his way through the crowd, nodding at people who were now smiling and waving at him, and frog-dived onto his case. He missed his footing a little and ended up moving along the carousel with his case for a beat till he managed to pull himself and it back upright. The woman was still there, giving him a conspiratorial look.

'I get it,' she stage-whispered. 'You have to be discreet, for the cameras. Is she meeting you later?'

He pulled his case to him, slamming it into his own leg and wincing with pain. He looked down and noticed a thin line of blood seeping through his cream linen trousers. He rubbed at it, which only sent a fresh wave of pain searing through his calf and caused the blood to smear. The woman never noticed, having sped off to collect her own baggage. He pulled up the handle of his case and took his opportunity to leave, pulling his carry-on man-bag onto his shoulder. He was feeling very confused and sweaty. Why would she think he was on his honeymoon? Surely the media machine had got wind of the story? He might not be famous by some modern reality TV standards, but in the North he was photographed a lot, normally because of his former shenanigans in the South with various IT girls and supermodels.

48

Drunken nights out in the right places. Or tumbling out of hotel rooms the morning after. And on one occasion, being papped jumping out of a mansion bedroom window when his date for the night's footballer husband arrived back early from practice with a pulled hamstring. Lucky for him, because the man was livid. Even with a limp, he had been within a cat's whisker of catching him.

He pulled his dejected self around the corner and gasped. Held back by several security guards and the barrier was a wall of journalists. He looked behind him momentarily, but there was only a couple with a small boy behind him. He didn't recognise them. Were they here for him? He turned back round and they started snapping away. *It might be me they're here for, after all*, he thought to himself.

'Darcy, mate – where's the girl?'

'Darcy, Darcy – over here, mate – can you flash your ring finger for us?'

Bemused, he looked down at his own hand, which was still sporting the small gold ring Maria had bought him when they got engaged. She had joked that it was to chase away the skanks, but knew it was just a thoughtful gift. Which he had forgotten to take off when he ditched her. *Shit balls of fire.* He went to shove his hand in his pocket, and was setting his head and body into battering-ram mode when a hand linked through his. A blonde woman, dressed in white linen trousers and a pink bustier, smiled at him, as though she expected him to just smile back in recognition. She covered his ring with her fingers and, bringing it up to her lips, dropped a kiss on it, winking at the cameras. Darcy was about to object when she leaned in and kissed him full on the lips. She had both hands rammed around his face, and it was all he could do to grip his bags and breathe. She tasted of cinnamon, which reminded him of the cough drops his grandmother sucked. He resisted the urge to gag as she pulled away, linking arms with him again and pulling him to the exit doors.

Security held off the paparazzi, but they were still hollering and whooping, shouting questions at him as the pair were ushered through security.

'What the hell was that?' he asked her, incredulous. 'Why did you do that, in front of them?'

He recognised her then. She had done it before, on the beach. He had been walking along, minding his own business, when she had appeared, grasped his hand, said hello and then disappeared. He had seen her loitering around the place, eating dinner near to him, sitting nearby at the pool.

The woman ignored him, gripping him in one hand and her case in the other as they headed to a driver holding a placard saying 'MR WHITE'. The bracelet she wore on her wrist jangled, annoying him.

'Here, honey,' she said, pointing at Darcy. The driver nodded and took both their cases, walking off towards the exit. 'This is us, let's go. We need to avoid them.'

She pointed a pink-painted talon back towards the arrivals area, and Darcy shuddered.

'Okay, okay, but I'm not Mr White. I'm—'

'I know who you are, Mr Burgess. I'm under orders to take you straight to the office.'

Darcy's heart sank into his designer shoes.

'Oh God, did my bloody father send you?' He clenched his fists in impotent anger. 'Argh! Will he never leave me be!' he demanded, shouting up at the white ceiling of the airport. The woman just ignored him and motioned for him to keep walking. He followed behind her, feeling like a man on his way to a firing squad. Then he remembered. The name on the placard. Mr White. *Oh God.*

'The driver, that sign? Was it really for me?' She nodded, raising a brow as if to say '*of course, dum-dum*'.

The colour drained from his face. She bloody loved *Reservoir Dogs*, and one too many *Godfather* binges had sent the old dragon over the edge.

'Bloody hell,' he exclaimed in his plummy Hugh Grant tones. 'I'm done for, aren't I?'

They had arrived at the waiting car now, and the driver opened the door. He looked inside, half-expecting the gates of Hades to be inside, not the plush leather interior he saw.

'Yep,' she said, bundling him into the back. 'Your mother sent me.'

Chapter 8

'So, you going to call him, or what?' Cassie asked, passing her a coffee and getting into bed next to her. 'Eugh, I hope you changed your sheets!' She wrinkled her nose in pretend disgust.

'Cass, your sheets are that cruddy they'd drag themselves to the washing machine if they could. Of course I changed them. You changed yours?'

Cassie looked embarrassed and Maria nudged her. 'You haven't! Really?'

Cass, housework?

'Yeah, well – they stank of Australian beefcake, so I kind of had no choice. Anyway, we're not talking about me, are we? Did you ring Mark or not?'

'Ring him? I'm trying to forget he exists altogether to be honest. It's never going to go anywhere, and it's probably a fake number anyway. He probably doesn't even remember my name, let alone our night together.'

'Was it worth remembering?' Cassie teased, waggling her eyebrows suggestively. This was rewarded by another jab to the ribs, nearly making her spill her coffee.

'Hey! Your clean sheets, remember! Just ring the number, then you'll know for sure, get a date on the go. You don't have to bloody marry...'

Cass stopped and winced. Maria sank down into the sheets a bit, the weight of the pain in her chest blindsiding her again. A wave of fresh pain. Each time it felt like she'd been hit by a truck, but at least the trucks were getting a bit smaller. More midsized van, less Optimus Prime. It was disbelief she felt now. She still couldn't get her head around the fact that the man she had agreed to marry had turned out to be a cheating bastard who'd left her crying at the altar wearing a stupid pouffy dress while he went on their honeymoon with his girlfriend. Even saying it out loud to herself didn't make it real.

'I'm really sorry, Maria. I didn't mean to say that, really. I'm an ass, you know that. I just want you to stop moping. You're so stressed with the business, it's not good for you. I can help you, lend you some cash, you know that.'

Maria was already shaking her head. 'No way. It was a good business before, it will be again. I can get this going, once things blow over. I just have to get the electrics fixed and get through winter. I can move in above the shop.'

'No way,' Cass retorted. 'You're staying right here. I know what you'll be like on your own, working and stressing 24/7. Besides, I like you being here. Stay with me.'

Maria smiled at her friend. She had to admit, she didn't fancy living on her own. She could foresee too many nights, Bridget Jones-style, listening to sad songs, eating her body weight in cheesecake and getting far too tiddly.

'Okay, but only if you try to keep things a bit tidier. The Australian has set a standard now.'

Cassie blushed and Maria's eyes boggled.

'Oh my God! I know why you changed your sheets! You're seeing him again, aren't you! What was he called, Terence, Tubby?'

'Tucker.' Cassie's cheeks burst into colour. 'His name is Tucker and, yes, he did demand I have lunch with him.'

'Oh my God, you like him!' Maria squealed and Cassie jumped out of bed, running towards her room.

'Nooo, I bloody don't!'

Maria dumped her cup and ran after her in her nightshirt. 'Yes, you do! Cassie and Tucker, sitting in a tree, k-i-s-s—'

'No!' Cassie screeched, trying to slam her bedroom door. Maria body-slammed her and the pair ended up on the floor. Maria tickled Cassie, just like she had when they were kids.

'Tell me, or I won't stop!'

'No, no, gerrroooffff!' Cassie giggled, squirming to get away. Maria tickled harder.

'Okaaayyy! I like him! Satisfied?'

Maria laughed her head off. 'Well, I never! Cass likes a boy!'

Cass lay on the floor, breathing hard. 'I know, I'm doomed. We haven't even slept together since. He says he wants to date.'

Maria lay down next to her, and they both stared at each other.

'I'm sorry you're so sad, Mar. I won't date him if it'll upset you. He'll probably run a mile soon enough anyway.'

'Don't you dare. You're going on that date. I'm okay.'

Cassie said nothing.

'I will be okay. One day. I'm… I'm working on it.'

Cassie scowled. 'I can still arrange for him to disappear, you know. My colleagues defend some pretty shady types. They could rip off his toenails and stick things to his testicles.'

Maria giggled. 'It's okay. I think I just have to realise for myself that I didn't know him. I won't make that mistake again.'

'And Mark?' she asked. Maria thought of the man she had spent the night with. Hardly the best start to a relationship.

'It was a mistake. I needed comfort, and he was there. I'm not proud of it, so soon after Darcy, but it's done now. I don't need to call him.'

Cassie nodded. 'Okay, I'll get rid of his number then, eh?'

'Take it, did you?'

Cassie gave her a 'my bad' look.

'I may have kept it in a safe place in case you needed it.'

Maria laughed. 'Trust you. Bin it. I'm okay on my own for now.'

Cassie put her hand into Maria's, squeezing it gently.

'You'll never be on your own, kid.'

Maria squeezed her back. 'It could be worse,' she quipped. 'I could be a messy bugger about to go on a date with a neat freak with a weird back tattoo.'

Cassie put her arm over her face. 'You haven't seen the one on his arse.'

Cassie's horrified groan had Maria laughing all the way to Happy Ever After, where James was waiting.

***

Lynn was staring wide-eyed, her mouth gaping open. Maria motioned to her from across the room.

'Lynn!' she stage-whispered. 'Stop it!'

Lynn jolted, looking at Maria sheepishly. 'Sorry, I can't help it,' she giggled, pretending to drool.

Maria shook her head at her, and Lynn dipped her head. She went back to scanning the *Westfield Weekly*'s announcements. James was humming to himself in the background, halfway up a ladder in a white vest top and work trousers. He was changing a light in the ceiling and sweating a little. Actually, a lot. The guy had walked in like he was dressed for the Arctic, but now he looked more like Magic Mike. Maria had even found herself wishing for an angle grinder and welding mask to magically appear.

Maria looked at all the births and deaths, scanning for people she knew, and made a few notes on the pad next to her. When local babies were born, she always sent a congratulations card with a discount voucher for her services. It worked well for getting suit orders, dresses for church, even the odd wedding booking.

The funeral notices were few and far between in a close community like this, so that was just to check no one she knew and liked had passed. She sent cards if they'd known her or her mother. Her mother always did it, every week without fail, and Maria had just carried on. The engagement announcements were next. They were the gold. She loved reading about people preparing to spend their lives together. They made a whole feature of it in the paper, complete with photos and backstories. Her mother used to say it was like reading love stories, with the endings yet to be written. She made a note of them all, relieved she didn't know any of them. She would send them all cards, with a business card offering her wedding services. She needed to get at least one booking for wedding season, if only to recoup the cost of the rewiring and keep the business afloat for another season. After that, she had no idea. She felt so stressed when she thought of everything Darcy's actions had cost her. It never failed to make her feel desperate when she thought of him. Lynn was looking over her shoulder at James again.

'Lynn!' she said a little sharply, making her friend jump. 'How about, since you're not busy, you go and get us some breakfast and coffee? James, bacon roll and a coffee?'

James stepped down from his ladder, lifting up his vest top to wipe at his brow. Maria could hear Lynn gasp behind her. He reached into his pocket and pulled out a twenty.

'That'd be great – I haven't had breakfast yet. I'll buy, you ladies get what you like. A bacon roll and a white coffee for me.'

She was just about to decline his kind offer when the door opened. Maria had barely turned to look when Lynn was out of her seat and pointing to the door.

'Oh no, sonny Jim, you can get out.'

Her voice was calm, collected even, but something in it made Maria freeze. She looked at the person in the doorway and blinked. Once. Twice. She resisted the urge to rub her eyes. For a beat, no one said anything. Maria turned to face him, James just next to her.

'You heard her, I'm busy.'

Darcy was dressed in one of his best casual outfits. He was tanned and looked good. Rested, aside from a slight darkening around the eyes. Probably from late nights playing honeymoon with her stand-in. He had on a pair of designer dark blue jeans, a pair of smart brogues and a cream sweater. He had had his hair cut, a little shorter than usual. Obviously not that heartbroken then. *He hasn't suffered at all, Maria. Make him leave.*

'You need to leave, now.'

Lynn stepped forward, making a shooing movement with her hands as though he was a stray cat that had wandered in. It made Maria think of the town goose they had been menaced by before he eventually found a mate. The little bugger had terrorised the shops and businesses for weeks, looking for a female. There had even been regular headlines about him in the local paper. She wondered who was watching this exchange now, and what they would say. *The business was barely hanging on. Was he here to end it completely?*

Darcy stepped forward, sidestepping Lynn and holding his hands out to her, palms down as if he was trying to get her to stay still.

It was then she found her anger. Lynn was moving towards him, and Maria turned to her.

'Lynn, you go and get breakfast, please.' She took the money from James's hand, giving him a quick nod of thanks. He was turned to Darcy though, a questioning frown on his face. The poor guy, he really was having the worst time ever working here.

'But—' Lynn tried, but Maria cut her off.

'Please Lynn,' she said, holding out the money. Lynn nodded, and came and took it, squeezing her hand as she did so. She glared at Darcy on her way out, and Darcy dipped his head.

'Why have you got your hands out like that? Scared I'll run or something?' She spat the words out, crossing her arms to stop him from seeing her shaking hands. She felt sick, shaky. He needed to leave, now.

57

'Can we talk?' he asked, one of his sickly-sweet smiles plastered across his chops. 'In private.'

He looked over her shoulder at James, and Maria realised he was still standing there, right by her side. She could have hugged him for not going back to work. She was pretty sure she was going to pass out, so at least she had him to catch her. A concussion wasn't going to improve her week.

'No, we can't. *You* can *leave*,' she boomed, jabbing a shaking finger at him before thrusting it back under her side. 'Now. You have nearly closed me down already. I don't want you anywhere near my shop.'

'What?' he said, looking crestfallen. He looked at James again. 'Listen, sir, we have business to discuss. Could you please leave?'

Maria clenched her jaw. He was still as polite as ever, thinking he could command people like he always did. She looked at James, and he was looking down at her. She pleaded with him with her eyes to stay. He nodded, just once, a barely there movement, and Maria let out the breath she was holding. James looked across at Darcy and, taking a step forward, put his arm around Maria. Maria sank into his warmth.

'I don't think Maria has anything to say to you, and she has asked you to leave.'

Darcy snorted. 'Really?'

'Really,' James said, pulling Maria in closer to his side. She felt his arm slide down hers, his fingers caress her own, and his hand wrap around hers. She held it tight, and James gave her a reassuring squeeze. 'Now leave, or we'll have a problem. I don't think you want that.'

Darcy stood open-mouthed for a moment, looking from one to the other, before composing himself. He nodded slowly, looking straight at Maria.

'Listen, I'll call you. Tonight. I know you're upset, but I can explain. I know we can sort this out. I'm not with anyone, the same as you aren't.' He glowered at James as he said it, but James didn't flinch. Darcy moved to the door. 'I love you, Maria.'

He left then, and James and Maria stood staring at the door, watching him getting into his car and driving away. Neither of them moved at first, watching till the car drove out of sight.

'I'm so sorry…'

James turned her and pulled her in for a hug. She froze for a second before wrapping her arms around his back and returning his embrace.

'Are you okay?' he asked, speaking into her hair.

'I'm fine,' she said into his chest, catching a whiff of his aftershave. He smelt nice. Comforting. *Getting awkward now, Mar. This is the electrician, remember?* She pulled away, but he didn't let her go completely, putting his hands around her face.

'Are you sure? You look really pale.' He was looking her up and down, his face a picture of concern. She pulled away, clearing her throat nervously. The poor bloke. He was only here to fix her electrics, and he'd been dragged into all this. 'Do you want me to call someone?'

Lynn bounded through the door then, a bag of food and tray of takeaway coffees in hand. She looked around the shop, putting the stuff on her desk. She looked at the pair of them, looking awkwardly back at her.

'He left? Are you okay?'

Maria felt both sets of eyes on her so she headed to the bag on the desk, pulling out the sandwiches.

'Food's ready,' she trilled as best she could. 'Let's eat. It's done now, and we all have work to do.'

Lynn nodded slowly and took a seat at her desk, taking a sandwich from Maria. James came and got his food, and Maria motioned for him to sit in the spare chair near her workstation. All three of them sat eating in companionable silence. She knew James was looking at her with concern, and Lynn was pretending to read a magazine at her desk as she ate.

She ripped into her own sandwich, her anger and adrenaline fuelling her sudden hunger. She swallowed a mouthful of delicious bacon and bread.

'Thank you, James,' she said softly. 'Thank you both for being there. He won't come here again.'

'Are you sure?' James asked, a look of doubt on his face, along with a blob of brown sauce. Maria chuckled and passed him a tissue from the box on her desk. 'He sounded pretty determined. He an ex?'

Maria nodded. 'Yep, he's my ex. I will make it clear he's not welcome.'

James nodded, wiping his mouth. 'What did you mean about the business? Are you struggling because of him?'

Lynn made a 'humpf' sound and covered it unsuccessfully with a delicate fake cough. 'Yes, in a way, and he needs to leave well enough alone now. Next time he comes, I shall get my sweeping brush.'

James looked at Maria, eyebrows raised in mock terror, making her giggle again.

'I take it this is a recent break-up?' James asked. 'My sister is going through one at the minute. I don't envy you, but for what it's worth, you're doing well.'

Maria smiled at him. 'Thanks. It's a lie, but thanks. I appreciate it. I just want to concentrate on work now and get through to the wedding season. If I can get any bookings.'

James nodded. 'Okay, well I'd better get back to work then, get this shop up and running. If you need any help though, if he shows up, let me know.' He threw his sandwich wrapper into the bin and wiped his hands.

'Thanks.'

She looked across at Lynn, and she was leaning on her hands open-mouthed at James as he walked into the back. As he passed Maria, he put his hand on her shoulder and gave her a reassuring pat and a squeeze. Lynn nearly burst into flames in her chair.

'Isn't he lovely,' she breathed. 'Did Darcy see him?'

Maria put her finger to her lips and walked over to Lynn.

'Yes, he saw him all right. It was weird actually, he kind of held my hand.'

'He did what!' Lynn shouted. 'What a total ba—'

'Not Darcy!' Maria whispered, shutting her up. 'James. He helped me, told him to leave.'

Lynn put her hand over her heart, smiling like a loon. 'That's wonderful. Oh, I wish I'd seen his face.'

Maria didn't answer, just sank to the floor, replaying the look on Darcy's face. He'd said he still loved her. He'd even made a dig about knowing she wasn't with James. He'd said something about being single too.

'What do you think he wanted?' she asked Lynn. 'Why come here? Why would he want to talk?'

Lynn shook her head, her expression pulled into a sad montage of itself. 'I really don't know, my darling. Really, I don't, but you can't let him in. You're doing so well. I don't want you to go backwards. Your mother would be proud. She'd give him a good smack too.'

Maria nodded, smiling at the thought. She was holding it together, just. If you didn't count the drunken one-night stand, or the drawer full of unsent letters to Darcy at Cassie's cottage. Or the zillions of scenarios she had run through in her head, reasons why Darcy had left her at the altar. She had considered everything from alien abduction to his being the next James Bond. None of which explained why he'd been on holiday with another woman, though. Or why he'd just shown up here. The only thing that added up was that Darcy was a snivelling coward. Either way, her heart was broken. She wasn't about to let him run over the tiny pieces that were scattered on the floor. Not again.

That night, as she lay in bed, having enjoyed an early bath and book while Cassie was working late, she heard her phone ring at the side of her bed. Sticking her hand out of her blanket fort, she saw his number come up on her display. She had already had Cassie delete it and every trace of him from her phone. It was odd seeing his digits flash across the screen. So different from when he was stored as hubby-to-be. She ended the call, opening the text screen and tapping out a quick message before he tried to ring again.

Don't call me again. I am not interested in anything you have to say. Stay away from me.

She read the text back to herself, feeling the sting of her own words. She hit send and slammed the phone back on the nightstand. It buzzed back immediately, and started to ring again. Reaching out, she held down the off button and shoved it into her drawer. It landed in among all the unsent hurt and venom and anger in her written notes. She turned over and cried herself to sleep.

Chapter 9

For the next two weeks, Darcy rang the shop every day, and every day Lynn hung up on him. He even showed up again one day, but James was outside installing a new doorway light and he turned the car around and left. Lynn said that if James had stared any harder, he would have seared the paint off Darcy's car, such was the Superman-style laser beam being emitted from his eyes. James had blushed and said he hadn't really got a look at the driver. Maria once again found herself grateful that her shop had the electrics of the Harry Potter Wand Shop. The job was nearly done now, but James had stayed on to finish the plastering, and Maria found she was glad of the company too. He was funny, and he made Lynn act like an awkward teenager, which was hilarious in itself. Cassie had even met him, having come to the shop at the weekend to look for a dress for her next date with Tucker. The woman could afford designer labels, but Maria appreciated her friend giving her some sorely needed business.

She was hanging on by a thread. She had been able to pay James and keep the shop afloat, but with the papers in overdrive about Darcy and his mystery woman, she just knew no wedding bookings were coming her way anytime soon. It was a miracle that the press had stayed away from her shop. Perhaps Agatha, matriarch of the village, had more clout than even the villagers gave her credit for. She ran Westfield like her own kingdom, and Maria was pretty sure she'd pulled up the drawbridge around her villagers. Hopefully it would last. They hadn't completely left her alone, though. The shop phone had been busy with nosy reporters, all despatched with a flea in their ear, and Maria had shut down all her social media, turning off the comments section of her website to avoid her business being deluged. Lynn was dealing with the shop's email, and since she hadn't passed any orders her way, she was pretty sure the shop was as dead as ever. Her inbox was no doubt filled with nosy reporters and supposed best friends wanting to check on her, or feed on her misery to make themselves feel better about their own situations. She would be the name on their lips when they uttered the words 'at least it's not as bad as…'

Once again it was Saturday, supposedly one of the busiest days of the week, and she was sitting in an empty shop, head in her hands. The shop phone and her mobile had been ringing every half hour since seven that morning, all the calls being from Darcy's mobile number. The man was insane. The irony of the fact that when they'd been together she could barely get hold of him wasn't lost on her either, and made every time he called feel like another knife in her heart.

The doorbell went and Maria looked up through her fingers in terror. James was standing there, toolbox in hand, and she sighed with relief. He went to open the door, and Maria ran to unlock it.

'You okay?' he asked as she practically dragged him into the shop and slammed the door shut behind him.

'I'm fine,' she said, clicking the lock back into place and rolling her eyes. 'Why does everyone keep asking me that? Cassie was the same this morning. I'm fine! I just didn't sleep well, and since every lowlife journalist seems to want to talk to me every minute of every day, I don't think I'll be sleeping any time soon.'

James stood staring at her, his face creased with concern. 'I mean it, you look really pale. You've lost weight too.'

Maria's jaw dropped. 'Since when is that a bad thing? I needed to lose a bit anyway. Since... well... since the thing, I've been spending too much time eating ice cream. I'm fine, I told you.'

He held his hands up in surrender. 'Okay, but you don't look well at all. I really think you need to go to the doctor's.'

She glared at him, and he raised his eyebrows at her, clenching his jaw.

'I mean it. It's not my business, but I consider you a friend now. You have to take care of yourself.'

Maria wanted to be mad, to tell him off, but she couldn't bring herself to be that way with him. The truth was, it was nice to have a friend. He had been there for her, and she had to at least admit to herself a little that it was nice to have people in her corner. She had been so used to it being her, Mum, Cassie and Lynn growing up. Losing Darcy had made her realise just how alone she was.

She reached up and chucked him under the chin with a loose fist.

'You are *the* most annoying friend on the planet, you know that?'

He snorted. 'I've met Cassie, so I highly doubt that.'

The shop phone rang, and Maria froze. James held up a finger and picked up the shop phone.

'Good morning, Happy Ever After?'

Maria sat down heavily at her desk. She really did feel sick. She hadn't even eaten that morning but she felt like she could vomit. She'd gone to make a coffee at Cassie's but the smell had turned her stomach. Which was odd, since Cassie's normally disgusting kitchen was now looking like a set design from IKEA. In case Tucker came around, she guessed, even though Cassie hadn't brought him home since. What was going on there was anyone's guess. Cassie was acting weird, though.

'No, she's not here.' James's tone had changed, and Maria mouthed 'who is it?' at him. He held up a finger and turned away from her. 'For you? Never. It doesn't matter who I am. All you need to know is she doesn't want you. Stop calling.'

Maria stood to get his attention but he moved further into the back of the shop. There was a sudden hammering at the door, and when she turned around a flashbulb went off in her face.

'What the he—'

Photographers were standing in front of the door to the shop, snapping away, tapping at the glass. So much for the Agatha bubble. It looked like it had just popped.

'Maria, Maria!' they were shouting through the glass. 'Do you have any comment about the rumours of Darcy Burgess getting engaged? Maria, talk to us!'

The cameras snapped again, a Mexican wave of light flashing across the windows. James was shouting down the phone, and Maria ran past him into the back office.

She slumped down to the floor, listening to James shouting at the photographers now to go away, threatening to call the police. She could still hear a voice shouting down the phone line, a tinny noise, like a bumble bee. Her stomach roiled and she got up and ran to the sink, heaving up the small glass of water she'd managed when she got up that morning. Her face felt like it was on fire, and she ran a washcloth over her face to cool herself down.

Engaged. He's engaged, already. She leant over the sink, suddenly wishing she had eaten something that morning.

'Are you okay?' James said, suddenly behind her.

She looked up at him and her head swam. 'No.' She started to cry, and fell to the floor. The banging still kept on. It sounded like they were going to come through the glass. James stooped to help her up, and she collapsed into his arms.

'Whoa, I got you, Maria.' He took her into his arms, pulling her tight to him. 'Put your arms around me, we need to get to the hospital. You don't look good.'

Maria tried to object, but her whole body felt like it was shaking violently. James strode to the back door and began fumbling with the key.

'James,' she said feebly, and he stopped to look at her, his eyes clouded with concern. 'Why is he doing this?'

She never heard his answer or felt him carry her out of the back of the shop. She had already passed out and couldn't hear anyone. Sweet oblivion met her, and she welcomed it.

Cassie was mumbling angrily, and Maria winced at the pain it produced in her head.

'Cass,' she murmured. 'Sshh.' The noise continued. It sounded like she was arguing with the telly again. Probably shouting at one of the actors on that soap she denied watching religiously.

Maria went to cover her ears, but something pulled on her arm, giving her a sharp pain.

'Darling, don't try to move, okay?'

The voice was silky, familiar. *Mum? No, of course not.* She felt the jolt of recognition and loss all at once.

'Lynn?' she croaked, peeling her eyes open. Lynn was sitting in front of her, smiling. She looked tired, drawn. 'What's wrong? Are you okay?' She tried to get up, but her head whirled again, making her dizzy.

'I'm fine, sit back in bed.' She settled Maria back down, tucking the covers around her gently. It was then that Maria clocked the fact that she was lying in a hospital bed, and Cassie was still shouting in hushed tones outside the door.

'What happened?' Maria asked. 'Where are we? Did they get in?'

Lynn shook her head. 'No, dear, you passed out, and James brought you straight here. To the hospital. He called me and Cass from your phone.'

She looked around the side room she appeared to be in, but there was no sign of James.

'Why is he arguing with Cassie? Tell them to stop fighting. Why are they fighting?'

Lynn frowned. 'He isn't, honey. He went back to the shop to cover for us, get rid of the stragglers. He's going to call in later on.'

'So who?'

Lynn didn't get a chance to answer, because the door banged open and Darcy barrelled through with Cassie on his back, punching him in the arms.

'I said get out, dipshit! Don't make me sue your ass!'

Darcy was hunched down like a turtle, trying to escape the blows and shrug her off. They were both still screaming at each other when the doctor walked in. He took one look at the scene and ordered them both to wait outside.

Lynn was furious by now and, patting Maria, she stomped off to sort out the 'quarrelling children'. Maria flashed the doctor an apologetic grin and sank back against the pillows.

'Sorry, Doctor, we have a bit of a situation.'

He nodded kindly. 'We've sent the reporters away; security are dealing with them. Mr Burgess and your friends can stay, if they behave. I just wanted to see how you were feeling. You gave us a bit of a scare, Miss Mallory. You'll have to stay in for the weekend, and we've put you on a drip for fluids. You need to eat something too; your recent weight loss has apparently been caused by stress, and you're a little dehydrated. Your blood sugar was very low, and we discovered you're anaemic too.'

Maria nodded along. She did feel rough, so it wasn't a surprise.

The door opened and then slammed shut again, and Maria could hear muted voices from behind it. It sounded like Lynn was playing bouncer. Maria sighed heavily, wishing she was still unconscious and not getting told off for being stressed while her life imploded around her.

'Of course, we can start you on vitamins and iron tablets, and you'll need to ring your doctor's surgery next week. This is a wake-up call, to take better care of yourself.'

She nodded along numbly. It was time to start looking after

herself. Lynn wouldn't let her do any different anyway, especially after this. The door banged again, and she heard Lynn shout 'no!' as though she was telling off a stubborn toddler. Which, in Darcy's case, wasn't far from the truth.

The doctor stepped in front of the door, closer to her field of vision.

'Maria,' he said. 'I need you to listen. I have to tell you that you're pregnant.'

There was another commotion at the door, and Maria stared at the doctor. The voices started shouting again outside, and they could hear other voices joining in now. The door was shuddering with the effect of being pushed and pulled. The doctor's beeper went off and he looked positively relieved.

'I have to go now,' he said with a look of such fake disappointment that Maria wanted to laugh hysterically. 'I'll come back later, after visiting hours, so we can discuss it better.' He motioned to the door. 'It will be quieter then. I'm sorry to drop all this information on you and run. You need to be aware, though, that with your current exhaustion, lack of eating and stress, your body won't be able to cope with the demands of pregnancy. You have to put things aside, if you can, and focus on your own wellbeing.'

Maria nodded at him dumbly, trying to process what he'd said. He had obviously got it wrong, the poor man. She knew they knocked the NHS these days, but he was obviously so overworked and stressed by the baggage she had brought with her that he had got it all turned around. He went to open the door, peering cautiously around it.

'Doctor?' she asked. She just wanted to explain to him, as kindly as she could, his error. 'You know my name is Maria, right? Maria Mallory? I came in today, a tall man brought me in? Probably wearing a tool belt?'

He smiled at her. 'I know who you are, Maria, and my diagnosis is correct. You had listed the lady outside, Lynn, as your next of kin, and we gained permission to do a blood workup. I'll be back later to discuss your options. The important thing now is to rest, let the fluids do their job.'

He slipped through the door then, and Maria was left alone. She shook her head. Dear Lord, that dude was going to be red-faced later. Granted, her life was a mess, but the worst thing she did was faint, not misdiagnose pregnancies. She turned on her side, away from the door, away from the noise, and closed her eyes. She just needed to sleep, and then she could go home and get back to work. Once the hospital realised their error, they would let her go. They would probably discharge her immediately, to avoid looking like idiots.

'Pregnant,' she said out loud. 'As if.'

Cassie came in, shouting 'bugger off, Burgess!' as she put a chair behind the door handle. The voices outside subsided. Maria faced away again, not wanting to talk. Cassie pulled a chair up to the bed and looked at her wide-eyed.

'What the hell happened? I had a garbled call from the hand-yman guy, telling me you were here. Did you not eat all day? I told you to take better care of yourself. You can't let *him* win.'

She jabbed in the direction of the door with her finger.

'I told him to leave, but he's refusing. He keeps saying he's going to talk to the press if we make him leave, make a scene. He wants to talk to you. He says he didn't say anything to the press yet, so that's a blessing.'

Maria shook her head, and Cassie patted her arm.

'Don't worry, I told him to drop dead. I'm just waiting for karma to strike him down, the big ponce.'

'Don't let him talk to the doctor, for God's sake. He thinks I'm pregnant.'

Cassie's jaw dropped. 'He what? He never said!'

'Not him, the doctor. What a joke, eh? I nearly told him, you have to have sex to get pregnant. Darcy and I didn't... before. I thought it was just us being busy, but obviously now I know different. Cold feet, icicle penis.'

70

Cassie shook her head. 'This is not a joke, Mar. You're pregnant? Really?'

'No, you're not listening! Darcy and I didn't have sex!'

'No,' Cassie said, moving in closer and flicking her gaze at the door. 'You and Darcy didn't, but you did have sex, remember?'

Maria had a flashback of a man, a tequila shot, a nightclub kiss. *Oh God. Mark.*

'Oh no,' she gabbled. 'Oh God, no.'

Cassie went to the door and pulled the chair away. Lynn was standing there, holding a bottle of orange squash.

'He's gone. The doctor threatened to call security. Is she okay?' she asked, bustling in. Maria started to cry then, and Lynn ran to her side.

'Oh baby, what's the matter? What did the doctor say?'

Cassie opened the window a crack and pulled the curtains open.

'It's okay, we can sort it. Don't worry. We'll all help. We're all here.'

Lynn started to cry too then. 'Please, honey, tell me what's wrong. Is it what your mum had? Is it—'

'I'm pregnant!' Maria blurted out. As soon as the words left her mouth, she knew it was true. She had been feeling really tired lately, and emotional. Which was what a jilted bride was, but also a pregnant person. She was late with her period, and in the chaos she hadn't even realised, so maybe the doctor wasn't as puddled as she'd first thought. 'The doctor just told me.'

Lynn's face lit up. 'Pregnant! Well, that's wonderful!' She looked at Maria's pale face. 'Isn't it?'

Cassie was scrolling through her phone, and she slapped Lynn on the arm.

'Good? Are you high? How is this good? She's having a baby!'

'I'm having a baby. OhmigodohmigodohmigodCassIcan'thav eababy!'

Cassie was pacing up and down, scrolling, scrolling.

'It's fine, we can do it. Don't worry, we just have to get you out of here, before the press get wind of the pregnancy.'

There was a knock at the door and a nurse popped her head round.

'Sorry, everyone, but visiting time is over for today, and the doctor has issued strict orders to keep the patient on bed rest till Monday.'

Cassie and Lynn looked at each other, nodding, and gave Maria a kiss.

'Don't worry, Mar, we'll sort this out. For now just rest, and don't speak to anyone, okay?' Cass said, her training kicking in.

Lynn squeezed her hand. 'We're all here for you, Maria darling, don't forget that. No matter what, you are not alone. Never alone.' Her eyes were bright with unshed tears, and Maria resisted the urge to burst into tears again herself.

They both left, and Maria could hear Cassie demanding that security keep Darcy and any photographers away. By the way she spoke, threatening legal action and using big legal words, and the way security simpered back at her, Maria guessed the rest of her stay would be somewhat quieter.

She looked around her room, taking in the stark surroundings. She missed her shop. She longed to be back there, where she felt some semblance of control. Where she could lose herself in her work, chat to the villagers, go back to normal. Pre-Darcy. Have a coffee with James, who was fast becoming one of her favourite people. The poor guy. She felt odd at the thought of him finding out she was pregnant. Like it would change them somehow. She couldn't bear that. The list of people she cared about was short, obviously, but still… God knew what he would think of her now. The man would probably run a mile rather than take another job from her.

Which was fine, because she was getting pretty used to the men in her life leaving. She lay on her back, looking up at the ceiling. The peace of the hospital had finally descended, the odd shuffle and bleep outside the closed door as people milled around.

She laid a hand on her stomach, trying to picture the baby that was apparently residing in there. A baby conceived in tequila. The poor thing was probably pickled. It would probably come out like George Best, clutching a bottle to its breast and asking where its father was. Which was a whole other problem. She thought of Lynn and her excitement. If she didn't keep the baby, what would happen then? Cassie would understand, but Lynn? Perhaps not. Thinking about Lynn's goodbye, something clicked. *You are not alone.*

It was true. What had this baby done, to warrant being evicted from its home? Fair enough, perhaps its conception was a rather shady story, to be airbrushed into a rose-tinted version later, but who was born in perfect circumstances? Out there in the world, there were many walking, talking products of too much drink, a sad event, a moment of passionate abandon, a weakening of rubber. Did that mean they meant any less, that they weren't as worthy as those born into love, heralded by perfect planning? It was 2018, for Christ's sake. There were sex robots. Actual sex robots. Not to mention bacon jam. Orange people in power, like the revenge of the Oompa Loompas. Another single mother wouldn't break society. She thought of her own mother, who had raised her single-handed after her father's death. Did they struggle sometimes? Yes, sure. The struggles she didn't remember so much, though; what she remembered was the love. She'd never felt truly alone till her mother died, and what Lynn said was true: with this baby, she would never be alone again. And really, what was she waiting for? She was single, with no prospects on the horizon or inclination to date again. Her business was struggling, but she was still fighting. Maybe she could do it. The thought of not doing this was just not for her. She was pro-choice, and this was her, making her choice.

She rubbed her hand in small circles along her flat stomach.

'I'm here, baby. It's not perfect, but we're together. We'll work it out. Just you and me.'

73

She thought of her mother, looking down on her in approval. She would say, 'You can do this, my girl.' And she would. They would see. She just had to get rid of Darcy before he found out. National coverage of the contents of her uterus was the last thing she needed. She didn't even know why he was sniffing around again. Hadn't he got a floozy to bed? Sunburn to soothe? He could just jog on. The last person she needed to see was him. She didn't want to have to explain herself to him. He would judge her, and she was the injured party here. Getting knocked up on a boozy night out wasn't the brightest move, but she didn't need to be told that by the lowlife who had deemed it acceptable to leave her at the altar in front of their friends and family, and hotfoot it away on their honeymoon, which she had paid for, with another woman. And tank her business in the process, which, let's face it, dealt in happy endings and eternal love. People never wanted to hear about jiltings and broken dreams; it didn't go down well with the cake tastings and flower arrangements.

But now, maybe it hadn't all been for nothing. Maybe this colossal nightmare of the last few weeks had been meant to happen. Maybe this was the plan from the big man upstairs. She looked up at the ceiling, resting both hands on her tummy as she went to sleep. Maybe this was just what she needed to pull herself out of her funk.

Hope.

Chapter 10

Cassie had eventually dropped a very emotionally overwrought Lynn off at home and was just pulling up to the cottage when the headlights highlighted the outline of a shadowy figure, near to her front door. Her heart thumped in her chest as she pulled up, instinctively flicking the interior locks closed on her car. *It can't be Darcy, he doesn't know where I live. He's never been here.* The thought of Darcy was in fact preferable to who else might be there, lurking. Through her job, she often encountered some disgruntled husbands who didn't take kindly to paying their ex-wives what they deserved, or to having their own fancy legal teams defeated by a young single woman. Things were out there on the net; people had a way of tracking people down. Would Darcy have the balls to come here? She revved the engine once, as a warning. *Come close, shadow in the darkness, and I shall run you over with my car.*

A figure shifted in the night, coming out from behind the large bush in the garden. Cassie reached into the side-door pocket for her car tool, an all-in-one thing she had bought once after reading about being trapped underwater in a car. She pulled it out and grasped it in her hand, feeling for the weight of it. It had a metal spike at the end, a small, stubby one, meant to smash a window, but she felt sure it could do some damage if she needed it to. She killed the engine, leaving the lights on, and drew a shaky breath.

TAP TAP TAP.

'Arrghhh!' she screamed as she saw a figure outside her car window. She grabbed the door handle and shoved the door open with all her might. 'You're not taking me down! Arggghh!'

She dived out from the car, grabbing her keys and bag and running for the front door, jumping over the writhing lump she had laid out with her door.

She had almost got to the door, keys shaking in her hands, when she heard a muffled voice from behind her.

'Cassie, it's me, Tucker.' He sounded winded, far away. She dumped her bag near the front door and turned.

'Tucker?' He stood up from the grass, looking like he was struggling to remain upright.

'Yep… it's me. Obviously that was my fault for surprising you. Lesson learned. We had a date, and when you didn't show at the restaurant… I guess I thought something might be wrong. Are you okay?'

She ran over to him, helping him to the front door.

'I'm so sorry, I totally forgot about our date. I thought you were some kind of crazy stalker. What were you doing in the bushes?'

'I wasn't in the bushes, I was standing near them. It's bladdy cold out here. I feel stupid now, obviously.'

She let him in and ran back to sort her car out and grab her things. Luckily, she had a good bit of peace and quiet here, so there weren't any concerned neighbours ringing the police or twitching the curtains. When she went back into the cottage, she looked at Tucker, who was slumped on one of her sofas, and gasped. His T-shirt was torn, and he had a deep cut on his forehead that was dripping blood onto his shirt and smart trousers, and her couch.

'Jesus, Tucker, we need to get you to the hospital.' Tucker turned to look at her, wincing at the movement.

'Okay,' he said, shallow breaths making his words come out short, stunted. 'I think that would be for the best. I feel like I just wet myself.'

***

Sitting in A&E, Tucker looked white. Deathly pale, if she were to allocate a shade to it. He hadn't said much in the car, and she had been too mortified and guilty to try to attempt conversation herself. So they had driven in silence, aside from the odd grunt of pain from him. She had wrapped some ice in a tea towel, and Tucker was now holding it to his head wound to try and stem the staunch of blood.

Cassie gave him a reassuring pat and headed to the reception desk.

'Er, hi,' she said through the glass to an eager-looking receptionist.

'Hi,' she said, smiling. She looked like Rosie O'Donnell, but on happy pills. 'Booking someone in?'

'Yes,' she said, pointing to a very white-looking Tucker. 'My er… friend… Tucker, he needs help. He has a nasty cut on his forehead, and I think he might have a cracked rib or two.'

The woman nodded, tapping away on the keyboard in front of her. 'Okay, address? Age? Date of birth?'

'Erm, have you not got a form we can fill in?'

The woman looked up at her. 'First date?'

Cassie's mouth dropped. 'Sort of. I actually stood him up.'

The receptionist looked over Cassie's shoulder. 'Point him out to me again?'

Cassie pointed at Tucker, who raised his hand weakly and gave them both a little finger wave.

'And what happened?' she asked. Cassie looked at a small fingermark on the glass screen in front of her.

'He got hit with a car door.'

'A car door?' Another tapping of the keys. 'Did he get run over?'

'No, the car was stationary at the time.'

'Did you notify the police?' Tapping.

'Er, no, not yet. We'll see how the night goes first. Listen, he might have internal bleeding, so if we can hurry this along…'

'No problem, you can give his details once you get seen. It shan't be long now. Are you staying with him, to take him home, or do we need to call someone?'

Cassie shook her head. 'No, I'll stay.'

The receptionist nodded. 'No problem.'

Cassie started to walk back to Tucker.

'For the record, next time a man like that wants to take you out on a date, it's probably better just to show up, not hit him with an automobile, you get me?'

Cassie turned to look at her and the receptionist winked. 'We see all sorts here, my dear. Let's hope it's something funny to tell the grandkids, not a parole officer.'

Cassie could hear her chuckling as she walked back to Tucker.

He still looked pale, green even, but he flashed her a gorgeous smile as he gingerly turned his bottom towards her on the seat. He moved one of his hands away from holding his torso to wrap his fingers around hers as they rested on her lap. She flinched but didn't move her hand.

'I am so sorry, I really didn't mean to.'

'It's fine,' he said, or rather whispered through gritted teeth due to the pain. 'I was just worried about you. Is someone after you? Are you in trouble?'

Cassie shook her head. 'No, sorry to have worried you. First of all I thought you were Maria's ex.'

'The lowlife jilter?' he checked. She nodded, loving him for not only remembering but taking her friend's side.

'Yep, and then I thought you might be a client's ex.'

78

His eyes widened slightly. 'I'm a divorce solicitor,' she explained. 'Some men are not happy with what I get for their ex-wives.'

Tucker was rubbing her hand supportively, and she had never felt so awkward. What were they doing here, like this? Were they a couple? A drunken fumble and a couple of dates didn't amount to much, but he seemed so relaxed in her company.

'So, did you mean to stand me up then? Should I take a hint?' He tried to laugh, but abruptly stopped and winced at the obvious pain he was in.

'Oh God, I'll go and chase them up.' She dashed off to reception, but the receptionist looked at her apologetically as she spoke on the phone. She opened up a low partition in the screen and passed out a clipboard with a form on it, and a pen. Reluctantly, Cassie took it and returned to her seat.

Tucker was sitting back in his chair, watching her walk over to him. Even with a tea towel wrapped around his head, he was pretty hot.

'Mr Tucker?' a nurse called from down the corridor.

'We're on,' he said and went to stand – went to, but didn't succeed. What he did instead was groan and moan in pain. And squat, halfway between standing and sitting. He looked sheepishly at Cassie.

'I might need a little help, then you can go if you like.'

Cassie looked at the doors to A&E, where her car sat waiting in the car park. If she left now, after seeing him in of course, that would be that. He probably wouldn't press charges against her for the whole car episode, and he certainly wouldn't bother her again. She looked at him, and then at the doors once more, before deciding. She strode straight past him, into the foyer. Right to the main doors, where a line of wheelchairs she remembered seeing were stationed. Grabbing one, she headed back into reception, where Tucker was trying to commando roll his way out of the chair, and the nurse was still shouting his name.

'Here, we're coming!' she shouted across to her, and stopping the chair in front of Tucker, she helped him into it. He looked surprised to see her but said nothing. She put her hand on his shoulder before wheeling him across the room, and he kissed it between his.

'I'll stay,' she said softly.

'Ya will?' he said, smiling through a split lip.

'You're peeing blood. It's the least I can do.'

He chuckled all the way down the corridor, wincing every time.

Maria woke up to the sound of humming. It sounded like a low hum, deep and full of bass. Can't be Lynn, she thought, in her half-asleep state. Darcy?

She opened her eyes and was relieved to see James. He was reading a book, some political thriller she had seen advertised, and humming away to himself.

'How did you get in here?' she croaked, making him jump. He closed the book and leaned closer.

'Sorry, do you want me to go? I just wanted to check on you.'

'No,' she croaked again, her mouth dry. She looked at her watch. 7.30 a.m. 'How come security let you in?'

He stood up and filled a beaker with water from a jug on the bedside table. She pulled a straw out of a small box nearby (Lynn thought of everything) and put it to her lips. She drank greedily and nodded when she had had enough. She was slumped on her side and tried to sit up.

'Oh, hey, hey, hey, let me help.' He put the cup down quickly on the overbed table and went to her side. She caught a whiff of his aftershave as he leaned in close, putting his strong arm under her and helping her to sit up.

'Better?' he asked, plumping up her pillows.

'Yes, much,' she nodded, suddenly feeling both grateful he was there and mortified that she was feeling a bit crusty, lying in bed with a nightie Lynn had brought in (frilly), scratchy big pants (think M&S kidney warmers) and a hairdo that looked a lot like something could nest in it quite happily.

'I'm a mess,' she said, trying to brush some stray tendrils back. They were starting to feel like dreadlocks.

'You look lovely,' he said, brushing her off. 'Do you want me to go?'

'No,' she said a little too quickly. 'I'm glad you're here.'

'Security have been told by the nurses to let me in; they apparently think I'm your new partner.'

Maria sank down into the pillows. 'Oh God, so not only did I pass out and have to be taken to hospital in front of the cameras, but now I'm apparently a slut as well.'

James shook his head, a deep frown furrowing his brow. 'No one thinks that, and if they said anything remotely like that, they would answer to me.' His jaw clenched. 'They know that Darcy bloke is your ex. Cassie filled them in and told them in no uncertain terms to keep him away, unless they wanted a lawsuit that would make their grandchildren's eyes water.'

Maria took his hand in hers, trying not to cry. Damn hormones. 'Thanks so much, James, for helping me.'

He opened his mouth to speak and was staring deep into her eyes when a nurse breezed in, holding a bedpan.

'Aw, you two are so cute together. You feeling better, honey?'

The pair looked sheepishly at each other, but then James winked, making Maria laugh.

'I'm much better, thanks.'

'Good,' she said, coming to the bed and thrusting the disposable bedpan at her.

'Sorry, love, but we need a urine sample. Check you and the baby are tip-top before we discharge you, okay? Does Daddy want to wait outside?'

Maria saw James's face change from happy-go-lucky to absolute shock in about two and a half seconds. She wanted to open her mouth, to explain, to the nurse, to him, but she was in shock herself. What could she say? Actually, this isn't the father, and the man stalking the wards isn't either? She was still digesting it when she felt James's lips on her cheek.

'I'll wait outside, darling. Just give me a shout when you're done.' She went to look at him, to suss out what he was thinking, but he was already out the door. The nurse continued with her business, pulling the covers back and making Maria feel even more undignified as she flashed her big pants during the walk to the toilet. She put the cardboard bedpan into the toilet seat and sat down to fill it.

At this point, another form of slight humiliation was just par for the course. She wondered when it was that her life had turned into a soap opera. When did life in the village get so complicated? Most of all, she wondered whether or not she should actually call the real father, or just raise the baby to think he/she had been magically conceived, by angel dust, or even sperm to your door. They did that now. That was modern life for you. If you had the money, you could order the sperm to be delivered to your door, to make the baby yourself. Like pizza delivery, but you didn't get it free if the sperm courier didn't deliver in thirty minutes or less. Or maybe you did, since temperature was as important to sperm as it was to pizza.

As she walked out of the toilet, bedpan of pee in hand, she wondered when her life had become so messed up. The nurse smiled and took it.

'I'll let you get back to your man now,' she beamed. 'Leave him out on that corridor for too long and you might just lose him to one of the staff.'

Maria laughed along with her. *Little do you know*, she thought to herself. *When you get out onto that corridor, you'll see the scorch marks where yet another man ran for his life to avoid me. And I'm not even with him!*

The nurse covered the pan with a disposable towel and walked out. Maria was just settling into her bed when she felt a presence behind her.

82

'Are you okay?' James asked, watching her cautiously. She looked at him, startled. 'Sorry, do you want me to go? You look tired?'

Maria shook her head. 'Er, no, no, I'm fine. They said I should be able to go home later. They said they need the bed, but I think they just want shot of my visitors.' She laughed at her own attempt at a joke.

James nodded slowly, wringing his hands together.

'Sit down, James, it's fine.' She pointed to the chair next to her bed and he sat down in it.

'Are you sure you're okay?' he asked again, leaning in.

'I'm fine, I'm sorry she thought…'

'Oh, it's fine.' James waved her concerns away. 'Don't worry, I won't tell them any different. It gets me in here. I'm just sorry the dickhead is still harassing you. I can't believe you're going through all this on your own. I want to hurt him.'

How much does he know?

'I'm sorry, I'm not one for gossip, but after the journalists and everything, I Googled you in the waiting room.'

Just what every girl wanted to hear. Sexy, eh? More modern life for you. A bit like Cluedo. Death by Google, with the smartphone in the hospital. She shuddered to think what would come up now by typing her name into the search engine. Before the failed wedding attempt, it was all about the shop, the happy clients, the love stories she had helped turn into that special day. Now, the best she could hope for was an alleged affair with Colonel Mustard.

James took her introverted, stunned silence as embarrassment.

'Hey, you have nothing to be ashamed about, it's all him. I get it now, why you were so upset. I've been talking to my sister and—'

'Your sister?' Maria blanched. 'Why?' Did the world need another person knowing her business? 'The baby?'

James clamped his hand onto hers. 'No, no, I didn't say anything

83

about any of this. I would never do that. No, the thing is she's getting married, and they had a bit of a false start, a wobble, and they broke up, so they cancelled all their wedding plans. They want to start afresh, and I recommended you for the job.'

Maria's eyes filled with tears. 'Really?'

James grinned. 'Yeah, of course! I saw your photo album in the shop. You've done so many amazing weddings, I thought you would be great. You'll really like my sister too. She's brilliant.'

Maria's face fell. 'Yeah, but once she sees the press...'

'She already has.' James stroked the back of her hand between his two meaty ones, soothing her. She was going to object, say she wasn't a child, that she didn't need to be mollycoddled, but actually, it was quite nice. Plus, she felt like she could burst into tears and fill the room with enough salty water to drown herself in, and the comfort kept them at bay. Closed the dam. Which was good, because she felt sure that if she started crying, she would never stop. Cassie would be here soon too, to pick her up, and she had already threatened to tit punch her if she saw any weeping or other sign of emotion. She was in full-on client PR mode, and she didn't want to give the 'blasted local paps any more fodder for the Burgess empire to twist around to their own twisted crapola version of the story'. She had a point, and her boobs were so swollen and tender that the thought of having a tit punch was less than pleasant.

James stopped his stroking and looked at her, puzzled.

'Where do you go when you do that?' he asked, and she rolled her eyes at being spaced out again.

'Sorry, I do that a lot, especially lately. My mother used to call them my dream talks.'

'When did she pass?' he asked gently. Maria felt the pang she always got when someone asked that question, and she was catapulted back to that bedside, but she pushed it away.

'A few years ago now. I still really miss her.'

James nodded. 'Our dad passed last year. Heart attack, mowing the front lawn. We're still all getting used to it I think.'

Maria turned her hand over and squeezed his. 'I'm sorry. It does get easier, with time. Less painful. Or less sharp, anyway. You feel able to look back more, once that eases. Remember the good times.'

'There were plenty of them.' He nodded, smiling. 'I'm giving my sister away, and I want her to have a really special day. Mum really needs it too. It might be the only wedding she has.'

Maria opened her mouth to ask why not him, but she closed it again. It wasn't her business. Time was, she would think anyone who didn't want to get married was crazy; that they just needed to find 'the one' to change their minds and get them high kicking up that church aisle, or on that plane to Vegas. But now it all seemed so futile. Someone once said life was what happened when you were busy making plans. No shit. Well, it seemed she needed this as much as James and his family did. She needed the money too.

'I'll do it,' she said. 'If your sister *really* doesn't mind me doing it, let's arrange something when I'm feeling better.'

James beamed, pulling out his phone and sending a text.

'There, I've let her know. No backing out now.'

The door opened then, and they both flinched. Cassie, looking pale, wrinkled and slightly shocked, popped her head around the door.

'Hey. Sorry, can I come in?' She looked from James to Maria, and they both nodded. Maria discreetly pulled her hand away, feeling a bit like a scarlet woman.

Cassie came in and gave her a hug, patting James on the shoulder as she passed.

'Hey, James. Maria, how are you feeling?'

'I'm fine. I think I can go home soon, but I haven't been discharged yet. More to the point, what are you doing here this early? It's not visiting hours. Did you flatter your way in, like James?'

'Nope,' she said, wincing. 'I brought Tucker in last night and they kept him in.'

'Oh no! Did something happen? Oh Cass, your date was last night. I'm sorry.'

Cassie huffed and flicked her hand backwards. 'No, it's fine. I forgot about our date, and I ended up smashing my car door into him.'

James stood up. 'Did he attack you? Where is he?'

Cassie gave him a gentle shove in his chest, pushing him back into his seat.

'At ease, Macho Man. No, he was coming to check on me, and he surprised me. A little too much, and I overreacted ever so slightly.'

Maria giggled. 'Oh God, I'm sorry. Is he okay?'

Cassie looked suitably ashamed. 'He has four broken ribs, a nasty cut on his forehead, a split lip, three broken toes and a broken left arm.'

'Toes?' Maria asked, confused.

'I may have stamped on his foot as I got out of the car too.'

'Jesus, how hard did you hit him?' James said, holding his fingers up to her in the shape of a cross. 'Remind me to never annoy you!'

'I know. Listen, he lives on his own really – his flatmate works away a lot – and he's pretty beat up, so the nurses won't release him till he has a carer. The man can't tie his own shoes at the moment, so I kinda said he could stay with us. That okay? I feel so bad. He's a chef at that fancy place, On the Square? He can't work or anything!'

Maria thought of poor Tucker, in pain and unable to look after himself.

'No problem – it's your house Cass. If you're sure he's not a serial killer, I'm fine with it.'

Cassie looked relieved. 'Good. I'm only doing it so he doesn't sue me, no other reason. I'll sleep on the couch.'

'No, you can't do that, I'll sleep on the couch.'

'Er, I don't think so. You're not well yourself.' She eyed James over Maria's head, being discreet for once.

'I agree, Maria, not in your condition.' Maria looked at him, and James just winked. 'You're not going to fit on it soon, anyway.'

Cassie slapped him across the back of the head, as Maria burst out laughing.

She was suddenly very grateful her crappy old wiring had given up the ghost. Having James in her life seemed so easy, and she was glad to have his friendship.

Chapter 11

Darcy was sitting glumly in the hospital canteen, listening to the clangs of pots and pans and ching of plate on plate from the kitchen. He had been nursing the same acrid cup of vending-machine coffee for the last hour, waiting for the staff to change over, so he could once again try to get up to the wards to see Maria. He needed to explain things, make her understand why he left. He hadn't meant to make her so ill, but obviously the stress and strain of losing him had just proved too much. He had tried to explain this to the doctors, but of course they wouldn't speak to him with Cassie interfering. He understood she was looking out for her friend, but still, did she realise that what Maria needed to get better was him? She was angry, sure, but still, they were going to be married. They could sort it all out, get back on track. His mother would have to understand, and given the news column inches they had been getting, perhaps she would relent, finally accept Maria as a good choice. The pressure sometimes was intolerable, but Darcy had soon realised that being without Maria was even worse. He took another swig of coffee and shuddered at the taste. The canteen had started serving breakfast now, and he could see coffee on the menu. Anything had to be better than the swill they sold in the machines. He would have to remember to mention it to his mother, for a future project.

He joined the queue, pulling up his jacket collar to try to stay hidden from the other people. Thankfully, at this hour, the canteen only had the odd exhausted and distracted-looking visitor in it, and a few tired hospital workers. Two nurses were ahead of him in the queue, chattering away to each other.

'So what happened then, in the end?' the nurse with long black hair tied into a French braid asked her friend, who had short red hair – shocking red in fact.

'You should have seen it! Vic from security came and tossed him out.'

Darcy's ears pricked up, and he hunkered his frame down in on itself. Thankfully there were a couple of people between them, equally caught up in their own thoughts.

'Damn, that poor girl. What's he even doing here anyway? Come back for the engagement ring or something? Cheap git.'

He wanted to tell them that, of course, she still had the ring, and he didn't want it back, but he just shuffled with the queue, trying his best to blend in and earwig.

'I know, right? I hope that big bloke who brought her in knocks him out. I think they're together. He likes her anyway, I can tell.'

Darcy bristled. What big man? Darcy had assumed one of the journalists had phoned an ambulance, or Lynn. Was this who they meant? He hadn't seen anyone hanging around, other than himself. Unless… there was that big pushy git from the shop that day, the electrician. He clenched his jaw, remembering seeing them together that day, his hands on her. They'd looked so comfortable with each other. Too comfortable.

'Oh well, that's nice. She deserves it.'

'I know, but—' she dropped to a whisper now '—she's pregnant. Don't tell anyone, or I'll be shot at dawn!'

The nurse's companion gasped, and her friend shushed her. 'I mean it, Karen, you can't tell anyone! If it got out, I'd lose my job. Her solicitor friend is some kind of crazy woman who threatened to sue anyone who opened their mouth.'

Karen nodded at her friend, wide-eyed.

'I promise I won't, Shar. What's she gonna do?'

'Shar' sighed sadly. 'I don't know, love. Men are total shits, aren't they?'

Karen nodded vigorously. 'Yep, that's why I have Brutus. I tell you, dogs are much more loyal. A dog walker, a place by the fire and a belly rub, and he gives me no hassle. Better off without them.' Shar nodded and they bought their grapefruit and muesli and moved to a table. Darcy was already leaving, hugging the walls at the sides of the canteen to avoid being seen.

Pregnant? he thought to himself. *I'm going to be a father!* The thought of what his mother would say, and the idea of having a baby seat in the back of his Porsche, had him running for the car park faster than Jack Flash. He needed time to digest this piece of news. Time to make a plan. What *would* his mother say? She had managed to spin the story of the jilting to suit the Burgess empire, but that suited her ends anyway, as she had never wanted the marriage to go ahead. His cold feet had been a delight to her, but this? Having a baby with a woman she didn't like, out of wedlock? After he had jilted her and gone on honeymoon with a mystery woman? This would take a PR whitewash, and no amount of spin could magically make a baby disappear. An heir to the Burgess empire. Imagine if it was a boy!

He pictured his mother, taking in the news, and decided to keep quiet. Just for now. He would keep a distance, watch from afar. Let Maria get better, get back to her life. Maybe then she would contact him herself, to talk about it. Then they could decide together.

Maria was a rational person, she would see sense. She knew what it was like to lose a parent, so surely she wouldn't deprive her child of one? And even before it was born? She just wasn't like that. Then, once he was there, at her side, it would only be a matter of time before they were back together. Then they could marry, and the whole thing would be put to bed. His mother would have to accept her then, given that his blood ran through her child. Their blood. Burgess blood. The little mite would be the next leader of the Harrogate tea empire. Little Darcy Junior. If it was a boy, of course. It might be a girl, which was fine. She could maybe take over her mother's little business. That would keep Maria happy, and then they could keep trying, till little Darcy Junior came along.

There, it was all arranged. By the time Darcy had left the car park to go and shower and sleep at home, he had arranged the next fifty years of Maria's life, and that of her many offspring.

Chapter 12

Late October – One Month Later

Maria polished the counter for the twentieth time that morning. Her shop was immaculate, the display showing party dresses and accessories for the upcoming festive season, and fancy dresses for Halloween. On a large rack in the back she had hung some of her best bespoke gowns, to show what she could do on the wedding front. She assumed Annabel would already have a wedding dress, given that they'd had a wedding planned but had cancelled it, but she had to cover all her bases. She hadn't wanted to quiz James too much; he had helped her enough. They had stayed in touch, and his texts had gone from concerned to cracking jokes. He was very funny, and she felt like she was going through his day with him. He was even going to come and look at the upstairs of the flat, to see whether anything could be done about creating a living space within her workspace. It was great living with Cassie, but it was two bedrooms, and with Tucker there it was pretty cramped. She couldn't make it worse by filling it with baby crap, and she was going to have to start buying some soon. If only to get used to the idea herself.

Today was the day James had arranged for his sister and her fiancé to come in and discuss their wedding. They had a date in mind, and even James had sounded dubious when he told her over the phone.

'It's a little close to your due date, though, isn't it? Are you sure you'll be able to do it?'

Maria looked at the dates in her academic diary.

'It will be close, true… but I can do it. I have to really, James. I haven't had any other bookings yet, and I can't really afford to pay for advertising either. I need to make enough to cover my being off. I plan to bring the baby to work anyway. I can work in the back making up the orders, and Lynn will do front of house, but I will have to pay her for the extra hours…'

'Okay, okay,' James said. 'Just take it one thing at a time, eh? Don't stress out over everything. Listen, I am here to help, honest.'

Maria had smiled down the phone. All he did was help her; it was nice, but she needed to do this on her own. She couldn't start relying on a man now, trusting him to be there, to be a part of her life for ever. Even as a friend. She had Lynn and Cassie, as always. That would be enough. She could rely on them, always. Besides, this baby didn't deserve to lose any more people. She hadn't had the guts to call the father, and eventually she had got the number from Cassie and flushed it down the toilet one night in a fit of tears and low-fat ice cream. What was she going to say? What did she expect him to do? She could only see problems, and as much as she hated herself for perhaps depriving him of something he might really have wanted to know about, she just couldn't take the chance. Growing up, she had seen too many families living in two parts. How many children lived with parents part-time? It was unavoidable. Relationships broke down, people fell out of love, new families were formed. She accepted that. The children were still loved, doubly so in fact. She just knew that handing over her child to a stranger for half the week, a stranger who would one day have a family of his own, complete with wife and kids, filled her with dread. She had been just fine after her dad passed, just her mother and her, and Cassie and Lynn. Who was to say this child would need any more? Besides, she hadn't been the only sad person that night. Not the only one needing comfort. Who knew what he was going through? If it was a fraction of what she was having to cope with, she couldn't subject him or the baby to any more.

All she knew was, her whole world had shifted in an incredibly short space of time. Without Happy Ever After, she would have felt utterly lost. So that was what she would cling to, making sure her business, and her mother's legacy, lasted, so she could provide for the tiny scrap of life growing inside her. The rest would just keep her up nights. She hadn't mentioned to Cassie about moving upstairs yet. She wasn't sure whether it would take too much money, or whether it would be big enough, but long-term she would need a place of her own. It would be ideal to live above the shop, since she owned it anyway. Then she could live pretty cheaply. If the business was still there of course.

She frowned, taking out her antibacterial spray and spritzing the till. Lynn had taken the day off, unpaid, and had agreed to drop her hours till the baby came. It was beneficial for them both really; Lynn liked to be indoors more in the winter, so the thought of fewer days trudging to work in the cold had appealed to her. She only worked there for the company, Maria knew, and extra 'fun' money as she called it. She would squirrel it away half the time. Last year she had booked an extravagant cruise with some of her friends, and had loved every minute. She said knowing she'd earned every penny of the trip made her feel accomplished, less retired and more alive. Westfield was definitely the place for that. If there were some places known as God's waiting room, this village was the opposite. The retirees around here had more adventures and went on more capers than the younger generations. Her mother had been just the same and would have been right there with them if she had lived longer.

94

For a sleepy village, there was never a dull moment what with one thing and another. It was only last month that Agatha, Dotty, Grace and Marlene from the craft and natter group at New Lease of Life had done a sponsored skydive to raise more funds for a swimming pool extension at the community centre. They were halfway to their target already, and the whole thing was going to be run by the villagers, independent of the council. How many villages had a silver brigade element like theirs? Not many. It was no wonder that not many people left. It wouldn't surprise her if the swimming pool turned into a scene from *Cocoon*.

She ran the cloth over the buttons on the till, running her nail between the keys to make sure she picked up every imaginary speck of dust.

She'd really gone to town cleaning up, but she still felt uneasy. Rattled. She hated feeling like everything was riding on this wedding, but it really was. This was her baby nest egg, the thing that would help her get set up, turned around, and keep things ticking over at the shop. She wasn't planning on having a lot of time off, but she didn't intend to struggle either.

The shop door opened and Maria took just a split second to get her game face on before she threw the cloth down on the floor behind the till and turned to face her visitors.

'Hi!' she trilled. 'Welcome to Happy Ever After!'

When she turned around and looked at the dark-haired woman standing before her it was like looking at a female version of James, which she supposed she was. She had his eyes, and Maria found herself genuinely smiling at the woman who was looking back at her nervously.

'Hi,' she replied. 'Maria, right? Wow, you're just how James described you! I'm so glad you could fit us in today.' She didn't look at her stomach, so obviously James had kept her secret. Bless him.

Maria motioned for her to take a seat on the couch she had at one side of the shop, all set up for their meeting with her folders of weddings and events she had done over the years.

'Is your fiancé coming? Sorry, James didn't mention his name…'

The door opened and Maria turned to it, her face freezing in pure horror as Tequila Man walked through it, dressed in a neat pinstripe suit and looking a lot less dishevelled than the last time she'd seen him. And with far more clothes on.

Maria stood up, the folder on her lap clattering to the floor.

'I'll just be a minute!' she squeaked, as she dashed over to the man. *What the hell was he doing here? Had she told him where she worked?*

'Oh, it's okay,' Annabel said cheerfully. 'This is Mark. My fiancé!'

Mark stood there, looking between the women so rapidly Maria thought his head might fall off.

This can't be happening, she thought to herself, subconsciously putting one hand on her stomach. *How is this my life now?*

'Hi!' she said, somehow making her legs walk over to him the rest of the way, arm outstretched to shake his hand. 'I'm Maria Mallory, owner of Happy Ever After!' Mark's eyes widened even further and she pulled a 'go with me' face at him.

'Say hello, Mark!' Annabel said, laughing. 'I'm sorry, Maria, he's a little socially awkward at times, I swear.'

'Er, um… Mark Smith, pleased to meet you.' He put his hand out, recovering a little. She didn't take it.

'Shall we sit down?' she asked, eager to get this thing over and done with as soon as possible. Her dreams of getting money for her baby were gone now. She couldn't do this wedding, obviously. Or maybe they already knew? Was this something they'd planned? To confront her? Did James know? She took a seat on the sofa opposite Annabel and busied herself with picking up her folder off the floor, straightening up the contents.

'Come on, darling, sit down!' Annabel said snappishly, and Maria flinched. Her hands were shaking so much she was making the folder jiggle on the table. *Well, this was it.*

She straightened up her clothing, a pretty black-and-white,

polka-dot, longline skirt and a cream silk blouse. She smoothed the skirt down over her knees and then looked up at the pair.

They were both looking at her, with very different expressions on their faces.

Mark looked like he was planning his own funeral, and Annabel looked… joyous. Maria couldn't look away from her face. It was one she had seen many, many times in this shop, on that couch. It was the look of a bride, a happy woman in love. Hell, it wasn't so long ago that she had sported that very look herself. Annabel Chance was here to plan her wedding. She had no idea. Maria felt ill. She wanted the very earth to split open, right in Westfield, right in the middle of her shop, and suck her and her unborn child into the very core of the earth.

'So…?' Annabel started, looking at Mark in bemusement. 'Sorry, I don't know what's got into him. We were thinking spring, next year? I know James told you some dates. We were thinking a country estate somewhere, maybe something a little different? Both of us have been to enough big weddings lately to be bored by the whole cookie-cutter church-wedding scene, so I thought we could maybe think of something else?'

Maria nodded, trying to turn off the screaming voice in her head that was telling her to run for the hills. She picked her notepad and pen up off the tabletop to take notes, and avoided looking at Mark. She could feel him staring at her, and she didn't trust herself not to do or say something stupid the moment she looked at his face. She just knew the guilt and shock she felt would be mirrored in his own features.

Business, Maria. Business. Just get through the meeting, then you can fob them off later. He will no doubt want another wedding planner to plan his upcoming nuptials. Just this one awkward moment, then you never have to see or think about them again.

'Okay,' she said, nodding away. 'And in terms of colours, themes?' She had to go through the motions. Maybe if she took some details she could pass them on to the next wedding planner, at least help a little, so as not to let James down. *James*. The thought of her new friend being caught up in this made her feel sick. She would lose him now. There was no other option. The twist in her gut hit her far harder than she thought it would. Optimus Prime-truck hard.

'I'm going to be honest with you, Maria,' Annabel said in a small voice. 'We did have a wedding planned. I don't know how much my brother told you…'

Maria finally looked at them both, and they were looking at each other. Or rather, Annabel was looking lovingly at Mark, and he looked like he was considering leaping over her to dash to the exit.

She took his hand in hers, and he seemed to sag into her touch. His eyes crinkled at the corners as his whole face smiled at her. *He loves her*, Maria thought. *That's good. Right?* He wasn't a mess, he was just a man hurting that night. Just like she was.

She levelled her gaze back to Maria, James's open, honest eyes in her head.

'We broke up, so we cancelled our wedding. We'd been fighting a lot, and had let things get on top of us, I guess. We spent some time apart, and then we realised that we really wanted each other. We love each other, and we want our wedding. Just not the one we'd already planned. So when James told us you had a space, we knew we had to see you.'

Maria felt like she was going to burst into tears, but she held it in as best she could. Bloody hormones weren't easy, on top of her horror and guilt. She had messed with this woman's life, and the poor girl didn't even realise it.

'Okay, well, I have some ideas for venues, locally.' She handed over her business card to Annabel. 'You two have a think about colours and themes and tell me what you had planned – then I can avoid it. Email everything to me, and I'll check my diary and get back to you, okay?' She stood then, holding her shaky hand out to Annabel as a way of dismissal. Annabel's smile dulled, but she, being all polite and lovely, stood too, dragging Mark up with her by the arm.

'Thank you so much,' she said, shaking Maria's hand enthusiastically. Maria stepped out, making moves to show them out, but Annabel didn't move.

'So, you'll take us on?'

Maria kept walking to the door. *Nearly there.* 'Well, email me, and I'll see if I can fit it in. I am very busy around that time, so I'll have to think about it.'

She turned, opening the door, and giving them both her best 'meeting is over' smile.

Mark gave Annabel a little nudge to get her moving and, linking arms with her, half-marched her to the door. Seemingly, he and Maria had the same idea. Go figure.

'Annabel, darling, we'll send the email, okay? Then we'll know if it's possible.'

Annabel looked like she wanted to object, but Maria jumped in. 'I'll be in touch. It was lovely to meet you both.'

Mark mumbled a goodbye and practically threw Annabel out of the door. Maria closed the door behind them both, smiling like an idiot through the window until they got into a white car and pulled away. With a slight screech of tyres.

Maria went and sat back on the couch, looking at the folder of smiling couples in front of her.

'Well, Mum,' she said to the room. 'That decides it. The father definitely does not need to know.'

She reluctantly stood up and went to get her phone. She had to call Cassie, tell her what had happened. And get back to work. Every penny counted even more now.

***

Annabel Chance was a woman who was used to getting just what she wanted. Not because she was ruthless, or evil, or selfish.

99

Because she was good. Snow White epic proportions of goodness, sweet temperament and light. She put good things out into the world, believing the universe would pass them on, spread them around, and give a little piece back to her. She was the type of person who recycled, picked up her dog's poop on walks *and* put it in a wastebin, never littered. She always had change for homeless people, volunteered when she was in college, and now worked as a nurse at Harrogate Hospital. She believed in the good in life, and now she was on the verge of having her dream wedding once more, but yet again it was feeling out of reach, at risk.

'She doesn't think we fit together as a couple,' she said, looking across the car at Mark as he drove them back to Harrogate. He had abandoned his tie as soon as they got into the car, and was now trying to undo his top button.

'Is it hot in here?' he gasped, speeding just a little too fast through the village.

'Mark, slow down! The office can wait, surely!' She flicked on the air con and buzzed her window down slightly. 'We can't do the wedding on our own, not again. We broke up last time. We need a wedding planner! I've been looking into her, and she's amazing. I really want her. I'm willing to wait even, for her to have a space.'

Mark shook his head. 'I don't want to wait, Annabel. We can get another wedding planner. I'll have a look on the net this afternoon.'

Annabel was already shaking her head. 'James said she had space, and…' She bit her lip, a sure sign that she felt bad. 'I can't tell you, because it's not my business, but she's had a bit of a bad time lately, and I think James really wants to help her too.'

Mark said nothing, wiping his forehead with the back of his hand and staring straight ahead.

'I don't mean to be pushy, but I really do think it would be great. Please, Mark, can we try? It was awful when we split up. I never want to go through that again. Please?'

Mark groaned. 'Let's just send the email, okay? We'll see what happens then.'

Annabel clapped her hands together. 'Thanks, darling! Oh, it'll be great, I promise!'

Mark smiled. At least, he tried for a smile, but it was more like a gurn.

'I know, darling, it will be. Let's just see what happens.'

Annabel sighed contentedly, sitting back in her seat and resting her petite manicured hand on his lap.

Annabel, always so nice. She just knew it was all going to work out, because she had dreamt about it for years, wished for it. Yearned. This was how she was going to be married, and she wasn't going to give up without a fight.

Chapter 13

Cassie pulled up at the cottage and dragged her tired body out of the car. Reaching into the backseat, she pulled out a box of files, her satchel and her handbag. She had been working for eight hours already and she could probably work another eight tonight and still have lots to do tomorrow. She rested her box on the top of Maria's car and locked her own up.

'Hi,' she called, levering the front door open and pushing herself and her baggage through it. She was greeted by a warm blast of air from the heating, and a truly heavenly smell. Her mouth watered, and she heard her stomach gurgle in delight. Having only managed to throw down a salad from the takeout deli and a million cups of coffee all day, she was starving.

'Hey,' Tucker called in reply. 'In the kitchen. Won't be long.'

Maria appeared in the hallway, wearing a long dotty skirt and slightly dishevelled blouse. She was holding a large glass of white.

'Hey, Cass!' She waggled a finger at her, motioning for her to come into the lounge. Cass dropped the box and her bags in the hall and, kicking off her heels, followed her friend. Maria pushed the door closed a little, thrusting the glass into her hand.

'Here, that's for you. Tucker has been on one today. I swear, I came home and the grocer was here!'

102

Cassie took a slug of the wine and digested the news.

'The grocer? Was here?'

'I know. Tucker had called him. I swear, there is so much food in the kitchen, it's mad. He's been cooking all afternoon I think.'

She sipped from her own wineglass.

'Maria!' Cassie spat. 'No drinking!'

She rolled her eyes. 'It's grape juice. Tucker bought it.'

Cassie took another deep slug. 'I feel like I walked into the twilight zone.' She sank down into the sofa cushions. 'You okay?'

Maria shook her head. 'Nope. Annabel has already emailed me with all the wedding details, and begged me to take them on. I can't believe it, I really can't.'

'I can.' Cassie snorted. 'Men are shits. I blame Darcy for all this. Dudes just can't keep it in their pants.'

Maria blushed, and Cassie could have kicked herself. 'Sorry, mate. The baby is good, of course. I've just had a bad day at work, that's all. A bad month actually. Why people get married I will never know.'

Maria said nothing, sipping at her juice, seemingly deep in thought. Cassie slapped herself on the forehead.

'Shit! Sorry, I did it again.'

'Did what again?' Tucker asked, walking slowly into the room with a bottle of wine and a bottle of grape juice, one in each hand. 'Top up, ladies?'

'God, yes,' they said in unison.

He filled their glasses accordingly and chuckled.

'Dinner won't be long. I felt better, so I decided to get out of that bed and do something. I can go home tomorrow, get out of your hair.'

He was standing there bare-chested, a pair of grey joggers hanging loose on his hips.

'Tucker,' Maria said kindly, 'I heard you trying to put a top on this morning, and it sounded like you were in pain. Since you currently don't have a shirt on, I'm guessing it still hurts, right?'

Tucker shrugged, wincing. 'Maybe,' he said sheepishly.

'And you still have your cast on,' she added. 'Just stay, right, Cass?'

Cassie shrugged. 'Sure, I'm fine on the couch.'

Maria glared at her, and she groaned.

'Okay, okay. Tucker, please stay. Honestly, it's fine. You can't go home with no shirt on anyway, you'll freeze.'

Tucker smiled then. 'Well, if you're sure? I was thinking I could make myself useful, clean up a bit, make some meals? I've made a curry tonight, homemade naans. I was gonna do a beef Wellington but I'm not up to pastry yet.'

Both women looked at him with big grins on their faces.

'What?'

Maria giggled. 'You had us at clean, Tucker, honestly. Thank you.'

Cassie was looking at him with a daft grin of her own.

'Yes, thank you. Do you need any help?'

Tucker looked at her, and Maria thought she saw something pass between them.

'You can, if you like, in the kitchen?'

Cassie nodded, and they both headed in together. Maria made a kissy face at her behind Tucker's back, and Cassie picked up a couch cushion and threw it at her.

***

'Morning!' Lynn said a week later, bustling into the shop with her furry boots and warm coat on. A blast of cold air came through with her, and she closed the door firmly behind her. 'You okay, my lovely?'

Maria nodded, smiling as best she could with a needle in her mouth. She was sitting stitching up a customer's order, a beautiful red party gown she had made from scratch. Agatha had ordered four dresses the day before, completing with matching boleros and cardigans, bustling into the shop with Taylor, her husband, in tow. She was the unofficial leader of Westfield, living in the huge manor in the village. Nothing got past her, and she had been a good friend of the family. Maria knew it was more than just an order; it was a show of support. She knew Agatha would tell anyone who asked who had made the outfits, and send them her way. She could expect more business to come from this order, so she had to get to work right away.

'I'm fine. Agatha placed a huge order this morning, and Taylor is coming in tomorrow. He wants a couple of new suits. Do you think you could see to him, do his orders?'

Lynn hung her coat and scarf on the coat rack and hurried over to her.

'That's lovely,' she said, fingering the fabric. She pulled a chair right up close and practically bumped knees. 'Now tell me, how did the wedding appointment go? I've been dying to know all week! I thought you'd have called me!'

'Ah, well, yes, I did get it, but...'

'But what? That's fantastic!' She jumped up from her seat, moving over to the calendar hanging on the back wall.

'Did they book it in? A specific date?' She was running her finger along the laminated paper.

It was like watching a child look for a present on Christmas morning. All excited, hopping from foot to foot, jiggling with excitement. Except Lynn had nothing under the tree, because Maria had been a naughty girl, and Santa didn't give out presents to naughty people.

'Lynn, I didn't book the wedding. I can't book the wedding, so if they call, either of them, we can't do it, and I am out at an event.'

Lynn turned around, crestfallen. 'Why? Can't you work it round the baby?'

She looked so worried. Maria wanted to kick herself for making her colleague worry. She knew how stressed she had been since the wedding. Another thing to blame Darcy for. She really hated him sometimes, but not as much as she'd hated herself since that meeting.

'No, Lynn, I can't take the wedding. I just can't. The groom, Mark? He's the—'

'Hi,' the door opened and there was James. He looked at both women and smiled nervously.

'You haven't been answering my calls, so I just thought I'd check on you. I brought breakfast.'

He raised a brown bag. 'Fruit salad, bacon rolls, fruit juice.'

'Lovely,' Lynn started to say. 'That's lovely, isn't it, Maria?'

'I have to work, James. Did you want something?'

He lowered the bag, and Maria went back to work stitching. She could hear Lynn tutting at her, and she did her best to pretend to be oblivious. She heard footsteps and the shop door close, and she looked up.

James was walking over to the sofa area, bag in hand. He laid himself out over it, feet on the coffee table, and, opening the bag, pulled out a bacon roll. He noticed her watching him and gave her a little wave.

'Oh, sorry, did you think I left? I was just closing the door. There's a bit of a draught. I'll be fine here. I'll just eat my breakfast and wait for you to take a break.' He beckoned to Lynn, who was now sitting at her workstation, watching in amusement.

'Come on, Lynn, come and grab a bacon roll. I have plenty.'

Lynn looked at Maria and got up, heading to the kettle.

'I will join you actually, James love. Fancy a cuppa to go with it?'

James nodded, mouth full of bacon. 'That would be lovely, Lynn. Thank you.'

Maria glared at the pair of them. Why couldn't people just leave her alone to live in her little bubble? God knew, when she started showing, the villagers would all know about it. She kept working, trying her very best to ignore them, but James was humming and singing along in the corner.

'I am trying to work you know,' she said huffily. He waggled a plastic container at her.

'Come on, you have to eat. Fresh fruit.'

Maria pouted at him.

'Please,' he said softly. 'Just ten minutes?'

Maria sighed and put down the dress.

'Five,' she said, wandering over to him. Lynn came over with some tea on a tray.

'I'm just going to go upstairs, sort some fabric samples out for Mr Taylor.'

Maria went to object but Lynn was already hotfooting it out the back. She slumped down into the couch opposite James and took the container from him. The fruit did look nice. She looked around for something to eat it with and James waggled a fork in front of her face. She took it without looking at him. 'Thanks.'

'You're welcome. So, what's happening with you then? Are you mad at me for something? I was supposed to be coming to look at upstairs, but you haven't been answering my calls.'

Maria forked a piece of melon into her mouth, her eyes closing at the taste. She hadn't eaten much that morning, other than coffee. Not the best breakfast. She needed to take her iron tablets too. Not exactly following doctor's orders. She had struggled to concentrate on anything since meeting Annabel.

'See, baby needs fruit.' His face dropped. 'The baby is okay, right?'

Maria grinned. 'All good, yes. Hungry perhaps.' She stabbed another piece of fruit.

'Good,' he said, looking relieved. 'So what is it then? Are you cross with me? I know it's weird, but I did think we were friends now. I don't get what's wrong.'

Maria felt awful. She had just assumed James would get mad at her for turning down the wedding and give up. She could just shut herself away, work hard, get someone else in to deal with upstairs. Simon, the handyman in the village, could help. She didn't need James. She didn't need a damn thing. She just wanted to live in her own little cocoon. Why couldn't people realise that? She couldn't let James in; she couldn't lose anyone else. If she didn't let him get any closer, it wouldn't hurt when he left. Her pregnancy hormones had turned from tearful despair to fuelled anger, so she had been clinging to that to see her through the day.

'Nothing's wrong, James, I'm just busy. I don't really have much cash spare, so I can't do the upstairs yet.'

'What about the wedding booking? Annabel said you turned them down. Why?'

'I just can't do it, James. I'm sorry. It's just too much work and—'

'I'll help! I'm part of the wedding anyway, so I'll be around. I'll help with everything, and Annabel says she'll leave it all to you and not interfere. To be honest, she got a bit bridezilla and it caused problems for her and Mark. They were stressing over everything, and money, but now Mark's family have stepped in with some cash. They really love Annabel, which is nice.'

Maria's heart squeezed when she heard James talk about his sister. He really loved her, Maria could tell. Here he was, doing what he did best, putting himself out there to help others. The man was a damn saint, and she felt a little like a devil in disguise these days. Leading all those around her down the path to hell and eternal damnation.

'I can give her some other numbers. I emailed her a couple of other planners. Did she not call them?'

James frowned, taking a big draw of coffee before answering.

'Maria, she wants you. They can get married before the baby comes, you'll have time.'

Maria gasped. 'You didn't tell them, did you?'

James smiled kindly. 'Of course I didn't, I didn't tell anyone. It's your business, no one else's. Has he contacted you?'

Maria could feel her heart thump in her chest.

'Who?'

'Your ex, Darcy.'

Maria opened her mouth to speak, to tell him some version of the truth, but his phone rang in his pocket. He looked at the screen and groaned.

'Sorry, it's Annabel. I swear she doesn't know I'm here.' He held a finger up to tell her one minute, and she nodded.

'Hey, sis, how's it going?' His face darkened, his features clouding over. 'Don't, Bel. Listen, stop stressing. We can sort it. Listen, er…' He looked apologetically at Maria. 'Can we talk later? I'm on a job at the moment… yeah, give me an hour, okay?'

'I'll do it,' Maria heard someone say. Someone that sounded suspiciously like her. *What am I doing!* 'I'll do the wedding.' *Oh great, you've really gone and done it now.*

James looked at her in shock. 'Just a minute, sis.' He covered the mouthpiece. Maria could hear Annabel squeaking tearfully at the other end. 'Are you sure?'

Maria nodded. 'Yes, I'll do it, but we'll need to discuss my fee.'

She had to make this right somehow. Having James here had decided it for her. She would do the right thing. Help James, help Annabel and Mark have their perfect wedding, and earn the money she needed for her unborn child. Then she would just be out of their lives. If Mark asked, she would tell him the baby wasn't his, and that would be it. She could tell him she'd had more than one drunken encounter, that it was another one which had resulted in her falling pregnant. Not the classiest answer, to be sure, but what else was she going to say? He hadn't been in touch, so perhaps he wouldn't even ask when he found out. It wasn't like they had feelings for each other. It was just one night; two lonely people doing something to ease their pain.

James gave her the biggest, daftest grin, and stood to go and talk to Annabel. By the sound of it, she was very happy to hear the news. Now Maria just had to get through it. Make everyone happy, and then get back to her bubble.

***

The bubble burst that evening as she was about to leave the shop to go home. Lynn had already left, and she was just heading to the door when a face at the window made her jump. She looked at the figure for a moment, and he smiled. An awkward smile that made his whole face look nervous. She slid back the locks on the door, allowing him inside.

'Hi,' Mark said, ruffling his unruly hair back off his forehead with his hand. 'I didn't mean to just turn up, but…'

'Annabel told you I said yes to the wedding, and you're here to tell me to turn it down.'

'I… it's not that, it's…'

He sagged a little and Maria took a step back, figuring he could probably use some more oxygen. She felt the same way. Being alone with him, especially here, among the dresses, shoes and dreams… it felt so wrong. So awkward. And oddly, it made her feel guilty when she thought of James. There was a baby elephant in the room, and Maria felt its trunk breathing down her neck.

'I'm not this man. I don't cheat. I don't hurt people. I just don't know what to do, and with you doing the wedding now, I just wondered whether…'

He looked stricken, terrified, and the penny dropped in Maria's mind. He felt guilty too.

'You were wondering whether I was madly in love with you, and planning to sabotage your big day.'

Her plain speaking made his eyes bulge, and she shook her head kindly at him.

'I know what type of man you are, I think. I was sad, you were sad, it was a mistake. As far as I'm concerned, it's not an issue. I don't mean you any harm. I need the money too, in all honesty,

110

with one thing and another.' *You know, my failed marriage, public humiliation, secret baby...* 'I just want to help James really.'

She couldn't help but smile when she thought of his goofy face, the way he made her laugh and feel safe. She really did want to repay him for his kindness, even if this was a warped way of doing it.

'Really? You're really okay with this?' Mark was looking at her sceptically, and she saw what Annabel saw in him. The man was in love, clearly. Adoration and sheer panic crossed over his facial expressions like raging storm clouds.

She took a step forward, placing her hand on top of his momentarily, without thinking. They both froze, and she dropped her hand.

'Sorry, that was a bad move. I seem to be making a few of those lately.'

His eyes crinkled in the corners as the tension in the room broke a little at her joke.

'I know the feeling.'

'I meant what I said. This is just about the wedding, doing the job and helping James. That's it. I like Annabel, Mark. You're both so happy. I don't have anything nasty planned. If you really don't trust me, I get it – believe me. I'm willing to drop out, but I just think we can get through this, and then we'll be done.'

He looked around the shop, his eyes flicking from one display to another.

'Annabel wants you, and James trusts you.'

Maria nodded, relieved he didn't seem to be so wary anymore.

'I can do the job, I won't let you down.'

Mark turned to the door.

'I trust you too, Maria. Goodnight.'

'Night,' she said, watching him walk away through the window, into the darkness.

So many people to please, to make happy, to keep safe from the truth. Placing a hand on her stomach, she flicked off the lights. This was going to be some wedding.

Chapter 14

Mrs Burgess was reading the papers in the sunroom when Darcy walked in. She was still in her dressing gown, her silk nightgown matching (of course) and her hair already neatly coiffed. She was sitting at the cream dining table, the papers of the day spread out all around her as she perused the business section with her usual Early Grey (Burgess brand TM) tea in the smoking pot next to her.

She looked down her glasses at him and he shuffled in, squinting at the bright light coming in from the numerous high, thin windows. The sunroom was his mother's favourite room. She spent much of her time in here, or in the conservatory that led off it at the bottom of the room. It was light and airy, a stark contrast to the bright, white, marbled family rooms, and the dark wood rooms his father occupied. In here, it was all florals, pretty cream furnishings, wall-to-wall bookcases full of colour-coordinated books. It looked like the perfect room for his mother, as she sat there, looking so at leisure, but Darcy knew different. The room had been designed by her for photoshoots, the woman behind Burgess Tea. People wanted to believe the homely image, the successful businesswoman, pride of Yorkshire. It was what she traded on, even enjoyed being from time to time. What they didn't see was the rod of steel that ran through her womanly features. Especially when it came to her family, her children. She ran the Burgess Tea empire like the Queen of England ran the monarchy, and she never let a thing escape her notice.

'I see the papers are finally dying down about your wedding farce,' she said, her soft tones sounding like slippers brushing along a deep-pile carpet. 'I think our PR girl really did earn her money this time.'

Darcy rolled his eyes but said nothing. 'It's not over yet, though. I told you, I can make things right with Maria, if only you'll let me. Sending that godawful publicity girl to pose with me on the beach wasn't the best idea either, was it?'

His mother folded the paper in half, dropping it back onto the table.

'I told you the day you left her standing at that altar, and again the day you came home from the hospital, we need to manage this situation, which means staying the hell away from her and letting the gossip rags calm down. She's done the right thing, now why can't you?'

'What do you mean, done the right thing? She didn't do anything wrong!'

His mother picked up an envelope from the pile of post she had on the table and waggled it at him.

'Charity ball in Leeds this weekend; I thought you could attend with me. Your father wants to stay at home – you know how he hates those things. I thought this could be good PR for you. Some bloody good women going too, by all accounts. Perfect for casting your net out again, discreetly of course.'

'Mother, what do you mean the right thing? And I'm not casting my net anywhere. I don't want to go.'

Beatrice huffed. 'The right thing by keeping quiet – quite dignified of her, I thought. Besides the rather dramatic hospital dash. That smacked of desperation a little. Did you ever find out what was wrong?'

Yes, mother, she's carrying your grandchild. Heir to your throne.
'She was exhausted, low blood sugar, dehydration.'

Beatrice tutted. 'These young waifs, they never look after themselves. Never mind, at least it's over now.' She took a sip of her tea. 'Your black tuxedo, I think, for the dinner. Have it dry-cleaned, won't you?' She smiled at him sweetly. 'A haircut wouldn't go amiss either.'

She picked the paper back up, seemingly dismissing him. He cleared his throat.

'Mother, I am going to see Maria again. We have things to discuss. I shan't be going to the charity ball either. I plan to get back with Maria, and marry her. I know I messed up, but without you constantly in my ear, telling me how unsuitable she was…'

'Who do you think you're speaking to?' Her tone was icy. 'You will be going to that charity ball, and yes, you did mess up. I had you meeting every eligible lady in the county, all with breeding, and money, and you go to some backwoods community event and meet a bloody shopgirl!'

'She's not just a shopgirl, she owns the place! She's a successful businesswoman, just like you.'

'Me!' Beatrice snorted. 'She is nothing like me! I married a man with a two-bit business and turned it into *the* most successful tea company in England, and I did it all while raising a family!'

'Well, actually—'

She cut him off before he could drop his bombshell. Her usual trick of raising one hand and pinching the bridge of her nose with the other. It had never failed to silence him as a child; she didn't even need words. Just that hand to silence him, and the action to convey her annoyance and pain at what he was saying. She used her migraines like warnings.

'Don't do that, or Mummy will get a migraine.'

'Keep the noise down, Mummy has a migraine coming on.'

Darcy realised he was never going to get out from under the shadow of this woman. He loved her, but everything he was and everything he had were down to her. Dependent on her. His job, his apartment, his lifestyle, all paid for by Burgess Tea. His mother would see him married off to some other heir to some other throne. She was already talking about the daughter of a local biscuit factory owner. Imagine the headline then. Tea and biscuits down the aisle? Dirty Darcy dunks into married life again for a second bite of the biscuit?

It didn't bear thinking about, and he already had a blossoming family out there, waiting for him to man up.

'Mother,' he said, ignoring his mother's wince. 'I will go to that ball, but as for Maria, that door is most certainly not closed. I'm taking the rest of the day off.'

He didn't dare wait for an answer. He was out of there, his expensive Italian imported shoes squeaking as he half-ran across the marble hall to the front door. Once in the car, his mobile rang in his pocket. He didn't need to look to know who it was. He had to get this sorted now, once and for all, before his mother called the dogs in.

***

December

'Is this the place?' James asked as they saw a sign half-obscured by the roadside. They had been driving on this road a good few miles, and the sat nav was no help at all, other than binging at them every now and again.

'I can't really see the sign clearly,' Maria said, frowning, trying to see the words through the thick brush around it. 'They should really cut this back, get some better signage in. How do the guests even find the place?'

He indicated, turning the van down past the sign. The road was narrow, well-maintained, with thick trees at either side. The light in the van darkened as they drove, the weak winter sunlight failing to crack through the thick branches above them.

'Be nice here when it snows, I bet, as long as you don't mind being holed up.' Maria nodded to herself, smiling at the thought of being in a hotel while the snow fell outside. Would she ever have that again? It was hard to think of someone whisking her off for a romantic weekend with a baby in tow. Who would take that on? She rubbed her tummy, feeling guilty for thinking of the baby that way. Her mother never had, and she wasn't about to either. She was happy with her decision, despite the circumstances.

'You okay? I told you I could have come here on my own, you know. I could have FaceTimed you.'

Maria shook her head, tapping the clipboard she held in her hands. 'So you would have gone through my checklist, all on your own?'

James looked at the pages and pages of typed notes she had printed off and winced.

'Maybe not. I would probably have just checked they did a nice beer on tap, and what time the bar closed.'

'See? You need me here, with you.'

She looked out of the window, marvelling at the beautiful countryside. Westfield was beautiful, but this place was lovely, right on the outskirts of Harrogate.

James looked at her, her tiny bump just visible through her long coat, and smiled.

'Yeah, I do,' he said softly.

The venue, Keane Hall, was gorgeous, despite the obscured sign, which of course Maria mentioned. The owner, Mr Hugo Harrison, was more than accommodating and agreed to cut down the foliage before the big day. Everything else had passed muster so far, and now they were sitting in the main dining hall, waiting for their starter. Mr Harrison had insisted they dine at the restaurant there, to taste the food, and of course Maria had agreed, being the professional. She was pretty hungry anyway, but her stomach was complaining of more than hunger.

116

Being here, in this hall, sitting at this table, she could now imagine the wedding she was planning, and it was making her feel nauseous. She had managed to pretty much avoid Mark altogether, and he certainly hadn't tried to contact her. Annabel kept in touch with emails, but she was trying to stay away, Maria knew, for the sake of her own sanity and to keep the bridezilla tendencies at bay. James had been a godsend, helping her, but the closer their friendship got, the more Maria worried about the big day. And when it was over, what then? Would she finally be able to relax, when the Chance family, and Mark, were in her rear-view mirror? The thought of not speaking to James filled her stomach with knots of dread too. It had to happen, though, she knew that. Especially when the baby came. There would just be too many questions. She couldn't risk it all coming out, and James hating her. Especially if he got to know her child. That wouldn't do at all. She couldn't let anybody into her child's life she wasn't sure would be there for good.

No, she would stick to the plan.

'So, what are your plans now?' James asked, pouring iced water into both of their glasses. The table was set up beautifully: candlelit candelabra and shiny silver cutlery on white linen tablecloths. The hall itself was bright and welcoming, with a large feature window on one wall, letting the light flood in. They did the bigger events – like the Smith-Chance wedding – in here. It would be lovely, she could see it now.

'Plans?' she asked, taking a sip of water to collect her thoughts. *Did I speak out loud?*

'Yeah, I know you said you didn't want me to help with the upstairs, but I just wondered if you had any plans for when the baby comes. Did you ring someone to help? Have you thought about where you'll live?'

'I… no, not really. Cass says I can stay with her, of course, but with Tucker still recovering there, it's a bit awkward. She's still on the couch because I have her spare room. I offered to share my bed with her, but apparently I'm a kicker in my sleep these days.'

James nodded. 'So no plans to move above the shop?'

Maria frowned. 'I haven't really called anyone yet. Lynn has been clearing things out up there, but it's not really ideal. Pushchairs and everything are going to take up space.'

'Why not rent somewhere?'

Maria shook her head. 'I can't really afford to rent a house round here, and there aren't many flats in Westfield. I'll sort something out. Once the baby comes, I plan on getting back to work, and hopefully this wedding will start to bring some bookings in, once word gets around. I can bring the baby to work with me in the shop, and Lynn said she'll help when I have an event.'

James nodded. 'I have a house, you know, in Harrogate.'

'To rent out? I couldn't afford to rent a house, James. Especially not in Harrogate.'

'No,' he laughed. 'I mean I own a house, I live in it. Our grandmother left us a decent bit of money when she passed, and I bought before the housing bubble burst. Annabel lives with Mark again now, so it's just me. It's a three-bedroomed house, Maria. I was thinking that if you needed somewhere, you could come stay with me.'

The waiter chose that moment to bring them their melon starters, making a fuss of asking if they wanted to change their minds about the wine, checking they had enough bread. James was polite, answering the waiter's questions, thanking him. Maria had a flashback to when she had last dined out with Darcy. The waitress had been a bubbly girl, eager to please, probably warned by her boss to give them the star treatment. Darcy had been dismissive from the start, lowering himself to downright rude by the time the dessert trolley was wheeled out. The poor girl looked close to tears several times, and she remembered how embarrassed she had felt, how ashamed her mother would have been of his treatment of that girl.

Everyone has to earn a crust, she used to say, echoing the words her late husband had used. *Don't treat them like they aren't even worthy of your crumbs.* It was something that was ringing in her head all through the meal. How had she forgotten that? His sneering attitude sometimes, the looks of derision he gave some of the people they met. It was the part of him she hadn't liked, but often overlooked. The side that came from his mother.

'Maria, you need anything?'

James and the waiter were both looking at her expectantly.

'No,' she said, shaking her head. 'Thank you very much. It's lovely.'

The waiter smiled and moved away, dealing with one of the few other diners in the room who were just now coming in.

'So, they use this room for weddings on a weekend, and they will, of course, accommodate all the guests, and the honeymoon suite will be included.'

Maria glanced at her clipboard, wondering if she had covered everything the couple wanted.

'Did you hear me?'

Maria sighed. 'Yes, I heard you, James, and it's incredibly generous, but I can't—'

'Don't answer yet. Think about it. Come and see the house, if you like. You have time yet.'

She pressed her lips together. She couldn't do it, even if she wanted to. How would that be? The baby was related to him, in a loose, by-marriage way. Or soon would be. It would be far too weird. She wanted to tell him, thanks, but no thanks. Explain to him why she couldn't do it, why she had to keep her distance, because one day soon they would have to part ways, and the thought of it was more than a little sad to her. She felt tears prick at her eyes and blinked them away quickly. Bloody hormones. No wine, and she cried at the drop of a hat. Hard to keep a 'lying to everyone' poker face up with that. Not very *Ocean's Eleven*, snotting over everyone you had to fib to.

'Okay. I have time.'

He smiled at her, his pearly white teeth flashing between his full lips, and her heart bumped a little extra beat. *Shame*, she thought to herself, pushing the thought away.

After dessert, the owner had arranged for one of the porters to show them the rooms where the guests would be staying, and the honeymoon suite, which was on the very top floor of the hotel.

Maria was still feeling full from lunch, and more than a little bit tired. Apparently, at this stage, she should have started feeling full of energy, but she was pretty sure the info she'd read online was actually a crock of shit. She felt like she would never feel bright-eyed and bushy-tailed ever again. Her boobs were swollen and sore, with huge veins starting to show under the surface, and her clothes were all starting to feel the strain of her expanding waistband. Not helped by Tucker's cooking, which was wolfed down by her and Cassie every night. He cooked low-fat meals, but there were always seconds, and thirds. She was grateful, of course, because without him still living at Cassie's, she would have ended up giving birth to a pizza baby. But still… She couldn't get rid of the niggling feeling that, soon, both the men helping her in life would be gone, and that left her alone. Lynn and Cassie were there of course, but Lynn had her own life, and Cassie was as busy as ever. Soon enough, it would be her and a small, defence-less child. She needed to pull herself together.

The three of them – James, Maria and the porter, an affable young lad called Gavin, with mild acne and bright ginger hair – all headed in the lift to the top of the hotel, where the honeymoon suite was. As soon as the lift doors closed, Maria suddenly felt very claustrophobic, and lightheaded. She started to fan herself with the clipboard, using the half-ream of paper attached to waft around the stale air. The lift trundled along, the lights for each floor pinging ever so slowly.

James looked at her, his face full of concern.

'Maria, you okay?'

'Yeah,' she said, waving her hand to reassure him. It flicked lethargically in his direction. 'I'm just gonna... er... nap...'

She passed out cold, the clipboard clattering to the carpeted floor as her legs gave way under her. James grabbed for her, just catching her before she hit the deck.

'In here,' she heard a voice say. She was floating and giggled at the sensation.

She saw a white door in front of her, and she was cradled in something warm, and strong. She could feel the power beneath her, but she felt protected, safe. The door opened, a flash of red in the corner of her eye. She tried to follow it, but soon regretted it.

'I don't feel so good,' she murmured, and felt the cradle around her tighten.

'I've got you, it's okay,' James said softly. His voice sounded strange, not the usual relaxed tone she had got used to. 'Call an ambulance, now.'

A vision of the hospital, the stark white room, the photographers, Darcy, sprang Maria from her stupor.

'No!' she shouted, trying to stand. 'No ambulance, please.'

James sat down on the bed, with her still in his arms. She was coming round fast, her body feeling hot and sweaty, her hip hurting from where she had banged it collapsing in the lift.

She tried to stand, but James's grasp was firm.

'Just give it a minute. Gavin, forget the call for now. Can we just have a glass of water, please.'

Gavin, looking white as a sheet and obviously cursing his job choice today, garbled something at them and ran off down the corridor.

'I think I scared him,' she said glumly, feeling her body come to. 'I'm fine, honestly. I think it was just the heat. My mother warned me about this. She was just the same with me, but I never really imagined what it would be like.'

'You scared me. Again,' he said, looking straight into her eyes. 'I bet you haven't been taking your iron tablets and had no breakfast. You need to let people take care of you, Mar, and look after yourself and the baby.' His blue-green eyes were quite a bright green close up. They were really pretty. Sparkly, even. She could see her own face in them, her dazed expression mirrored in an emerald sea.

'Your eyes are lovely, do you know that?' she blurted. His brows lifted, making them pop all the more.

'Yours aren't so bad either.' She could smell the chocolate from the pudding they had just eaten. It tasted sweet, mixed with his aftershave, a lemony scent that reminded her of when her mother cleaned the house in summer. A homey smell that centred her.

'Are you really okay?' he pressed, adjusting her slightly in his arms so she could sit up a little. He didn't let go of her legs, and she made no move to sit up.

'I will start looking after myself, I promise. I just need to get this wedding taken care of. I'm fine, honestly. I'm sorry I'm such a drama queen. I bet you rue the day you took my call.'

He stroked his fingers along her back, and she felt her nerve endings come to life.

'No, not at all. I'm glad I answered. Maria, I—'

Gavin burst into the room, slamming into the already ajar door with such force that the doorstop sent it flying back into him, bopping him on the nose.

'Ouch! Here, I got you some water, and I brought the first-aid kit. Mr Harrison is on his way.'

He held out a large green box and a bottle of Evian, hands trembling. The poor lad looked like he was about to join her in keeling over. James reached for the water, and Maria took the opportunity to slide her legs from over his and take a seat on the bed next to him. Mr Harrison came into the room then, casting a confused look Gavin's way before putting his best beaming smile forward.

'I heard you were unwell, Miss Mallory. I do hope you're okay now?'

He was obviously panicking, and she clicked why. Of course. Her name had been all over the papers since the wedding and her dash to hospital. The poor man had started out looking forward to a nice, easy wedding booking, but now his hotel was going to be plastered all over the papers.

'I'm fine. I just got a little hot, that's all. Nothing you did. You and Gavin have been lovely, and the meal was gorgeous. I think we will be booking the wedding here; I just need to confirm with my clients. I'll be in touch.'

Hugo Harrison's shoulders sagged with relief and, stepping forward, he shook her hand.

'Excellent, that's all wonderful news. Well, I shall leave you to look around. Gavin, will you see them out when they're ready?'

Gavin nodded, eyes wide in terror. 'Yes, sir,' he squeaked. Poor kid.

Mr Harrison nodded to him to follow him out of the door, and they both left. Hushed voices could be heard in the corridor.

James passed her the water and she took it, taking a big glug.

'Oh, thanks, that's better.'

James put the first-aid kit down on the bed, looking around at the room for the first time. The suite itself was lovely, a big four-poster bed in the centre of the room, ornate furnishings in light, airy colours. Just off the bedroom, an open archway led to the bathroom. Maria could see a claw-foot tub, a trolley full of high-end toiletries and plush towels filling it.

'Nice, eh?' James said, slowly pulling her to her feet. He'd picked up her bag when he caught her, and he passed it to her now. She pushed the bottle of water into it and nodded.

'It's lovely.'

'I kind of carried you over the threshold into here, you know,' he said, his expression suddenly mischievous. 'A bit romantic really, if you think about it. Minus the fainting on me, of course.'

123

'Oh, really?' She walked over to the bathroom, peeping her head around the corner to check the rest of the room. She felt sturdy on her legs, thank God. Her dizzy spell had passed. She was going to have to stop getting so stressed. The next time, she might not be so lucky. The last thing she wanted was to be back in hospital on a drip.

'Yep, I full-on carried you from the lift, like a scene from *Backdraft*. I always fancied being a fireman.'

She giggled, till the image of him striding out of a burning building all sweaty and covered in soot sprang into her mind, and the laughter turned into a strangled gasp in her throat. *Mamma Mia!*

He opened the closet doors and they both peered in together. 'Yep, I really did. Till I decided that being an electrician and rescuing damsels in distress was much more important.'

Maria rolled her eyes. 'You're such a goofball.'

He grinned, waggling his eyebrows. 'And you love it.'

She looked away, busying herself with her clipboard. This was getting too friendly. *He carried me over the threshold?* She remembered the feeling she'd had when she came to, in his arms. Had Darcy ever made her feel like that? If he had, she was hard pressed to remember it now. James had sat her down on the bed, in his arms, after carrying her into the honeymoon suite. She needed to get the hell out of there.

'Right, I'm done. Shall we go?' She pushed the clipboard back under her arm, all business when she looked back at him. He looked at her for a long moment before replying.

'Sure, Mar, I'll take you home.'

***

Maria was lying in the tub that night, the suds high all around her as she contemplated her day. She had called the midwife about her dizzy spell, and she was due to go in to the doctor's

124

the next morning to have everything checked. She felt fine now, but she didn't want to risk anything happening to the baby. She knew what they would say: too much stress, not enough food or rest. She hadn't been taking her iron tablets as she should have either. She needed to sort herself out.

She was already imagining the little thing here now, getting used to the tiny button that had invaded her body, making it swell, stealing her food. There was a knock at the door and Cassie's voice rang out.

'Mar, can I come in?'

'Yeah,' Maria said, and Cassie came through the door, shutting it behind her and sitting on the closed toilet seat.

'I've had an idea, you know.'

'Oh?'

'Yeah, well, I had a client today, and they're getting divorced because he won't get the kids christened. She really wants to do it before they get too old, but he's refusing to give consent.'

Maria looked at Cass, who was looking rather relaxed for once, a large glass of white wine in her hand. Her normally severe hairstyle had been blown out, her hair long and cascading down her shoulders, and instead of her usual sharp suit she was wearing a more feminine-cut, short-sleeved blouse and a pair of plum slacks.

'You look nice. Are they really divorcing because of that?'

Cassie looked down at herself, shrugging.

'Oh, thanks. Tucker picked it out. Not just that, no. He'd also been slipping one of the godmothers a bit of special attention, but still, it got me thinking.'

Maria was baffled. 'About what?'

'Kids' clothes! You could make them, Mar, for the shop. No one in Westfield does them really. New Lease of Life does the knitted stuff from the nana knitting club thingy, but not clothes. You do the Halloween children's stuff already, so why not do more? People have to do mail order or go into town. You could even make christening gowns! They're just like wedding dresses for babies anyway, aren't they? I bet they'd sell well, and Lynn could help you, and you could make a load for the baby too, save money.'

'Oh my God, Cass, that's bloody brilliant!'

Maria sat up quickly, sending bubbly water flying over the end of the bath. Cassie grabbed a towel from the rail and mopped it up before Maria could even make a move.

'Wow, I'm living in a parallel universe, aren't I? What the hell are you doing?'

Cassie looked up from wiping the last of the water away one-handed, throwing the towel into the newly acquired laundry hamper that now sat in there.

'What?' she said, swigging her wine. 'Tuck cleaned up today; I'm just giving him a hand. He still can't quite bend right.'

'Tuck, eh?' Maria knew her friend too well to let her off the hook. 'And what else do you do for our little Australian friend, eh?'

Cassie knelt down near the top of the bath, her voice dropping to a whisper.

'It's not funny. I don't know what to do, Mar. I think I might actually like him, but what am I going to do? I hit him with my car door and really hurt him. He's been off work for ages. He's got to be skint, but he's too nice to say anything. He keeps buying food and cleaning stuff too! Do you think I should offer him some money, to help him? He won't take any shopping money from me; I've tried. He might lose his digs!'

Maria shook her head. 'No way. I think Tucker would really hate that. He doesn't strike me as the kind of guy who would agree to that. You might offend him.'

Cassie rested her head on the side of the tub, and Maria stroked her hair, leaving a little trail of bubbles on her black locks.

'Tell him how you feel, see what he says. He's recovering well now; he knows you didn't mean to batter him with your car—' Cassie groaned. 'I think you might be surprised.'

Maria had watched the pair of them skirt around each other every night, laughing at each other's jokes, sitting on the sofa together, close enough to touch but not quite. She had been expecting to hear the pitter-patter of tiny, horny footsteps across the landing, but obviously that hadn't happened yet. Perhaps Tucker wanted to be fighting fit before he started round two. Knowing their luck, he would probably sneak onto the couch and scare her to death, getting a throat punch for his trouble. She couldn't blame him for wanting to be able to make a quick getaway from the lioness that was Cassie.

Cassie stood up, moving to the door. 'Maybe, I don't know.' She drained her glass, waving her arms out wide. 'I don't do this, Mar, I don't know how! How on earth did you do it?'

Maria laughed. 'I didn't do a stand-up job, did I? Left at the altar, knocked up on a one-night stand a month later, and now I'm planning—'

Cassie's face dropped. 'I thought you weren't telling him? Mar, you can't!'

Maria sank back down into the bubbles.

'I'm not! Planning his wedding is bad enough. I feel awful, Cass. James's sister – poor Annabel. Her Mark is my Mark. THE Mark. I still can't believe it. James would be so upset, and he's so lovely. I mean, today he—'

Cassie walked out of the bathroom door, slamming it shut behind her. Maria was still looking at it in shock when she came back in, bottle and glass in hand.

'Tucker says dinner will be an hour. Roasted peppers and chicken something.'

She sat on the floor, pouring wine to near the brim of her wineglass.

'You have to tell me everything, and you have an hour. Spill, now. Tell me about James.'

The roasted peppers were gorgeous, and the dinner was lovely. Tucker and Cassie were their usual selves, skirting around each other and making each other laugh with their daft jokes and sarcastic humour. Cassie was quite merry from the wine and, being exhausted from her day of passing out and gossiping, Maria headed off to bed early, leaving the two of them alone.

Cassie had grilled her, as only a solicitor could, asking her every little detail, who knew what, what happened next, whether Darcy had been in touch.

'I haven't seen him since he came to the hospital, and I don't answer his calls. I think he's got the message.'

'And James? What about him? Does he really not know?'

The very thought twisted in her gut like a knife.

'No, of course not. I'm doing it for him. He wants his sister to be happy, and so do I. I can do the wedding, save money for the baby, and then be out of their lives.'

She had thought of lying in James's arms today, and a feeling had stirred in her that she squashed down. *Nope, not today.*

Cassie had looked dejected. 'Can you do that, though? Not see him again?'

Maria had risked a look at her friend; she knew Cassie wasn't daft.

'Cassie, he's Annabel's brother. Mark's brother-in-law. They're family, not me. I have to get out of their lives as soon as the wedding is over, let them be happy.'

'Do you think James will be happy, you not being his friend anymore? Because the way I see it, he's got quite used to you being in each other's lives, and so have you.'

Maria swallowed hard. 'I have no choice. There's no other way to do this. Besides, I have the baby to think of. That's my priority.'

Cassie nodded. 'Just remember, Mar, how lonely you were when your mum passed, even with Darcy. I haven't seen you this happy in a long while, even with everything you have going on. It's not a coincidence that James came along when he did.'

The words rattled around in her brain half the night, till she eventually passed out in a heap, her quilt wrapped around her. She dreamt she was trapped in a burning building, a tiny little bundle in her arms. She was screaming for Cass, for Lynn, calling her mother's name. Then she saw him. A man, striding through the fire, fireman trousers slung low on his waist, showing the deep V of his taut muscles. His jacket was open, showing a bare, sticky-with-sweat chest, glistening in the bright, crackling flames of the fire. He took her into his arms, the baby in hers, and started to walk to the exit, through the flames. She looked at his face, and was met with Darcy's.

'I'm sorry, my love,' he said. And then he was gone, his face morphed into Mark's. His straggly, unkempt hair stuck to his head with sweat.

'I'm here,' he said. In her dream, she looked away, pushing her face closer to the bundle in her embrace.

'I've got you both,' a voice said, tickling her ear. She looked back at her rescuer, and it was James, smiling down at them. 'I'll always be here to carry you over the threshold.'

She woke up with a start, looking around her wildly before realising she was still warm in bed at Cassie's house. She punched the pillow beside her, feeling more than a little flustered. It was going to be a very long pregnancy at this rate.

Christmas Day came, and Maria awoke in Cassie's cottage to the sound of carols and the smell of bacon. Tucker was in the kitchen, clad in a pair of tracksuit bottoms and a Santa hat. Even his kangaroo tattoo looked festive.

'Morning, mummy-to-be,' he said, tipping his spatula towards her. 'Happy Christmas!'

Maria, clad in a nightie and slippers, dressing gown wrapped around her against the chill of leaving her bed, grinned at him.

'Happy Christmas, Jesse, you okay? Where's Cass?'

Tucker grinned. 'She's in her bed. She got a bit pissed last night and forgot she was on the sofa.'

Maria's mouth formed a perfect O as she gasped.

He shook his head. 'Nah, mate, I was a perfect gent. I came into the lounge.'

Maria sagged, disappointed.

'You two need to sort it out.' Tucker nodded earnestly.

'Tell me about it. Once I get better, I plan to. It's just…'

He sneaked a peek into the hall, to check Cassie wasn't listening.

'Your mate is a complicated woman. I would rather things happen sober next time, then she can't palm me off.'

Maria nodded, smiling at him. Cassie might just have met her match in Jesse Tucker.

'Besides, she's a bit handy with strange weapons, so I have to be careful.' He raised his potted arm and she laughed. The doorbell went and she froze, looking at the door in terror.

Lynn was with her sister, sunning herself in Jamaica for the festive season. And Cassie's parents were also in the Caribbean, no doubt making their private butler earn every penny of his wages and forgetting they had ever spawned a child.

Tucker went to the door, throwing a tea towel over his shoulder. 'That'll be our guest, right on time.'

Maria looked down the hallway, wondering who on earth would be coming here on Christmas Day. Tucker walked back into the kitchen, waggling his eyebrows at Maria.

'Santa's here,' he said, and Maria found herself looking into James's bright blue-green eyes, as he stood there, gift bags and a bottle of wine in hand.

'Happy Christmas,' he said, and she grinned.

'Happy Christmas, James.'

***

January

Lynn took one look at her the first morning back at work and headed for the kettle.

'Decaf coffee, love? You look awful!'

Maria pulled a face, taking off her hat, scarf and coat and slinging them onto the shoe rack. She kissed her fingers and touched her mother's photo frame and her father's hat on the way to the biscuit jar.

'Thanks, Lynn. I didn't sleep much, but the midwife says everything's still fine. My iron levels are better, and my blood pressure is good.'

Fine and dandy. And apparently she was now a baby-making machine and a sex maniac. Over Christmas, the dreams had intensified, somehow including James dressed in nothing but a Santa hat. She couldn't look at a Santa image now without blushing. Thank God it was back to normal business now.

'Aww, that's amazing! Did you hear the heartbeat again?'

Maria grinned. 'Yeah, I did. It was so fast! I recorded it on my phone; I'll send it to you. Amazing to think a little person with a little beating heart is in my tummy, isn't it? I'm so glad everything's okay.'

Lynn grinned. 'Feeling the pregnancy bloom now, are we?'

Maria nodded. 'Yes, I really think I am.' She opened the biscuit tin.

'Oh my God, where in the name of cock have all the friggin' biscuits gone?' She rounded on her work colleague, brandishing the tin at her and narrowing her eyes. Lynn was half-expecting a laser to shoot out of them and shrank back, shielding herself with a jar of decaf coffee.

'Have you eaten them all, Lynn? Why didn't you buy any more? I'm sooo hungry!' She slammed the biscuit tin down. 'Nothing goes right. Everything is so shit!' She burst into tears, reaching for the kitchen roll and blowing her nose loudly. Lynn started making the coffee, and Maria felt a pang of shame.

'I'm s-s-sorry, Lynn, I love you so much, I really do. I just really wanted a biscuit.'

Lynn nodded, passing her a coffee mug as though she was walking with a live bomb. Or towards one.

'That's all right, dear, I understand. You ate the biscuits, remember?'

Maria nodded, sniffing and trying to smile through her tears. She took a sip of her coffee and burst into loud tears again.

'Decaf coffee tastes like turd! Why do I have to do this? I never asked for any of this. I'm so depressed!'

She plonked her coffee down on her desk, cradling the empty tin to her chest.

'My life is over,' she said, in a very undramatic tone.

The door opened then.

'Whose life's over?' James asked, standing there with a tray of takeaway coffees from the café up the road, and a bulging carrier bag. 'I just came to see what the midwife said, and I brought coffee. It's not decaf, but I looked it up and you can have one a day without it hurting the baby. Also, the baby seems to like biscuits, so I brought some of them too.'

Maria burst into hysterical wails and Lynn ushered him in, giving him a hug and a peck on the cheek before taking the coffee with her name on it.

'Baby's fine, chicken, and I can honestly say I have never been so happy to see anyone in my life. I'm going to nip upstairs and do the online orders. Give me a shout before you go.'

James waved her off, taking a seat next to Maria, who was now sniffling into a huge wad of sodden kitchen roll. He put the coffees on her desk and, after a bit of coaxing, managed to pry the empty tin from the death grip she had on it. He opened one of the packets from the bag and filled it up. He held one to her lips, and she laughed through her tears.

'Open wide,' he commanded, and she bit into it, taking the rest from him. 'So, midwife go okay?'

He took a hanky from his pocket and wiped her tears away. 'Blow,' he said, and she squeaked at him.

'Eugh, no! I can't!'

He wrapped the hanky round her nose and gave her his best stern look, which was mildly cross at best and very cute.

'I've seen snot before. I work with big, burly builders. I've seen worse things come out of arse cracks, trust me.'

She giggled and did what she was told. He looked her over, seemingly satisfied.

'Better. So, what's wrong?'

'I got a bit upset. It was a biscuit thing. Hormones, I think. The midwife says it's going to get worse, and the rest of the stuff is no picnic either.'

'Rest of the stuff?'

She blushed furiously. Not the best time to let slip about how horny she was, or the fact that her dreams were about him as a fireman, a jolly red-suited man, and a go-go dancer.

'Nothing, just silly stuff.'

'You're both healthy, though, yeah?'

She told him yes, and he looked so relieved that her tummy fluttered. And then it fluttered again. Weird. She put her hand to her tummy, and she felt it again. A tiny little flutter. The midwife said she had felt it this morning, when she had the Doppler on, but Maria had discounted it as a hunger pain. Or maybe a suppressed fart. Another thing they left off the glowing-mum adverts on TV. The fact that your bum cheeks turned into the mouthpiece for a concerto of duck farts and foghorn toots.

Flutter flutter. There it went again. Definitely not flatulence.

'Quick, feel!' She grabbed James's hand and placed it on her stomach, under her own. His hand felt huge on her tummy, hers fitting snugly on his. She could feel the warmth from his skin through her T-shirt. It fluttered again, and James's face lit up.

'Wow, was that the baby?'

She nodded, too choked up to speak. It felt so weird being here with him, doing this. Right, but so wrong. 'I'm over four months now. The midwife said it would be happening.'

James leant in close, putting his other hand on her and cupping her belly.

'Hey, little Sparky,' he said softly. 'You all happy and healthy in there?'

'Sparky?' she asked, entranced by his interest. *Was this what having a baby with someone was like? She felt a pang for what she was missing out on.*

He looked embarrassed. 'Sorry, just my nickname. It's an electrician thing. I know you call it Button, but I just call her Sparky.'

'Her?' Maria and another voice said. Darcy was standing in the doorway, staring at them both with a look Maria had never seen on him before.

The air crackled with tension. Maria felt like she could physically hear the hum of it in the air. *Oh God, this is bad. He knows. Did he know already? Why is he here?*

'Her?' Darcy asked again, a little meaner this time.

'I… I… what are you doing here?' she stammered, standing up. James's hands fell from her tummy and he put them on his own jean-clad legs.

'It's a her? Our baby?' Darcy said, a hint of wonder in his voice now. *Our baby? Oh God, no. Why didn't he seem more surprised? Was that why he was here?*

'Her baby,' James growled. Darcy's eyes narrowed, his sculpted brows furrowing.

'Ours, I think you'll find. Last time I checked. Here again, are we? Who are you, exactly?'

Maria opened her mouth to explain, but James stood up, standing close enough to Maria's side to brush his arm against hers.

'I'm James, not that it's any of your business.'

Darcy snorted, a ridiculous, over-the-top sound he always made to show people his holier-than-thou contempt. Maria hated it, and she felt her skin bristle at the memory.

'Funny thing, business, isn't it? Being that this isn't yours… James.' He said James like a child might say Marmite sandwich, or extra homework. 'I'll thank you to leave now, so my fiancée and I can talk.'

'Fiancée?' James boomed, making Maria jump at his side. He didn't take his eyes off Darcy, but squeezed her hand gently in his as if to apologise, to check she was okay. She couldn't help but squeeze it back, keep it in hers for comfort. She could feel herself watching them distractedly, as though she was watching something she wasn't a part of. Like a telenovela, enjoying the drama from her couch. 'Mate, when you leave a woman at the altar, it's a pretty sure sign that the engagement is off. Maria, do you want me to kick him out?'

'Kick me out! How bloody dare you! You can leave, go on, go! Before I get really cross!'

'Oooh, really cross, eh? Well, we can't jolly well have you being cross, can we, you simpering douchebag!'

'Douchebag? How dare you!'

James let go of her hand and walked forward slowly, as though he had all the time in the world. Darcy shuffled back before he could get hold of himself, but then puffed his chest out in response.

'Go on then, make me leave. I dare you!'

James took another step, then looked back at her.

'Maria?' he asked, and she looked at him wide-eyed. 'Do you want him to go?'

Maria heard footsteps behind her and saw Lynn coming into the room. Maria looked back at Darcy, at James. What did she want? She was going to have to tell him it wasn't his, but in front of James?

She really didn't want to tell him the one-night stand story. She had to tell Darcy, of course. Leaving out the fact of who the one-night stand actually was. James hadn't asked about the father. Had he just assumed it was Darcy?

'I… er… er…'

'See?' Darcy jumped in. 'She doesn't want me to leave, so give us a minute, would you? I'm sure you have a light bulb to fit somewhere.' Darcy flicked his manicured finger at James's hoody,

135

which was emblazoned with his company name. James flinched, and Lynn came to stand at her other side, pulling her gently to the chair.

'Sit down, hun,' she said softly. 'It's okay.'

Maria felt pathetic. She couldn't get the words out! Her worlds were colliding, and she didn't know how to make it stop. She wanted to stop and get off the carousel that was her life now.

'Listen, posh boy.' James's voice was like something she had never heard before from him. It was as though his whole body was vibrating with tension, his words a throaty rumble from deep within his chest. No, his core. He looked and sounded a little like Wolverine. 'I won't tell you again. Leave, now.'

Darcy stepped forward, pushing his hair back with one hand, his cufflink glinting in the light of the shop. Maria knew it well; it was part of a set from her. A present one birthday, their initials entwined on the face of each. She had wanted him to wear them for the wedding, but his mother had insisted he would be wearing a pair of his father's. Family tradition apparently, which was fair enough. Maria understood the importance of family, if nothing else. She'd never got the chance to follow many traditions in her family, so she didn't want to mess with his, cause any trouble. She had only ever wanted his love, and to be a part of his family.

'I don't think so. We have things to discuss, and I don't understand why you're still here, arguing with me about something that doesn't involve you one iota.'

'I could say the same to you, young man,' Lynn said, stepping forward. 'You should just go. I'm sure Maria will call you if she wants to. But if she did, she would have done it by now, don't you see that?'

Maria sighed. Now even Lynn was sticking up for her. She really needed to put an end to this. Once and for all. Before the whole thing came tumbling out.

'Yes, please, Darcy, just leave. I don't want to talk to you.'

She looked at him for the first time, properly, in the face, and

136

was shocked when she felt it. She had thought about him so much since the day he had humiliated her, but now he was there, she wished him away. She felt nothing, nothing but shame. Looking at him had her straight back in that wedding dress, climbing out of the window of the side room to avoid her guests. Crying over her fries in the burger bar, her friend trying to pick up the dropped stitches of her ripped-apart life.

'You heard her.' James took this as carte blanche to turn into some kind of enforcer and folded his arms in front of Darcy. It was quite comical, James being a good foot taller than Darcy, but Mr Burgess wasn't used to being dismissed in such a manner.

He leaned to one side, looking at her with pleading eyes.

'Maria, we have to talk, I need to explain, and...'

He took a step forward and James reached out with one arm and placed his open palm square on the front of Darcy's head. Darcy tried to take another step forward, but James never budged and he was jerked back.

Darcy lost it then and, bending in half, emitted a strange 'weeeehhhh' sound and tried to slam into James's torso. James let go of his head and, catching him in his arms with an 'ooof', went straight in and tried to tackle him back. James's shove propelled the pair nearer the door, and then he was like a prop forward in a rugby scrum, lifting Darcy half off the floor and towards the door. Darcy started punching James in the ribs, the kidneys, but James slapped him on the behind hard and Darcy screamed. Actually screamed. Lynn was by now flapping her arms, running around the pair, saying, 'Stop it, stop it now, boys!' Maria was too scared to get close, in case a flying arm caught her. She was already feeling pretty off balance. One shove and she would be straight back in hospital. James kept flicking his gaze to her, as though checking she was okay, out of the way.

'Darcy, stop it!' she shouted, just as James roared and reared back, clutching his arm.

'You bit me?!' he said, looking at Darcy like he wanted to drop kick him through the shop window. 'You bloody bit me, you snobby wanker! What are you, a flipping toddler?'

'You can talk, you knuckle-dragging buffoon! What the hell are you even doing here?'

He turned to Maria then, realisation crossing his features. Maria steeled herself. This was it. Truth time.

'Are you shagging this gorilla?' he demanded. 'What is it, a bit of rough to get back at me? Classy move, Maria, I must say. I shan't have it!'

That was it. That was the moment she flipped.

'Have what? My life is nothing to do with you, Darcy! YOU LEFT ME ALONE!' she screamed at him, a howl of pure pain in her words. 'I was all alone! Get out, now! I don't have to answer to you! Go back to your bloody mother!'

Lynn came to her side, standing close to her and folding her arms sternly.

James went to push him again, but he held up his hands.

'Okay, I know, I know. I'll go, but we need to talk. You must realise that. We'll have to talk at some point. We have so much to talk about!'

Maria shook her head. 'No, we don't. I don't want to talk to you ever again. Just go. Don't come back, Darcy, I mean it. There's nothing here for you.'

He hung his head, and she took him in. His shirt was hanging out, one side torn, and his normally flashy hairstyle was a bird's nest on top of his head. She could see he was sweating, and she glanced at James. His back to her, his stance rigid, he didn't even look out of breath. The only evidence of a fight was the red teeth marks on his now uncovered arm, his sleeve pulled up to show the damage. She felt a pang of guilt. She had to tell Darcy Burgess the truth about the baby. He'd said 'ours' for a reason. This was bad. She had to get rid of him. Once and for all. What was it they said? Oh yes. *The truth will set you free. And get rid of the posh git who left you at the altar to*

138

please his mummy-kins. The sad thing was, it also put paid to dashing rescuers as well.

'I'll call,' he said, turning to the door. 'And you *will* answer.'

James took slow steps forward, punctuating his exit.

'Do me a favour, though,' he said in a low voice. 'Stop acting like a common slut, at least when you're carrying my child.'

Maria heard a bang, followed by a thud, and it took a good three or four seconds before her brain was able to process what her eyes had just seen. Without saying a word, James had taken a step forward, and then Darcy was on the floor, knocked clean off his feet. James had swung his right arm, and that was it. Hit-the-deck time.

James leant forward, right into Darcy's bewildered face.

'Don't you ever speak to her like that again, you hear me?'

'Do you know who I am?' Darcy spluttered through his rapidly swelling face. James laughed, an easy, carefree laugh. One Maria had heard many times before. It was at odds with his gait, which was coiled tight. The man was mad, she could see it.

'I don't care who you are. You will never, ever, speak to her like that again. Right?'

Darcy looked as though he might have trouble remembering his own name, let alone the horrible one he had just uttered, and he nodded reluctantly. James hauled him to his feet and out the door, leaving the two women standing there in silence.

'Well,' Lynn said, rubbing her hands together as though shaking off the dust of Darcy. 'Shall I make a pot of tea?'

***

Outside, Darcy was trying, very unsuccessfully, to keep his dignity, and his feet on the ground, while James marched him to his car.

'This yours, is it?' he said, pointing to the rather flash white Porsche. His weekend car. He nodded, trying to wriggle out of James's rock-hard grasp and gain some purchase on the pavement

139

with his Italian leather shoes. James suddenly let go, and Darcy windmilled his limbs to stay on his feet.

'Bye,' James said, turning away to go back into the shop. He needed to check everyone was all right.

'Tell me something first.' Darcy's voice stopped him in his tracks. 'Is she... are they okay?'

James closed his eyes, sighing deeply. When he opened them again, he could see Lynn and Maria talking, Maria sipping from a mug, one hand on her growing bump. He felt a huge surge of feeling slam into his chest once more, just as when Darcy had called her that name. He was in this, whatever it was, and he didn't know how, or in what way exactly. It was nothing he could put into words. He just knew he wanted to be there.

'They're fine,' he said, turning to look at Darcy, who was inspecting his rather swollen face in the wing mirror of his car. *Priorities, eh, Darce? Pretty boy.*

He turned to look at him then, jutting out his glass chin.

'I'm not going to go away, you know. I'm here to stay.'

James shook his head and went to walk back inside.

'Yeah, well, so am I. And I never left, either.'

Maria was just drinking a warming cup of herbal tea when James walked back in. She heard the roar of Darcy's car driving away. His weekend Porsche, obviously. She'd always hated that thing. It was like being careened across the road in a low toboggan, but he loved it.

James came straight over and sat next to her. Lynn was working in the back, singing along to Nina Simone on the radio.

'You didn't need to do that, James,' Maria said, looking at him coldly.

'I know, I'm sorry. I didn't think about it in all honesty. I just reacted so I apologise for my part, but no one speaks to you like that.'

'Why not? Why am I so special? He's mad, I get it.' She looked down at her lap, her hand stroking her tummy.

'He's mad? Why do you care how he feels? The man is a louse, Mar, pure and simple.'

Mar. Not many people called her that, and now James was one of them. She thought of the scene Darcy had walked in on. Them together, over her bump like that. So blissfully domestic. She didn't know what Darcy knew, but he'd obviously picked up on something Maria herself had been trying to ignore.

'James, you need to go too, I think.'

James's eyes widened in shock, and he reached for her hand, covering it with his over her bump.

'I really am sorry, I just lost my temper. You have to know, that's not me.'

'It's not that… it's not just that, anyway.' She picked up his hand and, after a moment, placed it on his own leg. He looked down at it, but said nothing. 'You've been so good to me, with the wedding and the shop and everything, but I really… I just need to get used to doing things on my own now.'

James frowned. 'Why, when I'm here?'

'I can't rely on you, James.' She stood up, stretching out her back and suddenly feeling very tired.

'What makes you think that? When have I ever let you down?' He looked so confused, aghast. She tried to summon up an occasion to strengthen her non-existent case, but of course nothing came to mind. He had always been there, her rock.

'Listen…' She looked at him kindly. 'I love your company, but you have a business to run. Surely you have things to do, besides bailing me out of my misery and being a bouncer. I just think maybe we should have a break from each other. We have all this wedding stuff to do together anyway, so it's not like we won't see each other.'

Maria noticed that the radio in the back room was noticeably quieter, and she knew Lynn would probably have something to say to her later.

He didn't say anything at first, and the look he gave her broke her heart a little. His hair was doing the tufty thing she liked, which meant he had probably jumped straight out of bed, and just wanged a comb through his dark locks. He always looked so eager in the morning. She imagined him jumping straight out of bed at first light, eager to get the day going.

'That's not an answer. So now, because of Darcy, in the space of a few weeks, we've gone from possibly living together to being strangers?' He stood and looked down at her. She caught a waft of his aftershave and had to fight the urge to tuck herself into his big arms. 'I don't want to do this. I'm sorry if I overstepped today, but that man...' He jabbed at the window and clenched his fists at his sides.

He fixed his gaze on her, and she looked away.

'He just gets me mad. He doesn't know what he had. He never deserved it in the first place, and he still threw it away.'

'He did know, and he left. That's the point, James. I need to concentrate on my baby and the business, and that's it. I can't deal with anything else right now. I need to move on.'

'I'm not asking for anything! I thought we were friends? Why do you need to move on from me?'

'We are friends, James, but I have Cassie and Lynn. I'm fine.'

She looked to the door, and she could feel her whole body shaking. 'I'll let you know when the next appointment is, okay? For the wedding, I mean. I need to go sit down for a bit.'

James clenched his jaw and strode to the door.

'I don't want to stress you out, so I'll go. Tell Lynn I said bye.' He slammed the door behind him, and the radio sang a sad song in the background. One she used to love, about true love and perfect partners. What a crock of utter crap.

Chapter 15

'Mr Atwood, one more outburst and you shall be taken from this courtroom! The case has been decided, any appeals should be discussed with your solicitor.' Judge Rothwell banged his gavel again and eyed the irate defendant over the glasses perched on the end of his nose. Judge Alexander Rothwell was one of the nicer judges at Harrogate County Court, but Cassie could tell that the slimeball ex of her client, a very mousy and kind woman called Joanne, was testing his limits.

'I don't give a rat's arse what you do with your little 'ammer, I ain't paying her nowt. She sat on her arse all day, while I grafted my arse off at work!'

Grafted meaning running a very successful engineering firm and banging any female he could, while his long-suffering wife raised his three children, did his books and cooked and cleaned for him. Not much sitting on your bottom with all that and three children under three, surely?

Cassie thanked the judge and was just ushering a very delighted and embarrassed Joanne outside when she felt her arm being grabbed roughly, pulling her off kilter. She felt another set of hands on hers as the solicitor for the other side tried to wrestle his client off her.

'Get off me *now*, Mr Atwood,' she said as nicely as she could. She wanted to rip his arm off and beat him with it, but it wasn't really the done thing. Not in the courtroom anyway. Had they been in the car park, she might have had an answer using her car door. It seemed she was a dab hand with one of those. Mr Atwood sneered at her, called her a 'feminist tramp' and, rearing back, went to spit at her. A hocking great loogy of a spit too. Cassie pushed her client back, spinning out of the way, and the huge wad of sputum landed squarely in the face of Mr Atwood's solicitor. A rather weakly but razor-sharp law-minded man who looked at this moment like he wanted to throw up.

Joanne shouted, 'Stop it, Michael! You owe me!' and passed the poor solicitor a pack of baby wipes from her oversized handbag.

Court security came and hauled Michael off, Cass waving and giving him her best 'eat shit and die' grin, which only inflamed him more and caused him to catch the poor guard, John, in the testicles with a flailing leg. He was still screaming about bra burners and his lack of money when they took him down to the cells to cool off. Cassie hugged Joanne, making sure she was okay.

'I can't believe it's over. I can buy a place of my own now, me and the kids.' Joanne looked elated, and Cassie felt elated for her. Another client happy, able to move on from a bloke who couldn't keep it in his pants and expected a woman to just take it without a grumble.

'Well, you earned it too, don't forget. I'm really happy for you and the children. I'll get everything signed off and be in touch, okay?'

She looked to the doors through which darling ex-hubby dearest had just departed.

'He'll be down for a while, but will you be okay tonight?'

Joanne waved her away. 'He's not that type. He'll just moan for a while. But he's a good dad, believe it or not. When he shows.'

Cassie nodded, satisfied. 'Well, any problems, you know where I am, okay? Call the police if he gives you any trouble.'

Her phone buzzed in her pocket and she went to take it as she waved Joanne off.

Her house phone number came up on the screen, and she smiled.

'Have you not got a phone yet, Mr Tucker?' she teased.

'I'm waiting for it to be repaired in the shop, remember?' Tucker's laughing voice came over the phone, warming Cassie's cheeks. 'Some psychotic legal eagle tried to crush it into my hipbone. How did the case go?'

'Good,' she said, making her way out of the court building to the nearby car park. 'We won. It didn't go down too well, but I'll tell you about it later.'

The line went quiet. 'Ah well, that's what I wanted to talk to you about. I think I'm ready to get back to work, and my flat.'

Cassie reached her car, but instead of getting in, she sagged against it.

'Oh?' That was what she said. What she actually wanted to say was *don't leave. Why are you going, now?*

'Yeah.' Tucker cleared his throat. 'My business partner has been coping pretty well, and fine about letting me have the time off, but he's wanting me back. Light duties of course, and I'm pretty sure all my plants are dead at the flat. Plus my roommate is a huge slob.'

'Really?' she said, thinking about how her house had been before he came to stay. 'What an animal. How do people live like that, eh?'

He chuckled. 'I know, right? Anyway, I was thinking I'd start back tonight, get out of your hair. It's quieter in January, it'll ease me back in. My shift starts before you get home, though, so I thought I'd better let you know.'

'No problem, thanks,' she said, pushing down the huge slab of hurt she felt in her chest, and digging deep from her tough persona. *Woman up, Cass.* 'I'll see you around then. I have to go.'

She ended the call, threw her phone and bags on the passenger seat and slumped down into her driver door. She looked around, but the car park was deserted, just empty cars around her.

Still, she waited till the first set of traffic lights had gone before she started to cry. He rang her phone again, the personalised *Crocodile Dundee* theme tune he had programmed in as a joke ringing out in the interior of the car. She drove straight to the off-licence and let it go to voicemail.

Yet another charity ball, and his mother was once again planning his life like a puppet show. He half-expected to see strings sewn into one of the suits that she forced him to wear, passive-aggressively sending his tailor 'suggested' designs for his bespoke clothing. He thought of the suit Maria had made him, how lovely it was, and how at the time he had been too preoccupied worrying about what his mother would make of it to thank her. He'd slept at his mother's that night, before the wedding, and left the suit there. No doubt it wasn't there now. His mother never would have kept it.

He was in his apartment in Harrogate now, and it was eerily quiet. He'd never been bothered by his own company before Maria moved in, grateful to be out of his parents' house, but he had got used to her being there, her humming as she sewed on the couch, the strangled garble of her singing Motown in the shower. He hadn't expected to feel her loss so much, given his urgent need to run away from her. From her, and their unborn child, it seemed. Did she know on the day? Was she planning to surprise him on the honeymoon? More to the point, the question Darcy kept asking himself, over and over, rattled around inside his skull. The question he knew he didn't like his own answer to.

If she had told me before the wedding, would I have gone through with it, or would I have run that little bit faster?

The buzzer for the foyer rang, and Darcy was brought back into his empty apartment.

'Hello?' he said, pressing the intercom.

'Your guest is here, sir. Shall I send her up?'

Darcy sighed inwardly. Another night out with the PR woman – Victoria Shaw, he now knew her as – to prolong this wounded-bachelor-finds-solace angle that bit more, till the press could focus on some other scandal. The new range of weight-loss teas would be launching soon, and then his mother might actually ease off him a little. Just a few more events. He had tried to call Maria, but her phone always went unanswered, and Lynn would just hang up if he rang the shop.

He went to answer the door, and there she was. Perfect blonde coiffed hair as usual, her boobs looking pushed up and perky in the red velvet gown she had been poured into. Darcy thought he saw the hint of a nipple but looked away quickly. Hopefully she would pull a fashion faux pas and wap one out just as a photographer came past. That would piss his mother off.

'Hey,' she said, looking him up and down. 'Your bow tie's not tied.'

'Full marks for observation, minion,' he said, ignoring her shocked expression and heading to the mirror in his bedroom to sort it out. She followed him, and he tutted his annoyance.

'I don't need a babysitter, I would have met you there.'

She went and sat on his bed, the slash in her gown showing off her tanned, muscular thigh.

'That wouldn't do, would it? We need to appear together. Your mother ordered a car to collect us from here.'

Darcy groaned. He'd been planning to take the Porsche, giving him an excuse not to drink and a means of slipping away early. Now he would probably end up getting battered just to have something to take the edge off the long night of being on show. His mother's prize specimen.

'Something wrong?' she purred, and he felt her behind him. She was looking at him in the mirror, a predatory stance. She wound her hands around him, her long talons stroking down his sides, till one rested on the bulge in his trousers. 'You seem so stressed. I can help, you know.'

147

She squeezed him, and he gasped involuntarily, making her smile triumphantly. She went to put her hand down the front of his trousers, and he stopped her, pushing her hands away from him.

'What's this, a bonus from Mother?' She rolled her eyes at him. 'For you, or me?'

'Oh, come on, we have to work together for a while yet. Why don't we both get something out of it?'

Darcy scowled at her. 'You get paid, and I'm a captive little performing monkey. That's the deal, isn't it? I don't need to be fed a peanut, thanks.'

She stood in front of him, changing tack, walking her fingertips up the button track on his crisp white shirt. 'Yes, but it's not like we can date anyone else, is it? We're supposed to be dating each other, remember? So why not just do it? It will make our public interactions more believable.'

She ran her finger along his jawline, her fingernail making a scraping sound along his stubble. He watched her, saying nothing, and she moved her thumb pad over his bottom lip, making him quiver. She smiled, moving closer, till their lips were almost touching.

'Just another little piece of the puzzle,' she whispered seductively. 'Like a jigsaw, fitting together. Don't you think we would fit together well?'

She leaned in, just that fraction of a bit closer, and flicked her tongue out to taste him. He considered kissing her back for half a second, before he saw their reflection in the mirror. *No.* It didn't look right, and he thought of Maria. How they had looked together. A photo on the nightstand taunted him in the reflection. A picture of the two of them, post-coital in bed, looking pink-cheeked and happy, laughing into the camera, wrapped up in his bedsheets. He pulled Victoria's hand away, taking a step back. His erection betrayed him, pushing against the fabric of his trousers painfully. Her face dropped, turning to a thunderous look.

'No,' he said. 'I'm not free.'

She jutted her jaw out, fluffing her already perfect hair with one hand.

'Oh, baby, I think you'll find you've already been bought. I'll wait in the car.'

She waggled out, her Kim Kardashian arse leaving a good few seconds after her cleavage.

Darcy sighed with relief, looking down at his waist.

'We'll have no more of that,' he scolded. 'It's time to pay the piper, I think.'

Chapter 16

March

Walking back from Foxley Street, huge bunches of daffodils in her arms, Maria smiled to herself. Lily had been on top form at Love Blooms, giving her the best flowers for the shop window, laughing along with Roger, and asking about her growing baby bump. She had suddenly popped, her belly making her do that waddle thing all expectant mothers did at some point, and her ankles were often swollen after days in the shop. Add to that the fact that her appetite was that of a pro boxer, and she wanted to pee every five minutes, and she was definitely feeling pregnant these days. Happily pregnant, in fact, despite herself. Taking all of her vitamins, and no more dizzy spells, thankfully.

She had been keeping herself busy, and the shop was full of clothes. Racks and racks of clothes, and her christening gowns now hung alongside her wedding dresses. She had even started renovating upstairs. Simon, the handyman in the village, was coming most nights after helping his dad in the shop, and he had managed to separate out a small room, aside from the flat, so they could store her stock. He was doing it ridiculously cheap, not that he admitted it, and she was really grateful to him. Their families had always been kind to each other, so now she was in the process of making him some clothes to thank him. He wasn't really the suit type, but Lynn had knitted him a few nice warm jumpers from some Aran wool, and Maria had made him some nice shirts based on the latest designer trends, minus the designer label and price tag of course. She hoped he liked them. Money was still a little tight, but after she had started stocking the baby clothes in her online shop, things had started to improve. Cassie was a bloody genius. Maria had even had a couple of bespoke orders for wedding gowns and christening gowns. She had also had the brilliant idea of offering to match wedding gown designs to christening gowns, and her online enquiry service had gone bananas. Lynn was a machine, sitting at the laptop most mornings dealing with customers, leaving her to sit in the back room and get on with the orders. Media-intrusion-free, touch wood. Her social media had gone quiet. She was still hiding, and she knew it, but since the day she had told James to leave, Lynn hadn't tried to push her any further.

She walked slowly back to the shop, enjoying the fresh air as she left Foxley Street, turning onto Carrington Street and finally onto Wexley Street. As she turned the corner, her heart stopped, and she almost dropped the flowers. A van she recognised well was outside. Chance Electrical. Her heart thudded in her chest. *Why was he here?*

She couldn't escape. Her handbag and car keys were in the shop, by her desk, and he had parked right next to her. Lily always invoiced her for the flowers, so she hadn't needed any money. He knew she was there, or had been. Why hadn't Lynn sent him away?

He'd left her alone since that day, but she had the feeling Lynn had been less than impressed with her behaviour. Maybe he had just come to see Lynn? They were friends too. She couldn't stop that. It wouldn't be fair.

She sighed and, keeping a tight hold on the flowers, walked slowly across the road.

She couldn't see James through the window. Perhaps it was a coincidence. Maybe he had another job on the street, at one of the cottages, or the shops. She went to walk in and was startled by a voice.

'Maria?'

Spinning around, she saw James, opening his van door and stepping out.

'Hi,' she said, for lack of something better to say. He looked a bit pale, a bit less than the wall of man he usually was. 'Are you okay?' she asked, suddenly worried.

His lips twisted into a rueful smile.

'Not bad. You?'

He looked her up and down, and she flushed, knowing she looked very different from the last time they had seen each other.

'You look beautiful,' he said, and her guts twisted. The baby kicked then, as if saying hello itself.

'I doubt that, I'm getting so big.'

He looked straight at her, his blue-green eyes fixed on hers. 'You look great. Are you both okay?'

She nodded, shifting the flowers into one arm so she could rub the spot where the baby was kicking madly.

'Here, let me,' he said, taking the flowers from her without giving her chance to object.

'Thanks, the little one is kicking me like mad.'

His face lit up. 'Aww, little Sparky!' He put a hand out towards her belly, then dropped it back to his side. 'Sorry,' he muttered. 'Habit.'

Maria tried to slow her heartbeat down. She wanted to cry, hearing his nickname, seeing his happiness about the baby.

'You had a job nearby? Is that why you're here?'

He looked awkward for a moment, and then nodded, glancing into the shop momentarily.

'Yeah, something like that,' he said. 'I'd better go actually.'

She took the flowers back from him, and their fingers brushed against each other's. The baby went for a hat-trick in her uterus. *Sure, move now, little one. You haven't made a peep all morning.*

'Okay, well, nice to see you.' She swallowed down the torrent of unspoken words she could feel threatening to erupt from her throat.

'You too,' he said, looking at her once more, just a beat too long, before getting into his van. She watched him pull away and then walked into the shop.

Lynn was sitting at her desk, tapping away on the laptop. She rose, taking the flowers from her.

'Kettle's on,' she said, pushing a large plastic bag under her desk discreetly with her foot. It went unnoticed by Maria, who was trying to fight the urge to run after the van and its occupant.

'Thanks,' she said. 'James was outside.'

'Oh, really?' Lynn said, busying herself with arranging the flowers into various vases.

'Yeah,' she said, flumping down on the sofa. 'He had a job nearby, I think.'

'Mmm,' Lynn replied noncommittally. 'Simon coming tonight to work on upstairs again?'

'No, he's out with Elaine tonight. He's coming tomorrow instead.'

Lynn nodded, saying nothing further.

James drove through Westfield, looking at the people in the village going about their day. It really was lovely here. The people were friendly, vehicles were secondary to walkers, and he felt less stressed every time he came here. He thought of his home in Harrogate, a lovely family home, with no family in it. Every day he went home and sat on his own, his neighbours all having their own busy lives and families to occupy themselves with. He always felt like the odd one out on a weekend, while their children played in the street, and they washed their family cars. He was normally on the couch with a beer in his hand, contemplating going to the pub for another pint and a solo carvery dinner.

He thought back to Christmas, the dinner he had shared with Maria and her friends. He wondered what Maria would be doing this Sunday. He pulled into a side street, turning off the engine and reaching for his phone.

Dialling a number from his contacts, he braced himself.

'Tucker?' he said. 'It's James, James Chance. Listen, do you fancy a beer tonight?'

Cassie finishing dictating her letter and put down the Dictaphone. She sagged in her wingbacked office chair and looked out of the window at the view outside. She normally kept the blinds open just a crack, but lately she had felt stifled in her little office, choosing to open them wide and let the light in. She was antsy, and had been for a while, but she couldn't put her finger on it. She was on the case-closing streak of her life, billing mega hours for her firm and settling case after case, all in favour of her clients. The men of Harrogate were quaking in their designer shoes when they even heard her name, and Cassie should have been in her element. She was, for the most part, but then she had to leave work. Just the drive home to Sanctuary Cottage filled her with dread, and she was terrified Maria was going to move out when the baby was born. She'd been working on the upstairs of the shop, and Cassie knew that eventually she'd have to make a home for herself and the baby, and that was fine. She wanted Maria to be happy and God knew, after the last few months, she needed some stability.

She knew she should feel glad to be getting her home back, after months of pregnant jilted brides and injured Australians, but the thought of going back to living on her own depressed her.

She would be fine, she knew that. It wasn't like she needed anyone else, and she would still have Maria, even when she was a new mother. Best friends for ever, that would never change. She was even looking forward to being an auntie. She was used to being on her own, and she was a master at it. The difference was that now she wouldn't necessarily choose to be. That was the difference. The fact was, when her little cottage was full of life, so was she, and she wasn't very happy at the prospect of going backwards.

John, one of the senior partners, knocked and she turned to greet him.

'Hi, John,' she said, sitting up straighter in her chair.

'Hello, Cassie,' he said, rather formal as always. He looked a little awkward, sheepish even.

'Is there something I can help you with?' she asked.

'Er, well…' He rubbed a nervous hand down his spotted tie. 'There's a delivery for you, in reception.'

Cassie gasped when she walked into the reception area. Gerald from accounts was grappling with a large floral arrangement, and Brad from the mailroom was shouting, 'Move it left a bit, bit more!'

John placed a comforting hand on her shoulder.

'They're trying to get it into the mailroom out of sight till we can get the florists to pick the damn thing back up.'

Cassie nodded, walking forward to inspect it more closely. Written in flowers, in a large floral arrangement akin to the ones you had for funeral cars, was written one word.

TRAMP.

'I'm sorry,' he said. 'The florist is refusing to hand over the details of the sender; apparently it was anonymous, and they paid cash. God knows why they even took the damn booking. We should sue. Shall we call the police?'

Cassie shook her head. 'No, John, it's fine. Just another unsatisfied ex of a client. I'll phone her now, check she's okay. I'm pretty sure it's him, given the wording. It's the spitter from court, remember?'

John nodded. 'I do, and I am sorry,' he said awkwardly. 'Some awful people out there.'

Cassie nodded, brushing it off and heading back to her office. 'Comes with the job, John. Thanks.'

She waited till she got back to her office, door closed, before she allowed herself to show any emotion at all. Here, the sharks could smell blood in the water, and word soon got around.

The saddest thing was, it was the closest she'd come to a man sending her flowers in a long while.

Once she had pulled herself together, she got her mobile out and texted a number. She had to do something to improve her day. Maybe she should try making the next move.

'So you stood her up, for me?' James asked, shocked. 'You didn't have to do that, mate.'

Tucker wiped the beer froth off his lip and shrugged. 'I'd already made our plans, and besides, I don't have a plan for Cass yet. I don't know how to play it.'

James frowned, taking a sip of his own lager. They were in a pub in Harrogate, one that had missed the hip trend completely and stuck with the Yorkshire 'old man' feel. Slightly sticky carpets, quiet atmosphere, sports on the big screen, and the most important thing of all: a decent beer. Qualities both men valued, they had found out at Christmas. They had bonded over many things, including the troublesome women in their lives.

'What plan do you need? I got the impression you were sort of seeing her already?'

Tucker shook his head. 'Nope, we had sex once, after a night out. I came back to her house with Maria and another lad.'

James jolted at his words, but Tucker didn't notice, one eye on the football match on the big screen.

'A lad, for Maria? You never said.'

Tucker nodded, not looking his way.

'Yeah, a one-night thing.' He seemed to realise what he had said then, wincing as he looked at James.

156

'Sorry, mate, I didn't think. It was a one-night mistake. I remember Maria being cut up about it. It wasn't long after the wedding thing, and she wasn't herself.'

He looked down at his pint, slapping himself on the forehead. 'For God's sake, don't let on I told you. It's kind of a big deal.'

James shook his head. 'It's okay, mate, it's not my business. She seen him since?'

Tucker snorted. 'Nope. His name is not allowed to be mentioned at Cass's. Women, mate, I tell you.'

James nodded, trying to ignore the feeling that someone had just kicked him in the stomach.

'What was his name, out of interest?' Tucker looked at him, his eyes narrowing. 'She mentioned a bloke a bit ago. I just wondered if it was the same one. Darcy?'

Tucker shook his head. 'Her ex? Nah, mate, not him. Mark something, I think. It was just that one time, that's it. I never really met him. We were all smashed, and he was gone in the morning.'

James nodded, relieved. The thought of her spending time with Darcy after what he'd done made him feel like punching his face again. Hard. Maria wouldn't have wanted him to know that anyway, he guessed. He remembered her comment the day they met, something about an awkward sexual encounter. It clicked into place, and he pushed it out of his mind. He wasn't a virgin himself. Besides, it wasn't like they were even friends now. He had no right to the jealousy he was feeling.

'It's all irrelevant anyway. She's told me to stay away. I have to just give her some space.'

Tucker nodded. 'She's got a lot on. Cass helps her, but she's busy with work a lot of the time. I'm still in shock that she texted me today.'

'Mate, I saw her at Christmas. I think she likes you. Maria hasn't mentioned anyone else, so go for it.'

'I want to, believe me. Even with a car door, she's pretty special.'

James laughed and Tucker held his ribs, as though reliving the memory. 'Did you tell her you were meeting me?'

Tucker shook his head. 'Nah, don't worry.'

Both men looked glumly at their pints.

'So, they're out there, living their lives, and we're comparing notes here, trying to figure out how to get close, yeah?'

Tucker put his head in his hands. 'Oh God, we're like lovesick teenagers, aren't we?'

James patted his mate on the shoulder, heading to the bar.

'Yep, that's us, dude. I'll get the shots in.'

Tucker got his phone out of his pocket, sending Cassie a text asking her if she fancied meeting up the next night. Plan or no plan, he was going in.

He had barely had chance to dissect his text with James when a reply pinged.

You're on, was all it said, but it was enough to make Tucker whoop loud enough to pull a still-recovering rib.

Chapter 17

Cassie was pacing around and around the living room and Maria was starting to feel slightly sick. She was ensconced on the sofa, her sore and swollen ankles perched on top of a cushion on the coffee table, swaddled in PJs, dressing gown and a patchwork blanket her mother had made her. She was planning to sit in front of the TV and read her pregnancy books. Enjoy the peace of the empty house while Cassie was out on her date, but now she seemed to be witnessing a freak-out.

'What the hell am I doing?' She was walking from one side of the room to the other now, her heels wearing holes in the carpeted floor. 'I asked him out! I mean, why?'

Maria put down her book. She had read the same paragraph about labour stages five times, and it looked like she was going to have to talk some sense into her mate.

'You like him, you nursed him back to health, you've lived together, you've slept together, and been on dates. This is normal, Cass.'

Her horrified look made Maria want to laugh, but she managed to keep it in.

'Look shocked all you want, but in all the years I've known

159

you, a man's never got under your skin like this. He makes you laugh, he puts up with your weird moods. He likes you!'

She looked around at the cosy living room, which was now all dust-free and welcoming. Waving her hands around the room, she made her point.

'Plus, your house is actually habitable now, and you can't tell me that's not a good thing. He makes you want to be tidy, Cass – the man is a miracle worker. If I could fly, I might even have jetted off to Australia to see whether they clone people like him over there.'

Cassie tittered. 'He does have a brother.'

Maria rolled her eyes. 'I think I'm off men for life.'

Cassie frowned, but said nothing. 'I'm supposed to meet him at the restaurant; he has to go through the menus with the staff. I asked him out for last night, did you know that? He stood me up to go for a drink with one of his mates! It's ridiculous. Then he asks me out for tonight, and I have to go! What the hell am I doing!?'

She was waving her arms around, windmilling them in panic. Maria was starting to get mad. Why could people never sort their lives out?

'Cassie! Will you just shut up and go tell him you like him!'

Cassie stopped walking around, almost falling over the coffee table in shock.

'What?'

'You know what!' Maria clenched her fists, shaking them at her pigheaded friend. 'Sometimes, for a big, independent woman, you are a massive dick! You brought the man home, then dated him, then ignored him, then hit him with your car! You've lived together for weeks, and anyone can see the man is mad about you, and now you actually want him, and you're still moaning!'

Maria started to cry, cuddling her bump in her arms. 'I have no one, and my baby has no father, and all I want is—'

'James,' Cassie said, looking past her.

'Oh God, I can't—'

'No,' Cassie said, stopping her. 'James is here.' She pointed to the doorway.

'Hi,' a deep voice said behind her. Turning to the door, she saw him standing there, carrier bags in one hand and a large, rolled-up sheet of paper in the other. He looked Maria up and down.

'You weren't expecting me, were you?'

Cassie leant over Maria, taking a tissue from the box on the coffee table and wiping her face.

'I'm sorry, I might have forgotten to pass the message on.' She didn't look for one minute like she had meant to pass any message on, and Maria glared at her. 'Thanks, mate, I have a man to go talk to.'

She hugged her, whispering 'stop crying like a loony' in her ear, and then, patting James on the shoulder, she was gone. James hadn't moved from where he was standing awkwardly in the doorway and as Cassie's car drove away the silence in the room grew deafening.

'Sorry, I did leave a message. Annabel wanted to go through the seating charts for the wedding, and the rehearsal dinner? She sent me as a proxy. Cassie called me back, told me to come tonight.'

He lowered the things in his arms, shoulders sagging. 'I can see now that you had no idea, I'm sorry, I'll go.'

He went to put the plans on the coffee table and Maria reached forward to touch his hand. Or tried to, anyway. She actually rocked forward awkwardly, reaching her hand out and just managing to stroke his arm.

'Don't go, I'm sorry. I didn't know, but it's fine. We should go through the plans, of course.'

'You sure?' he said, pushing her legs back onto the cushions when she tried to get up. 'Stay there, I'll get what you need.'

Maria pulled the blanket off herself and went to stand.

161

'I need the bathroom, I'll be a minute.'

James stood back a little, and she shuffled awkwardly past him.

'Make yourself a drink, I won't be long.'

She headed straight up the stairs, walking into the main house bathroom and shutting the door quietly behind her. As soon as the door was shut, she grabbed her mobile phone from her dressing-gown pocket and dialled a number.

'Hi,' a sheepish voice answered.

'Cass,' she whispered in a murderously low voice. 'I am going to kill you! How could you do this to me! What the hell am I going to do? I—'

'I'm sorry, I know.' Maria could hear the crackle from the car phone. 'I'm just so sick of you moping, and Lynn said James is sad too. I just thought you needed to do the wedding stuff anyway, and you can't do it with the happy couple, so James is the contact. He makes you happy!'

'Oh God, I hate you so much!' Maria bent to use the toilet. She really did need to pee. As in, every five minutes. 'Why did you do this!'

'You just lectured me about being a coward. Now what about you! You like him, Maria, and you know it. The man hasn't left your side since the first day you met, and he's never let you down. Talk to him, tonight. See what happens, and… oh dear God, are you peeing?'

Maria flushed the chain and jammed the handset back under her chin to wash her hands.

'Yep, always peeing. Have we met? This little monkey thinks my bladder is a trampoline.'

'Do me a favour, go put your big girl pants on and talk to the man. And never, ever, ring me from the toilet again.'

'Maria? You okay?' James called from downstairs.

'Oh crap, I've got to go. Enjoy your date!'

'You suck! Enjoy yours!'

Both women hung up cursing the other, even though deep down they knew the other was right.

'I'm coming!' she said, looking at herself in the mirror. She looked okay, beside the fact that she was dressed in her PJs and her blonde hair was tied into pigtails at the sides of her head. She looked healthier these days, now the shop was finding its feet. The clothing side had really taken off, and she knew, even if she didn't get the wedding side back up to what it had been, they would be okay. She could keep Lynn on. This wedding would be cathartic, her way of repairing some of the damage she had inflicted on the Chance family. Damage they didn't know about, and hopefully never would. It would be proof that she could do this too, that she could do all of this, without Darcy. Without anyone.

She headed down the stairs, and into the lounge, but it was empty. The plans were on the coffee table, still rolled up. He'd left. *Oh God, had he heard?*

'Do you always take your phone to the bathroom?'

His voice behind her made her jolt. She could feel his closeness, and as she turned her tummy brushed against him.

'Sorry, you scared me. I thought you'd gone.'

James shook his head. 'I would never just leave, Maria. Do you have a grater?'

It seemed her baby was in food heaven. The little button hadn't stopped kicking since Maria had picked up her fork. In the bags, James seemed to have the contents of half the local shops, and he had proceeded to whip up the best spaghetti bolognaise and garlic bread she had ever had. It was so nice, she wasn't even bothered she was making a pig of herself. They were sitting in the lounge, watching a programme about people wanting to make a change in their lives by buying a house abroad.

'I always fancied doing that, you know,' James said, slurping a piece of spaghetti into his mouth. 'Buy some shack in the South of France, do it up.'

Maria smiled at the idea. She could just see him doing that, working on some little chateau, the women in the town falling over themselves to butter his baguette.

'Why didn't you do it then?'

He shrugged. 'I don't know. I finished renovating my house, and then I guess I just wanted to keep filling it. It's still not complete.'

Maria was stuffing a piece of garlic bread into her mouth, groaning with pleasure.

'Filling it?' she said through her food. 'Sorry,' she said, pointing to her mouth. 'This… is… goood!'

She swallowed it down. He grinned at her, wolfing down a bite of his own.

'Answer the question then.'

He looked at the television screen, at a couple sitting on a verandah, talking to the bubbly property expert.

'What do they have in common, the people on these shows?'

Maria took a swig of her hot tea and thought for a moment. 'Disposable income?'

James shook his head. 'Money doesn't mean much in life.'

'Says someone who has it.'

He raised a brow at her.

'I earn it, just like you do.'

She stuck her tongue out at him.

'The thing they have in common is that they're in something together. Life's scary, and exciting, but what's the point of doing it all alone?'

He gazed at her, his blue-green eyes boring into her, daring her to answer. She rested the plate on her bump, sitting back on the sofa. He leant forward on the couch opposite, putting his plate on the coffee table.

'I know you didn't want me here tonight, but I can't help but think we were meant to meet. Can't you see it?'

'I thought you had come to do the table plans, James. I told you, I need to concentrate on the baby.'

'I'm not asking you to do anything else, I'm just trying to get you to see you don't have to do it alone.'

164

Maria sat forward, pushing her plate away. 'I think we should get on with the table plans. I'm pretty tired, to be honest. I was planning an early night. I don't need anyone's help. I can do this without a father.'

She didn't look at him, she couldn't bring herself to.

'I'm not talking about Darcy, Mar.'

She wanted to ask him what he was talking about, what he meant when he said they'd been meant to meet. Did he just mean so that he could help her, or more? Was he offering to be part of her life? She wanted to ask him, but she was terrified of the answer. Would it be what she wanted to hear? If it was, she couldn't do anything about it anyway.

She spread the plans out on the table, shuffling forward on the couch and reaching for her sticky coloured dots, the ones she used to plan the seating.

'I just want to work, James, please? Shall we just get to work?'

He nodded, taking their plates and heading into the kitchen.

'I am glad you're here, though,' she said softly. He didn't reply.

Cassie pulled up in the restaurant car park and, turning her engine off, sat back in her seat and willed herself not to vomit in panic. She thought of Maria at home with James, and hoped she was having a better time. She had been watching them for months, and she just wanted Maria to have a good life. Why shouldn't she get what she wanted? James was great, and the baby would be cared for so well by them both. She had met enough lowlifes in her job to know that, sometimes, secrets were better buried, to protect people, and let them have their own piece of happiness. If her own parents had been more honest, she might have had a different upbringing herself. Or never existed at all. Some people were never meant to be parents, and some babies were just meant to be born, no matter their origin story.

She locked up her car, grabbing her purse and checking her reflection in the car door before setting off. The new car door, as the other one had a Tucker-shaped dent in it. She smiled at

165

the memory despite herself. Maybe her gung-ho attitude wasn't the best, but at least she had got to spend time with him.

She walked into the restaurant, oblivious to the stares and looks that half the diners gave her as she walked to the check-in.

'Hi,' she said to the suited man on the front desk. 'I'm here to see Jesse Tucker.'

The man's face lit up in recognition and he scurried around the desk.

'Right over here, Cassie. So glad to finally meet you!'

Cassie followed, wondering how much Jesse had said to the people he worked with. The man took her through to the kitchen area, straight past the stainless-steel worktops bustling with activity and inviting smells, and knocked on a side door marked 'office'.

'Jesse,' he said cheerfully, 'your date's here.'

The door opened, and there he was. Cassie looked at the man and he winked at her, scurrying off.

'Hey,' Tucker said, his lopsided smile making her stomach flip. 'Come in, I won't be a minute.'

She walked into the neat office and immediately felt at home. It was Tucker all over, photos on the desk, everything neatly arranged, colour-coded files on his shelves. He motioned for her to sit down on the sofa at the back of the room, but she moved to the desk.

'This is so you,' she murmured, picking up a photo frame bearing a younger-looking gappy-toothed Tucker and two people who were obviously his parents.

'Mum and Dad?' she checked, running her finger along the faces.

'Yeah,' he said, and she could feel his breath on her cheek. 'You'd love them.'

She resisted the urge to take a step back, to feel his chest against her. 'I doubt that. Parents don't really take to me. Apart from Mar's, of course.'

166

He wrapped his arms around her, making her flinch, and took the photo frame from her hands.

'That's because you never met any that weren't related to clients, and your own parents don't count. Mine would love you to bits.'

He dropped a kiss on her cheek, giving her a squeeze.

'I'm due to go back soon, so maybe next time you can come with me, have a little holiday.' He must have felt her tense up, because he squeezed her that little bit tighter.

'Don't freak out on me, not yet. We have a date, remember?'

He put the photo frame back on the desk, pushing her body forward with his to reach the desktop. She could feel the solidity of him against her. It felt oddly right.

'I'm pretty much done here. I'll just nip and tell the chef for tonight we're off.'

He released her then, walking to the door, and she felt the loss of his body warmth. He reached for her hand, lacing his fingers through hers and pulling her gently to the door. It was as though he couldn't bear to be far from her, and she was shocked to recognise that she felt it too. She had missed him so much. Too much. It scared her.

He closed the door to his office behind her, leaning in to her till they brushed cheeks.

'I can't wait for tonight,' he murmured into her ear, and she shuddered despite herself. *Great*, she thought to herself, *I'm turning into the heroine from an Austen novel. I might as well buy a petticoat and practise my swooning.* She cleared her throat and took a sidestep to get some distance from him.

'I'll er… wait at the bar,' she said, flashing a quick smile and not meeting his eyes. She could feel him looking at her, but she turned and walked as well as she could on shaky legs. Reaching the bar, she flicked her gaze back to his office door, but he was gone.

The bar was quite busy, couples and groups of people engrossed in their own conversations while they waited for their tables. The woman next to her was raving about the food here to her friends. Apparently there was some hot Australian that had come in, bought the place and vamped up the menu. Riding the surge of pride that rampaged through her body and flushed her cheeks, she asked the bartender for a Chardonnay. A large one. She needed to drown the butterflies in her stomach, or at the very least get them a little buzzed to chill them out.

She was just handing over a note to the barman when she felt a sharp pain in her side. Turning, she saw that a man had jabbed her with his finger, digging into her shoulder blade to get her attention. She fixed her face into her best scowl and looked straight into the eyes of Michael Atwood, the slimy, flower-sending ex of her lovely, timid client.

'Hey, tramp, what you doing in a nice place like this?' He spat the words at her in a low growl, making great effort to enunciate every consonant like he was trying to hit her with the violence of his words. At the use of the word tramp, she bristled with anger. The message sent to work. She'd known it was him. She also knew how to deal with bullies like this. Bullies who used their masculinity and 'I am far better than you, little female' attitude to keep women small and manageable.

'Good evening, Mr Atwood,' she said sweetly, looking at the barman directly while she sipped her wine. The barman had obviously heard his comment, and he was looking at her companion intently. She hoped Jesse wouldn't see him. She didn't want to have to explain things to him. She'd just cost him weeks off work and she didn't want to tank his business by causing trouble the minute she walked through the door.

'Don't good evening me, you little bitch! What are you doing here? Shouldn't you be out chasing ambulances?'

He was standing next to a blonde woman, a very pretty, petite woman who was wearing what was essentially a slip. She had her arm linked through his, but she was looking decidedly uncomfortable. Cassie smiled at her, and she smiled uncertainly back.

'Well, Mr Atwood, we all have to eat. You have a good evening now.'

She wanted to add *thanks for the flowers, dingleberry*, but she didn't want to cause a scene, or let on that she had even seen them, let alone been affected. She turned her body slightly away from him, closer to the bar, and sipped again at her wine. The other customers were oblivious, but Cassie could feel the crackle of tension in the air. The woman he was with withdrew her arm slowly, and Cassie knew she felt it too. Another lamb to the slaughter.

He was glaring at her, panting heavily, and she could smell the alcohol on him every time he breathed out. She felt like it was invading her skin, his nasty, drink-fuelled thoughts sneaking in through her pores. She fought the urge to rub the skin on her arms. She looked good, and she felt good. This man wasn't going to ruin her night. She was still praying for him to get bored and go away, before Jesse was ready to leave, when she felt a yank on her arm. The barman leant over the bar, grabbing his hand.

'Hey, mate, you need to let go and leave.' Cassie tried to prise his fingers off her hand, and looked to the girl, but she was gone. His fingers were tight, gripping her skin and piercing it with his sharp fingernails. 'Mate!' The barman raised his voice, but he was invisible to Michael as he tightened his grip.

'Dining out on my money, are we?' He had spittle forming at the corners of his mouth, his whole face twisted in a truly grue-some way. She thought of his ex-wife and kids, so lovely, normal, and never to be fully rid of this man.

She was suddenly very grateful that she was who she was, and had never taken any guff from men like this. She was also glad Maria had insisted she have her nails done for her date at the fancy Harrogate salon near her office. She turned on her heels, facing him with an eerie grin, and putting her hand over his arm she squeezed. As hard as she could. She felt her nails rip through the top layer of his skin, and she pressed harder. The barman let go, stepping back.

'Mr Atwood, get the hell off me before I have you arrested for assault as well as threatening behaviour. I earn my own money, defending women against filth like you. Your date left, join her.'

He released his grip on her arm, and she took a subtle step away from him. Her arm was smarting, but she would check it out later. He looked over his shoulder as though checking the veracity of her statement, and then she saw Jesse. He was standing behind Mr Atwood, looking at him as though he wanted to rip his arms clean off his body. Mr Atwood didn't notice in his drunken stupor and turned back to her. He raised his arm as though he was going to touch her again, but Cassie raised her hand.

'Don't,' she warned. 'Just leave, now.'

'I'd do what the lady says,' Tucker said behind him. The barman was still serving drinks, but tipped his head to Jesse. She realised he must have told him somehow. She burned with shame at making a scene at his workplace. Dear God, why did she always feel so vulnerable, so gawky around him? She never usually had men making her feel like this.

Jesse had his arms crossed, and she could see his muscles pulse and flex under his shirt, his fists clenched tight under his elbows.

'Oh really,' Mr Atwood said, not even bothering to look over his shoulder. 'Come to fight her battles, have you?' He snorted, and the spittle sprang from his mouth, like a trapeze artist on a ribbon. 'I wouldn't bother if I were you. Tramps are never worth the effort.'

She heard Tucker suck his breath in through his teeth, but he didn't move.

'I don't need to fight her battles, fella, trust me. Paul, mate, you might wanna move back a bit.'

The barman chuckled and went off to serve the rather bemused drinking crowd.

170

Cassie looked at Tucker, and he looked right back, as if to tell her he was there, he had her back.

She focused once again on her aggressor and flicked her hair back off her shoulders.

'I'm leaving now, Mr Atwood, and if you bother me again, I will press charges for assault against you. I have witnesses—' she pointed to the people around her '—and you will be dealt with to the fullest extent of the law. Let's go, Jesse.'

She went to walk around him, and Jesse took a step forward to take her hand, but he was there again, between them.

'Who said you could leave, tramp? You ruined my life!' He was so close, so in her face, that her nose pressed against his. She grabbed him by the shoulders and rammed her raised knee straight between his legs with as much force as she could muster.

'Urrgghhh!' Mr Atwood dropped to his knees, holding his privates.

Jesse took her hand and pulled her into his arms. He grabbed her face between his hands and searched her face.

'You okay?' he asked, his tone calm but his demeanour showing he was raging on the inside.

'I'm fine,' she said, and dropped a kiss onto his lips. His face broke into a huge grin, and the two stood there, looking at each other intently as the staff were carting Mr Atwood to the door, still bent on his knees, crying in pain.

Paul shouted to him from behind the bar.

'You weren't kidding about your girl, Tucker!'

He wrapped his arms around her, and she snuggled into him.

'You should see what she can do with a weapon, mate. We're off.'

Paul gave him a salute and got back to work, and they headed to the exit.

'Thanks for letting me deal with that, Tucker.'

He led her outside, and to the car park, stopping by her car.

'You okay to drive?'

She nodded. 'Where are we going?'

He looked a little blindsided by the question.

'I, er, figured we'd be going to yours after that. Don't you need to call some people?'

She suddenly thought of Michael Attwood's wife, and her boss at the firm.

'You're right,' she said reluctantly. The truth was, after that kiss, all thought of work was lost.

One of the waitresses ran out to them, a huge picnic basket in hand.

'Here, Tucker, we put this together for you.' She was only a young lass, eighteen if that, with a bright pink streak in her blonde hair. Tucker took the basket from her, his eyebrows raising when he looked at the contents. The girl hugged Cassie fiercely.

'Michael's been coming here for years. With his wife. You did us all a favour. Enjoy your date!'

Tucker waved her goodbye and tucked the hamper into the boot of her car.

When he looked at her, she was watching him.

'What?'

'Thank you for letting me deal with that on my own, and not stepping in.'

'I think I get the measure of you now, Cass. You don't have to thank me. You just have to let me in.' He went and opened her car door for her, raising an eyebrow. She rolled her eyes and went to get in, but he pinned her in the open space.

'I will open car doors for you, Cassie, and I will always protect you, but I get that you don't need me to. You've never relied on anyone for anything, and I get that. I'm here, though, and I'm not going away. Not unless you ask me to.' He leant on the car door with his right arm, leaning in and brushing his lips against hers. 'Are you going to ask me to, or are you actually going to give me a chance? Give us a chance at being together? Equal partners?'

He kissed her again, and she didn't protest. She kissed him back, enjoying the feel of his lips.

'That a yes?' he asked. 'You going to let me date you, and be there for you? Be there for each other?'

She covered his hand with hers, over the car door, and he nuzzled his stubble against her neck.

'Okay,' she said. 'Let's try.'

Chapter 18

Maria drove up the long, winding road, thinking of the last time she'd been here, the excitement and tension in the van when she'd driven up with James. Now it was almost here. Two days and it would all be over. Mark and Annabel would be married, and her secret would get easier to keep. Darcy had stayed away from the shop but constantly sent her letters and rang her. His messages were mostly about his mother, how he was going to tell her to mind her own business, that they could work it out. He didn't mention the baby, just how he felt, how sorry he was. All about him. She hadn't replied, except the time Cassie got hold of her mobile and texted back BUGGER OFF YOU NAMBY PAMBY DIPSHIT before she could wrestle the phone from her grasp. He'd stopped calling the shop too, since Lynn had taken to blowing a whistle down the line every time she knew it was him. Short, but very effective at getting rid of nuisance callers. This weekend would be another part of her closing the Darcy file, planning the perfect wedding to prove she still had it in her, even if her own marriage was a non-starter. She just wanted to see Annabel and Mark happy, then she could have that in her head as a good memory. The knowledge that she hadn't screwed up anyone's life. James was respectably cordial, but he was keeping his distance too. She had seen his van in the village lately, even on Wexley Street itself, but when she looked again, it had always disappeared. Maybe it was a pregnancy mirage. Given her current near-to-delivering condition, it wouldn't be much of a surprise.

She drove her car into the car park area, as close as she could to the hotel while still being tucked away out of sight. The hotel was gorgeous, and there was even a nice big visible sign at the entrance now, so at least the guests wouldn't have any problems finding it.

She grabbed her bag and headed to the boot to pull out her overnight case. She had just waddled to the end of the car when someone opened the boot, pulling the case out.

'You look nice,' James said, pulling out the carry handle and reaching for her bag. She let him take it, and his lips twitched as though he was ramming a smile back in. 'Getting big now.'

'Thanks,' she said sarcastically, rubbing her bump. James's blue-green eyes ran over every inch of her, making her feel like he was trying to scan her for any changes.

'You know what I mean.'

'Maria!' A screech behind him heralded Annabel's arrival. 'Look at you!'

Annabel slammed into her and James winced.

'Anna, be careful!'

'Sorry,' she said, shooting him a glance. 'I can't believe you kept this a secret from me!' She pulled back from hugging and put both hands on her bump. Maria shrank back before she could stop herself. James appeared at her side and removed his sister's hands.

'Anna, you don't just touch pregnant women like that.'

Maria grimaced inwardly, thinking of the times James had touched her stomach, felt her child kick, and spoke to it about the shop, the wedding, a rude customer he had had that day. The baby did a little kick, as always reminding her on cue of the good times with him.

'Sorry!' Annabel trilled. 'It's just so exciting, and you kept it quiet!' Her face fell. 'Oh God, sorry. I guess I get why. I found out from James, though. He had a pregnancy book in his van!'

Maria looked sideways at James, but he kept his eyes on his sister.

'Er, shall we go in then?' He picked up the case like it was a piece of paper and held out his arm for Maria.

She looked at it, at Annabel, and at the rather steep set of stone steps that led up to the hotel. She put her arm in his, and they all walked in together.

Annabel kept up a constant stream of chatter until the checkout desk was free, and Maria found herself flagging with the small talk. It was lovely to see her so happy, but she was fast realising that doing this wedding was going to be the hardest thing ever. Especially with her secret on show for everyone to see. Her bump was like a telltale beating heart.

'Hello, can I help?' the chirpy receptionist asked, and Annabel finally drew breath. James took the opportunity to grab one of her girlfriends from the bar and take them off together.

'Hi,' Maria said, sighing with relief. 'Maria Mallory, I have a suite booked for one night.'

'One?' James asked, appearing beside her again, still carrying her luggage. 'Two, surely?'

Maria ignored him, taking the key from the receptionist and heading to the lift. James went to follow, but she turned and held her hands out for her bags.

'Mar, stop being ridiculous! Let me help you.' He grabbed his own hair in his free hand, as though he was ready to rip it out.

'It's fine, honestly. I'm just going to freshen up.'

He didn't move, or give her the bags. The lift pinged as the doors opened, and a bellboy was standing there, looking at them expectantly.

'Hi, can you possibly take my bags?' she asked him. James tutted behind her but gave the bags to the lad. She followed him

176

into the lift, and turning to face the doors as they closed, saw that James was gone.

'Cassie, I don't think I can do this. James is here, and I don't know... Mark is going to see I'm pregnant. What am I going to say?'

Cassie was lying in bed with Tucker at the cottage, and he gave her a kiss and headed downstairs to make them both breakfast. Cassie pushed her long black hair off her face, tousled from Tucker running his hands through it, and sat up straight.

'You do the job, Mar, and get out of there. Do the dinner tonight, the wedding tomorrow, and then get your stuff in your car and come home. Don't tell Mark anything. You have to act normal. Let them think it's Darcy's baby, just for now, then you can sort it out after. Tell the simpering git the truth and get rid of him and his dragon of a mother for ever.'

'What about James, though?'

Cassie sighed down the line. 'I don't know, Mar. You know I think you should tell him how you feel. I know it's impossible now, but maybe after the wedding...'

Maria looked in the mirror in the hotel bathroom. She was wearing a neat little sky-blue maternity dress, her hair swept back behind her ears.

'I could wait for ever, but the baby will still be Mark's. I can't lie to him like that, not while I'm in his life. I'm a bad person. I need to get away from him, so I don't ruin his life too.'

'You didn't ruin your life, or anyone else's! You had a one-night stand, you were both single, and now you're having a baby. Hell, without people like you, taking chances, living their lives... well, I'd be out of a job! Life is messy!'

Maria laughed.

'Great, thanks, mate. Great time to be a born-again bloody optimist by the way. I still can't get James involved in this. Ever. I have to let him go, let him live his life. He deserves better.'

'I get it, Maria, I do, but your whole stubborn independent

streak will shoot you in the foot before too long, and then it might be too late.'

'Takes one to know one,' Maria retorted, and Cassie laughed. Tucker walked into the room, holding a tray with breakfast on it, wearing only her apron. He had a flower from the garden between his teeth.

'Yeah, well, maybe it's time to let someone into our lives, you know. Maybe we can do that, and still be us.'

Tucker grinned at her words and snuggled back in next to her, tray on his lap.

'Love you, mate, speak soon.' Maria felt so happy for her friend. She had met her match, it seemed.

With Mr Atwood being dealt with by the authorities, and his wife taking out a restraining order on him, it seemed Cassie and Tucker had a lovely lazy weekend ahead. Maria just hoped she could get through the next two days in one piece.

The sound of laughter and the tinkling of glasses were music to Maria's ears as she came down from her hotel room to deal with the evening dinner get-together. All of Annabel's and Mark's families were in for the night, ready for the big day tomorrow. She stepped out of the lift and headed to the dining room where the hotel had sectioned off part of the large room to accommodate the wedding party. Time to face Mark. She brushed her hands down her black maternity trousers, smoothing her cream blouse down at the front as though she could hide her bump under a crease. If only.

She headed to the room and stood in the doorway to survey the scene. There was one long table with all their immediate family and friends chatting away as they waited for the meal to begin. The wine waiters were making their rounds, and the whole room looked perfect. So far so good. She scanned the room and saw Annabel, sitting next to Mark. They were laughing along with each other, and they looked so perfect together. Maria felt a twinge of guilt, wrapped in panic, but pushed it away. She surveyed the rest of the guests and felt her stomach clench. James was sitting at the table, talking with the head bridesmaid, a rather pushy woman called Liz. She and Annabel had gone to university together apparently, but Maria could tell that Annabel was the pushover in the relationship, someone who was too nice to stand up to her friend. Annabel was a sidekick.

Liz seemed to be looking for a leading man at the moment though, as she leaned in to James. Their chairs were smushed together, and she was practically dry humping his leg with her own while she ran her finger along the shoulder of his shirt. He was listening to her and smiling while she cooed over him. He was the brother of the bride, and there to give his only sister away, and she was the head bridesmaid. Maria had done enough weddings to realise this was never going to end well, not for her anyway. Weddings did funny things to people – the hormones, the life-affirming love, and the sense of for ever. It made people bonkers. Events like this always did. It wasn't a coincidence that birth rates went up after a horrible global loss of life. People reached out to people after funerals. It was human instinct to grasp for life, for happiness. Even if it was a skanky hook-up among the coat racks, it was still inevitable. Weddings were no different. The thought of Liz and James together made her feel physically sick and she rubbed her bump for comfort. She stayed where she was, leaning against the wall. She needed another minute at least.

'Well, who would fall in love, eh, Sparky?' she said to her tummy.

'I would,' a voice answered behind her. She whirled around and saw Darcy standing there. She walked over to him, trying to work out if he was a mirage, or actually there, on one of the most important days of her life. Déjà vu. She scanned the foyer, but it was thankfully empty.

'What are you doing here?' she asked him, moving away from the doorway to try to get him away from the wedding party.

'I'm here for you. I told my mother everything.' He looked down at her bump. 'Well, not quite everything, but I will. I want you to come with me, we can tell her together. Tell her we're getting married, that we're going to be a family.'

'A family?' she echoed. 'I'm not your family, Darcy, and I'm working, so please go. I need this job.'

He looked past her at the doorway. 'Well, tomorrow then. I saw on your business page you had this on – is the wedding over?'

Maria's anger flashed. 'No, Darcy, for once you actually arrived *at* the wedding, and early to boot. It's tomorrow, and you need to leave. Now. If the press are anywhere near here, I swear…'

He held his hands out. 'No, I borrowed Sis's car. No one knows I'm here. I wouldn't have come, but with Lynn at the shop and Cassie at the cottage… you don't take my calls. I need to straighten things out.'

Maria shook her head, pointing to the corridor, and glancing frantically around her to check for any guests that might be overhearing.

'Darcy, I'm not interested. It's over. Go back to your girlfriend. Leave and let me do my job!'

'No!' he shouted back, loud enough to make the receptionist look up and take notice. Maria flashed her a relaxed smile and she looked back at her computer.

'Darcy, leave, please. I don't want to see you ever again, don't you get that?' She moved closer to him, trying her best not to shout. 'Please, I need this job. There's no couple that will touch me, after you. I need to get my business going, so please, just go!'

Darcy pointed at her belly. 'I need to care for you and our baby, and I will. You don't need to work. I already told you that. We can hire someone to help out at Happy Ever After, Lynn will work more hours, and you can be home with our baby.'

Maria shook her head. How the heck she'd ever loved such a pigheaded man was beyond her. He had literally trampled all over her life, and now just expected to get back in and go back to where they'd left off. It was time to finish this, and quickly.

'Darcy, I don't need you. I never did, but I wanted you.'

He started to preen, pushing out his chest, and she swallowed down her revulsion, the sudden nausea she felt. Obviously the baby wasn't keen on him either. Smart baby.

'I wanted you, but you left me, and since you've been gone I've realised a few things. Family is very important to me, and I've realised you feel the same. For your family, for the trappings of your life. You let your parents get into your head and you left me humiliated and alone, for no reason other than your parents feeling I was beneath you. I will never forgive you for that, but I'm over it, Darcy.'

He took a step forward.

'I'm so glad to hear that, Maria darling. If we can just get over this, we—'

'Now leave. Don't come back.'

His face crumpled in confusion. 'But – but, the baby…'

'The baby isn't yours, Darcy. I'm sorry I didn't tell you sooner, but I never expected you to come into my life again.'

'Not mine? Don't be ridiculous. I demand a DNA test. You can't shut me out, lie to me!'

The receptionist was flicking papers now, obviously for effect, and Maria felt herself flush. This was her worst nightmare.

He was looking at her now as though he was trying to work her out. Trying to figure out what was going on in her head. The problem was, he had never really known.

'Darcy, I'm not kidding. I slept with someone else, after our wedding. It's his baby, not yours. Now please leave, I have to get back.'

She could hear a commotion behind her and knew the meal was getting underway. She needed to be there, to make sure everything was running smoothly. She had only glanced at Mark a couple of times, but luckily the Darcy-father cover story must have reached his ears, because he had just given her a panicked look and quick, awkward wave before scurrying back to Annabel's side. Just as she wanted. That was where he belonged.

Darcy didn't move, just looked at her with a sneer.

'Well, I'm just glad I didn't marry you then, if you were cheating.'

Maria clenched her fists by her sides.

'Darcy, just leave!'

He shook his head. 'I think I'll stick around actually. Is he here?'

She looked around her, feeling pure panic now. She needed him to leave, and to do her job.

'Is who here?'

'The father!' he boomed.

'What father?' a familiar voice said behind Maria, and she felt like her heart had stopped. Turning around, she saw James standing there, a drink of what looked like iced water in his hand. 'I came to bring you a drink,' he said, moving closer. 'Darcy? What are you doing here?'

Darcy sneered at him. 'I came to talk to Maria, but apparently you're the father. It makes sense now.'

James shook his head. 'Don't be ridiculous. You know you're the father. Don't try and wriggle out of it. Now's not the time, so leave.'

He put a hand on Maria's arm, passing her the drink. 'You okay? You look pale.'

'I'm fine, you go back to the meal. I'm so sorry about this, I'll sort it out.'

James shrugged. 'I'm fine here, thanks. Darcy, don't make me throw you out of another door.' The look he flashed him was enough to tell Darcy just what he thought about him.

'Oh, do shut up, Daddy. I'm going, don't worry.'

Maria stepped forward, pushing the glass of water back into James's grasp. 'Please, go back to your family.'

'Oh! Family wedding, is it? Nice, screwing the clients, eh? Nice one! Classy. My mother was right.'

Maria opened her mouth to give him what for but then realised he wasn't wrong. His mother would love this too. Well, bugger her.

She looked at Darcy and realised any feelings she had ever had for him were nothing really. A fondness perhaps. She had felt more love in the past few months than she had since her parents passed. Real love, for her child, and for a man who, in another life, she would have walked to the ends of the earth for. By contrast, she wouldn't wee on Darcy if he was on fire.

'I had a one-night stand, Darcy. The baby is his, not yours, or James's. It's my baby, that's all that matters. I don't care what you or your bloody precious mother think. I'm happy. For the most part anyway.' She glanced at James before she could stop herself and he showed her a little shocked smile. 'I wish you well, Darcy, and I'm going to go back to work now.'

She turned around to head to the dining room and bumped straight into Mark. He was standing there ashen, looking at her bump as if he expected an alien to jump out and attack him.

'Is all that true?' he murmured, his eyes bulging in his head.

'Oh God, I'm sorry... I'm so...'

'Oh God... oh God... Annabel...'

The two looked at each other, not knowing what to say. Darcy started to laugh, a haughty, ear-grating sound she'd always hated.

'Well, well, well... you can take the girl out of the village...'

He stopped talking when James charged at him, and the two tussled on the floor, James's knee on Darcy's chest.

'Gerroof!' he demanded.

Mark didn't even look at them. He was standing with his head in his hands, looking at Maria in disbelief.

'Why didn't you tell me?'

A tear fell down her cheek as she saw what she had caused. Two of the porters were separating James and Darcy, James screaming for him to be thrown out.

'I didn't want to ruin your life. I'm so sorry. I wanted to do the wedding to help you all, I was never going to tell you.'

He looked back at the dining room. 'I'm getting married tomorrow.'

'I know,' Maria said. 'I'm so sorry.'

James walked back over to them, Darcy being hauled out in the background. He took one look at Mark, and Maria started to cry as she saw the light of recognition cloud his beautiful, trusting face.

'Mark...' He put his hand over his mouth, running it down his close-set stubble. 'Tucker said you had a night with a man called Mark.'

Mark moved towards him.

'Mate, I didn't know. Annabel and I broke up, and I was drunk, and...'

'Don't come anywhere near me,' he growled, and Mark stopped dead. 'I will deal with you later.'

Mark shuffled away, back to the dining room, and then the two of them were alone. The foyer had descended into a deafening silence.

He focused his blue-green eyes on her, and she saw tears in them.

'Was all this some kind of plan? The wedding, the electrics?'

Maria started to sob. 'No, no, of course not. I didn't have any idea. He never told me anything, and I didn't know till they came to the shop. I said no, but then I wanted to help you, to help them, to make it right.'

'How can you make this right?' he shouted, crying openly now. 'You lied to me, Maria! Everything is one big lie. How could you do that? How could you do any of this?'

He crumpled in half, his palms on his cheeks as he hugged his elbows to his stomach.

'I just can't... Why didn't you tell me!' He stood up, holding his hands out to her. 'I thought we...'

184

He bit his lips together, his eyes looking like the ocean, sea glass reflected in the water of his tears. She took a step closer, and another.

'I'm sorry,' she sobbed, her face and top wet with tears. She felt like her heart was going to split in two, the pain was so physical. The baby kicked like crazy. Another person mad at being let down. She rubbed the place and the movement stopped. *Sorry, baby, Mama has made such a mess.*

He lunged forward suddenly and she was in his arms. He dipped his head to hers and kissed her fiercely. His tears mixed with hers, their pain and sorrow drying into salty tracks. She kissed him back, but he pulled away, pushing her away by her shoulders.

'I shouldn't have done that. I can't... I just can't. It's done... it's just done.'

He turned and ran across the foyer, smashing through the entrance doors and racing out of sight. Maria was left alone, weeping, her lips bruised and swollen from the kiss.

'I love you,' she sobbed. 'I'm so sorry.'

'Hang tight, I'll ring Taylor – we'll come get you.'

Lynn was already putting her coat on and shucking her slippers off, cursing her neat and tidy ways. Her shoes were in the hall closet as always, neatly on the rack. She picked up her keys and tried to stay calm as she listened to Maria cry her heart out over the phone.

'No, Lynn, I can't go. My car's here, and...'

'So? I'll ask Simon to come too, or Dot, or... I'll find someone to come and drive your car back, or we'll get it another time. I'm on my way.'

'No, Lynn, I can't leave. I have the wedding to do.'

Lynn stopped by her front door.

'Maria love, I don't think there's going to be a wedding. You need to come home, get out of there.'

'Lynn, I've been hiding for too long. I have to face this now.'

Lynn sat down on her staircase. She wished her dear friend was there with her, to help with her daughter. It broke her heart listening to her.

'Why didn't you tell me Mark was the father, love? I never would have let you do this, it's too much. You haven't done anything wrong, but planning the wedding was a bad idea.'

Maria was sitting on her hotel bed, lying back against her headboard, resting her swollen and throbbing ankles on the soft mattress.

'I wanted to help them, to get money for the baby. I thought I could at least help them have their happy ever after, and then I could raise the baby and leave them alone.'

'And James?' Lynn said softly.

Maria burst into tears at the sound of his name.

'Oh, Lynn, he hates me. He knows, and he kissed me and ran away.'

'He kissed you?' Lynn said, holding her hand against her heart. She'd always known it; that man had been lost since he'd first set eyes on Maria.

'Yes, but then he stopped and ran away. He literally ran out of the hotel, Lynn, and I don't blame him.'

Maria heard a knock at the door and her heart leapt out of her chest.

'I have to go, Lynn, someone's at the door. Don't come, okay? I'll call you later.'

She hung up on Lynn's protests and waddled over to the door. Annabel stood there, dressed in her wedding dinner outfit. She looked at Maria's bump and swallowed.

'May I come in?'

186

Chapter 19

Maria awoke on the day of the Chance-Smith wedding to Cassie talking quietly in the hotel bathroom. She tried to listen but couldn't make out any of the words. She rolled over onto her side – well, as much as she could – and looked out of the window through the gap in the plush curtains. It was sunny, and thankfully cloud-free. *Thank God for small mercies*, she thought to herself.

Annabel had come into her hotel room the day before as though she was walking into a dungeon full of vipers, and Maria had never hated herself more. The elephant in the room was about to be addressed, and she felt like one herself.

'I have one question,' Annabel said, looking at the carpet and nowhere else. 'Do you have any feelings for Mark?'

Maria shook her head vigorously.

'No, not at all. It was a huge mistake. I never... I didn't... I...'

Annabel finally looked up at her and she felt her whole body sag.

'I need to sit down,' she said, returning to her position on the bed and lifting her ankles up to gain some blessed relief. She placed her hands on her bump, and moved them immediately, putting them by her sides.

'Darcy left me at the altar. I lived with him. He was my family;

I don't have many people I can call that. I moved in with my best friend, Cass, and I tried to cope. We went out on a girls' night, and I met Mark.'

Annabel said nothing, but came further into the room, sitting awkwardly on the edge of the bed.

Maria took this as a sign to keep going.

'He seemed really sad, and I was too. We got drunk, and...' She didn't say the words. She didn't need to.

'In the morning, he was gone. We never spoke. I didn't see him again, not till the day you both came into the shop. I had already become friends with James by then, but I had no idea he was your brother. I didn't know you existed. We didn't talk about any of that.'

Annabel moved a little closer.

'I don't have any feelings for him. It was a mistake, two people needing comfort, I suppose. I tried to say no to the wedding, but then I felt so wretched, I wanted to help you.'

'What about Darcy?' Annabel asked.

Maria frowned. 'He was a mistake too, I think. He must have found out about the baby somehow and assumed it was his. I couldn't tell anyone, not till after the wedding. The press have been awful, and I didn't want anything to get out, for you and for me. I'm ashamed enough.'

Annabel stood and walked over to the window, looking out at the moon, which was full and bright in the night sky.

'James hates him.' Hearing his name felt like a knife in her chest.

'I know he does. They're so different.'

Annabel laughed, just once, but then her face returned to stone.

'He loves you, you know.'

The baby jabbed her in the ribs, and she sat forward a little, trying to get comfortable.

'He doesn't. He doesn't know what love is.'

Annabel turned from the window and sat in the chair by the bed.

'Not Darcy, James.'

Maria welled up, and she rubbed her eyes quickly.

'I never meant to hurt him. I was going to do the wedding and then go away, leave you all alone. I already told James that.'

'You know him well enough by now to realise that James never listens to anyone, and he never leaves anyone. The man is loyal to a fault.'

Maria started to cry, tears running silently down her cheeks as she tried to talk.

'I know. I hurt him, and I can't bear it.'

Annabel looked at her bump again, and Maria watched her.

'I'm sorry.' The words sounded so empty, so pitiful, even to her. 'I never meant for any of this. I just wanted to help you, and I've made such a mess. I can't begin to imagine how you feel.'

Annabel stood suddenly, and started walking towards the door. Maria hung her head, but felt the bed move next to her. Annabel pushed her heels off, crossing her stocking-clad feet on the mattress and sitting back against the pillows.

Both women sat in silence for a while. The baby started kicking and Maria rubbed the area.

'Is it moving?' Annabel asked, and Maria nodded.

'Would you... er... never mind. That's crazy talk.'

Annabel reached over and held out her hand. Maria took it and placed it over the spot. The baby kicked again and Annabel's face lit up.

'Oh my God, I felt that!' She moved closer, waiting for it to happen again.

'Do you know what you're having?'

'No, I wanted to wait.'

Annabel nodded and pulled her hand away, sitting up.

'I slept with my ex-boyfriend, the night after I broke off my engagement.'

She grimaced and Maria said nothing, listening.

'It was a mistake, and I felt awful after. I went and got the morning after pill and everything, and I never told Mark. Until today. I can't be mad at him for something I did myself, for something I kind of understand. I needed comfort too, and I ran back to my idiot ex like Mark meant nothing. I get it. I don't like it, but I understand. I understand why you did all of this.'

Maria didn't know what to say. James was right about his sister; she really was the most special person. Mark was lucky, if they could come through this.

'I don't expect anything,' Maria said. 'I never did. I wasn't even going to tell anyone. I was just going to go, and that would be it. You and Mark can do that, get married, get your happily ever after.'

Annabel shook her head. 'The Mark I know will never walk away from a child.'

She stood and straightened down her dress.

'I wouldn't marry him if he did either. So, Maria, if you want him to be a part of the baby's life, I'm okay with it.'

Maria went to stand, but Annabel came around the bed and sat down next to her.

'I always liked you, Maria, and now I think I understand you better. Don't punish this baby for all of our mistakes. We're all just pretending to be grown-ups who have it figured out, but really, it's all just a hot mess.'

'Are you going to get married?'

Annabel smiled, taking her hand in hers.

'Yes, baby mama, we are, if our wedding planner is still available. The rest is nobody's business, and we can figure it all out.'

Maria couldn't believe what she was hearing.

'What about Mark?'

'He agrees. We've had a long talk, and will probably talk all night, but we are getting married tomorrow, unless you have any objection.'

Maria squeezed her hand. 'None at all.'

Annabel hugged her.

'Well, it will be something to tell the grandchildren anyway.' She walked to the door, grabbing her heels on the way past. 'See you in the morning?'

Maria smiled at her. 'I'll be there.' Her face crumpled. 'What about James?'

Annabel shrugged. 'I haven't seen him, he won't talk to anyone.'

Maria felt her guts clench.

'He'll never speak to me again.'

Annabel opened the door. 'You're family now, Maria, he'll come around. Just make sure that when he does, you know what you want. Because if you don't, if you have any doubts whatsover, you need to let him go.'

The door clicked shut after her, and Maria was left alone.

She flicked her gaze away from the clouds and picked her phone off the nightstand. She had heard nothing from James, and she had texted and called him several times. His phone had been switched off last night. She pressed the button to dial him, sitting up as best she could in bed and holding her breath. The phone rang twice and then he picked up.

'Hello.'

It was him, a cold, distant voice, but his voice all the same.

'Hi,' she half-whispered. 'Can we talk, please?'

'No, I don't think so.' His clipped tones felt like they were chipped from granite. 'I don't have anything to say. Stop calling.'

The line went dead. Maria still had the phone cradled to her ear when Cassie walked out of the bathroom in her pyjamas.

'Mar? What's wrong?' She knelt by the bed, taking the phone from Maria and looking at it. Her face flickered in recognition.

'He'll come around, Mar. It's a lot to take in, and he'll be concentrating on today, for his sister. Are you really sure you can do this?'

Maria threw back the covers.

'I have to finish this, Cass, then we can leave.'

When Tucker had dropped Cass off last night, snacks and

tissues in hand, Maria had cried again. They had talked it all out, and finally dropped off to sleep at half one. Maria felt like she hadn't slept at all.

'Who were you on the phone to?' she asked, remembering the hushed voice in the bathroom.

'Lynn. She's nattering about not being here. She's going to come and kidnap you if you're not out of here after the first dance.'

Maria chuckled. 'Don't worry, the porter will have our bags in the car for a quick getaway. I can't wait to leave either.'

Cassie was wearing a pastel-green fitted dress, with matching heels and her black hair swept off her face in a pretty plait down her back.

'You look amazing.' Maria beamed at her. 'Thanks for being here, mate.'

She hugged her friend to her and breathed in her light perfume. It comforted her, always had.

'Listen, Auntie Cassie will always be here.' She pulled away and waggled a finger at the bump. 'But, little one, you ever pull the shit that me and your mum have over the years, and you are in big trouble.'

Cassie and Maria stood in the front-left corner of the large hall, watching the sea of wedding guests chatting to each other, laughing, telling stories, flicking their gaze to the groom and his attendants. Mark had avoided Maria, thankfully, and she realised he was probably still in shock. At the baby and what it meant, about Annabel's actions, and about the fact that he was still standing there, about to get married to the woman he loved, while the woman he'd knocked up ran the event. It was the stuff of Shakespeare, or Austen, or Brontë. Probably the Brontës: they really liked to ratchet up the emotions. Which meant that, today, James was Heathcliff. He had been moody, angry and silent all morning, and had pretty much pretended that the heavily pregnant woman in the room just wasn't there. Cassie had tried to speak to him, but he hadn't given her anything back. They knew he had spoken to Tucker but, Tucker being Tucker, he wouldn't break the bro code and tell them anything, other than that he was upset and angry. They didn't need anyone to tell them that; it oozed from his every pore.

Maria had kept herself busy all morning, making sure everyone was where they needed to be, finalising the little details in the rooms, taking delivery of the flowers, the cake and the wedding presents, showing the guests into the room after their champagne reception. There was always someone needing help, needing a question answering, but now it was all in place, and she just needed to watch, and troubleshoot when she needed to.

Mark was standing at the front of the wooden altar, and he turned and glanced at her. She smiled at him, mouthing 'congratulations' to him. He smiled back and she felt better. Maybe having him and Annabel in the baby's life could work, somehow. It would be family for the baby, and she couldn't turn her back on them now they knew. He had a right to know his child, and she wasn't going to stop that. She thought of her mother getting sick, all those years ago. At least, if the worst happened, the baby would have people who loved it, who would be there. She'd never had that, and she remembered the hard times. She wouldn't wish it on anyone.

Cassie was moving from side to side on her heels, and Maria tapped her arm.

'Stop fidgeting!'

'I can't help it, I hate weddings!' she mumbled glumly. 'My living depends on these things failing, don't forget. I don't get why anyone would ever do this.'

Maria rolled her eyes, and Cassie winced. 'Sorry, I forgot. Again.'

Maria took her hand in hers as the wedding music started and the doors opened.

'It's okay,' she murmured, seeing James standing in the doorway, Annabel on his arm. Everyone's heads turned to the bride, to take her in. She did look beautiful, her hair even darker against the white sparkle of her veil, her dress pooling at her feet like cream poured from a jug.

Maria couldn't see her, though. She was being held in place by a pair of blue-green eyes. The moment the doors opened, she had looked for him, and he for her. She saw his eyes scan the room, the crowd, only stopping their frantic search when he saw her. She looked straight back at him, trying to convey all the things she wanted to say, from her gaze right to his soul, his head, his heart. He never moved his eyes from hers, and she mouthed 'I'm sorry' to him. She couldn't tell him what else she wanted to say, not here, not today, not this way. He bit his lip and she saw his jaw clench, and then the march started, and he didn't look at her again.

It was almost over. Cassie had done front of house at the meal, with Maria choosing to stay in the kitchen, dealing with any problems that came her way and sending Cassie out as her face. She couldn't bear to see James again, and she was pretty sure the last thing Annabel and Mark wanted was to see her milling around on their big day. They weren't enemies by any means, but the situation was still raw, still strange. They had the honeymoon and the rest of their lives to talk about it, to make it work. Maria had a feeling they would too.

'It's almost over!' Cassie said, echoing the words that had been rattling around in Maria's head.

'The guests are in the bar area, the evening guests have started to arrive, and the preparations for the evening-do turnaround are done. The dancefloor is down, the DJ has set up; we just need the first dance over with, and we can go. That skinny porter has put our stuff in the car.' She leant in close. 'I might have bagged a bit of champers too, for Tucker and I later.' She winked, and Maria laughed.

'Well, you deserve it. Thanks for today.'

Cassie fist-bumped her. 'It's okay. It's good to see a bit of love in a room; makes a nice change from work.'

The DJ started talking bang on seven o'clock and the two of them headed out to the room.

He announced the couple for their first dance, and the whole room clapped as they took to the floor. Annabel and Mark looked like the quintessential newlyweds, and as the drums for 'Kiss Me' started, Maria found herself feeling very happy for them both. This was what love looked like. It wasn't always pretty, or perfect. It wasn't the good days that showed people how they felt about each other, but the worst days. The days when you wanted to leave, to throw in the towel, to rip your own heart out rather than feel any more pain. Getting through those days made the good days all the sweeter, with the right person by your side.

She had never had that with Darcy, and now he had no claim on her heart, or her head. She was free. They looked so happy, so carefree, and the day had gone without a hitch. Cassie nudged her, pointing to the entrance, and she slipped into the kitchen to check everything was okay before they left. The night manager was taking care of the buffet, and the bar manager was doing the rest.

Maria looked at the couple on the dancefloor, suddenly happy she had decided to do the wedding. She was glad she was here to help. To be family of sorts.

The DJ called for other couples to join the bride and groom, and the head bridesmaid of course made a beeline for James. He was sitting at the top table, beer in hand, looking decidedly the worse for wear already. He had been drinking steadily all day, but his mood hadn't improved.

He brushed her off at first. Maria saw him pointing to his pint glass as she moved away to the door, in the shadows, but the woman wasn't going to be deterred. She took the pint from him, placing it out of reach, and grabbed his hands, pulling him to his feet. They walked to the dancefloor to join the others as the song played, and she pulled him in close, placing his hands on her bottom. Maria felt sick. She saw Cassie coming out of the

195

kitchen towards her, but she couldn't look away. James raised his hands to her back and Maria felt a jolt of relief, till Liz moved them back into place and held them there for a moment. He swayed along with her, and she reached up to his neck, tilting his head to hers. James seemed to stumble a little, but recovered, and she went in. Moving her hands onto his face, she kissed him hard.

Maria felt Cassie put her arms around her and turn her away.

'Mar.' Maria tried to look again and Cassie pulled her back into place. But not before she saw they were still locked together.

'Mar!' she called. 'Let's go.' Maria looked into her friend's face and pressed her lips together.

'Okay.'

James felt like he was going to pass out, fall asleep, and/or vomit. It could go either way. He had cheap perfume tickling his nostrils, and he pulled away, breaking the kiss. She looked like the cat that got the cream, and she went to lay her head on his chest, but he stepped back.

'What's wrong?' she simpered at him. 'Too hot to handle?'

He pointed to the toilets. 'Won't be a minute.'

She rolled her eyes and pouted at him. 'I'll get us a drink, yeah?'

He mumbled a 'yeah, whatever' and walked away to the toilets. When he was nearly at the door, he turned to the bar, but she was busy giving her order to one of the staff. He walked straight past the toilet doors and headed to the rooms.

He walked up to the room he knew Maria was staying in. He hadn't seen her in the ballroom, and he hoped she had gone to pack with Cassie. He needed to see her, though in his drunken state he had no idea what she was going to say. Or what he was going to say for that matter. He just needed to see her.

He knocked at the door but got no answer. He knocked again. He didn't hear anything from behind the door and his swaying was getting worse. He sat down, or rather slid down the wall, his back against the wood.

'I'm sorry, Marihah, I really am. I'msho mad you see, at you. For not trusting me, you'shoulda know'n you could tells me anything, I'm always here for you. And Sparky.' He dipped his head onto his chest.

'Little Scparky, I love her too. It's a girl, ya know.' He struggled to keep his eyes open as he spoke.

'It's definitely a girl. With your hair, and eyes.' He started to fall asleep, right there against the door.

'I just wish you'da told me, Mar. I really do.'

Chapter 20

Due Date

Maria was a ball of energy, all mixed up in a streak of anger and excitement and fear – and needing to pee every twenty seconds. Cassie and Tucker were in the kitchen making a chicken and pineapple curry to try and get things moving, and she could smell the raspberry leaf tea that Cassie was brewing. She had to get out, so she hammered out a quick text to Cassie and, turning her phone off, half-ran like a sumo wrestler down the path of Sanctuary Cottage towards the centre of the village. The text read: OFF TO THE SHOP. FOLLOW ME AND DIE. BACK IN AN HOUR.

She kept up the pace till she was out of sight of the cottage, and then started to stroll slowly down to Happy Ever After. Things had picked up now and, with the new line of baby clothes and christening wear, the shop was out of danger. The money from the wedding was safely in the bank and she had a Moses basket ready in her room, along with enough nappies, nipple cream and baby crap to see her through the first couple of months. She had been taking it a lot easier since the wedding, staying at the cottage and reading books, watching slasher flicks, sewing, and pretending to Cassie and Tucker, who were now madly in love, that she didn't sit and cry every day over the image of James locking lips with the maid of honour. It was seared into her brain – tattooed on the inside of her eyelids every time she dared close her eyes. She hadn't heard from him, and he had been very clear about never wanting to hear from her.

Mark and Annabel had been in touch; they had been on honeymoon and even sent her a postcard. Cassie was going to draw up some kind of custody arrangement for them all, giving them visitation rights, so things were clear, but for the most part, the pair of them were oddly excited about the impending birth. Maria still marvelled about Annabel's attitude, but knowing James, it didn't completely surprise her. They never mentioned him, so she hadn't dared ask. Knowing her luck, he was probably engaged to be married and little miss 'put your hands on my arse' was working on a baby Chance of her very own.

She walked through the village, enjoying the fresh air and sunshine. She had had backache for days, and felt sure she was in slow labour, given the information she had gleaned from the books she had devoured, but she knew it would be a long haul. The midwife had said as much.

For someone normally so chilled, even Tucker seemed to be agitated. He had been up at six cleaning and he and Cassie had both taken the day off work to 'keep her company'. They obviously didn't realise it wasn't like in the movies, where a woman gave birth in five minutes flat and wore her normal jeans home from the hospital. She couldn't look at their expectant faces anymore without wanting to punch them, so she would just go to work. She had just passed the corner of Carrington Street, and was heading to Wexley Street, when something stopped her dead. James's van was here. Parked right outside the shop. She scanned the street, but there was nobody there. She waddled as fast as she could to the shop, flinging open the door and barrelling in. Lynn was sitting at one of the sewing machines and whirred to a stop.

'Maria?' She jumped up, shepherding her to one of the comfy sofas. 'What on earth are you doing here? You sound out of breath!'

Maria wheezed a little. 'I walked, from the cottage. I wanted to kill them both, so I left.' She looked around, but there was no one else there.

'James?' she asked, hopeful eyes flicking to Lynn, who smiled.

'He's here. He's been here most days, when you weren't. He's upstairs.'

Maria walked up the dark wood staircase at the back of her shop, ignoring the squeal of her back and the burning sensation in her lungs. He was here. Had been coming here. She felt better just knowing he was close by. She rubbed her bump, but the baby had slowed down over the last couple of days. Probably limbering up for the big finish, and the marathon it would have her running for the next few months.

She reached the top of the stairs and stopped to catch her breath. She felt so hot, clammy. She had a simple maternity dress on under her coat and comfy shoes on her feet, but she felt like she was standing in a blast furnace. She shrugged her coat off, hanging it on the banister, and walked into the main room doorway, standing on the small landing.

The furniture she had had delivered had all been put together and arranged nicely. It looked like a home. Her new couches, TV unit, desk, everything. All the things she had had delivered were here and in use.

The kitchen off the hallway was cleaned down, and she could see utensils sitting in a crock on the worktop. Peeking into the storeroom at the other side, she saw it had been cleaned down and organised. Lynn's handwriting was on some of the drawer fronts. In the corner, a small desk and chair were tucked away. Her favourite scan picture was sitting on the desk in a silver frame.

She walked further, looking into the now partitioned-off bedroom, and there he was. He was sitting on the floor cross-legged, staring at a piece of cherry-red wood, and occasionally looking at a sheet of instructions.

'I hate you.' His words rang out in the room and she took a small step back in surprise. Her back protested.

'Did you hear me?'

She was about to answer, when he spoke again, waggling the piece of wood in his hand.

'I detest you, instrument of torture. How the fecking feck can A go into B, when C is there? I swear, if your instructions were in Swahili, I would get more sense out of them.'

He looked up as though searching for another bit, and then he saw her. His eyebrows shot up into his hairline and he dropped the wood.

'Oh, sorry, I didn't know you were there.' He looked her up and down and, standing up fast, strode over to her. 'You okay? You look a bit red.'

She didn't say anything, just looked into the marble-like blue-green eyes she'd thought she would never see again. He frowned and, taking her by the arm, brought her over to a rocker at the other side of the room. She sat down in it gently, looking around the room. He placed her foot on a footstool that matched the rocker.

James didn't say anything, leaving the room and returning with a bottle of water.

The bottle was cold to the touch. 'Where did this come from? It's cold.'

'Lynn went shopping, stocked the fridge up.'

'Where did all this other stuff come from?' She cracked the bottle and drank thirstily. He knelt by her feet, still looking at her like she was going to collapse. 'I'm fine, just hot,' she said to soothe him, and his brow unfurrowed a fraction.

'It's your stuff mostly. Simon did the wall work, and the

plumbing, and I did the electrics. We sorted the stuff out that you had delivered, and the rest just came from well-wishers.'

She stroked the arm of the rocker. It was beautiful, dark wood with creamy cushions and upholstery. 'This is wonderful. Who bought this?'

He went and sat back down on the floor, not looking at her as he got back to work.

'I did. It's a nursing rocker. It matches the cot bed, if I can ever get the bloody thing to go together.'

He was studying the instructions intently again, but Maria could see his hand was shaking.

'Why are you here, James? Why did you do all this?'

He looked up and sighed heavily. 'You know why, Maria. We were friends, and I wanted you to have a place of your own, you and Sp... the baby.'

'Sparky,' she said, rubbing her bump. 'It's still Sparky, that hasn't changed.'

'Yeah,' he said sarcastically, 'but now I really am Uncle James, aren't I? By blood, not by friendship.'

'The baby isn't your blood, not really.' She tried, knowing that really, with family, blood meant nothing. It was down to more than haemoglobin. Family was much more than that. Ugly as it was sometimes, but that was life.

'You know what I mean.' His jaw clenched, and she could see he was still angry. She pushed the footstool away and stood up in as dignified a manner as she could.

'I'll leave you to it then,' she said, starting to head to the exit.

'Why didn't you tell me, Mar?' he asked her, and she felt him move behind her. She wanted to turn around, to look him in the eye, but she knew it was more than she could take. If she turned around now, even caught a smell of him, she would be lost for ever. She would never recover from this, she knew that now, but she needed to be strong, if only for the sake of the baby. Right on cue, the little one gave her a nudge, and she rolled her eyes. This little monkey was a smart one, that was for sure.

'I wanted to, but I just couldn't do it. I didn't know where to start. I knew I had to walk away, so I just focused on that. Doing the wedding and leaving you all to get on with your lives.'

'What about us? About me?'

She turned sideways, not looking at him but reaching for his hand. She felt his fingers lace around hers, and the warmth and comfort from him seeped into her skin.

'I was trying to protect you. You deserve someone who will treat you better. Someone without all the baggage and drama.'

He pulled gently on her hand, turning her to face him. She looked at the floor.

'You kissed me back.' He stated this but in a way that felt like a question. One Maria had been thinking about since their lips had met. 'Why did you kiss me back? Look at me!'

His urgent tone made her raise her head, and she dreaded what she would see in his eyes. Hatred, resentment, disappointment. She locked with those baby blues and jolted when she saw love and fear in them instead. He ran his gaze all over her then, taking in her face and landing on her swollen stomach. He reached out his free hand, ever so slowly, and placed it on her tummy.

'Hey, Sparky,' he said softly, and a tear ran down his cheek. He wiped it away, taking her hand with him as though he was afraid to let it go. She felt a drop of salty water run down her wrist, and she wiped at the moisture on his cheek. He moved his cheek into her palm and kissed it.

'Tell me, Maria, tell me once and for all, what is this?'

She ran her thumb along his bottom lip, thinking of all the kindness that had come from this mouth, the devoted friendship, the way he nibbled his lip when he was concentrating, the way he had growled and pouted at Darcy, the way his angry kiss had bruised her lips, her soul. She couldn't ever imagine not seeing this face every day. She had missed it so much.

'I love you, James,' she said. 'I just love you so much. I have no reason for you to stay, to be here, but I'm yours. I think I always have been, and I'm so sorry I hurt you.'

'What about the baby?' he asked, his eyes shining, his mouth slack with shocked surprise.

She laughed as the baby gave another nudge, right on James's hand, and he laughed too, bending to kiss her bump.

'I think Sparky loves you too,' she said, running her hands through his hair. He looked up at her, his cheeky boyish grin back in place, and she beamed back at him.

'Maria, I love you—'

There was a sploshing sound and James fell backwards. Maria looked down in panic and saw that the floor was wet, and James's trousers were soaked.

'What the hell was that?' she asked, just as a sharp pain erupted in her stomach. It felt like someone was squeezing her stomach hard. 'Ouch!'

James scrabbled to his feet, grabbing his phone out of his pocket.

'Oh my God, I think your waters broke. I'll call an ambulance!'

Maria leant over the bed, moving her hips from side to side as the contraction subsided. She could feel the water sloshing out of her as she moved. It was such a weird sensation; she felt a little like a water balloon.

'No…' She reached for him and he grabbed her hand, supporting her. 'I'm okay, it's going off. I've read all the books, it takes hours. I'm okay, I'll ring a taxi.'

James put his arms around her and raised her face to his. She could see him relax a little as he realised she was no longer in pain.

'You sure? No taxi, I'll take you in the van.' His face fell again. 'Oh shit, maybe not. Your car?'

She shook her head. 'It's at the cottage. I can't walk that far. The van's fine. You might just have to help me get in.'

He nodded, and they looked at each other as the adrenaline pumped.

'James, Sparky's coming,' she said, scarcely believing it herself.

He kissed her then, a soft, short kiss that told her everything she needed to know, and everything he needed to say.

'I love you,' she told him again, not wanting to stop saying it.

'I love you too,' he grinned. 'I fell for you the minute we met. I'm here and I will never leave you again.'

She smiled, just as the next contraction started to take hold of her.

'Good, because I have no intention of letting you down ever again either.'

They walked together arm in arm, slowly down the stairs, James rubbing her back and watching her like a hawk down every step. Lynn turned to see them coming down the stairs and clasped her hands together.

'You sorted everything out!' she exclaimed, practically flying across the room on her office chair. 'I knew you two would get together!'

She looked again at them, and her face fell. 'Maria, what's wrong?'

James smiled at her, half-carrying Maria to the door.

'Get the door, Lynn, Sparky's coming!'

'OH MY GOD! OH MY GOD, THE BABY!' She ran to the door, curls flying loose from her pins, and jumped from foot to foot in a panic. 'Get going, you need to get to the hospital!'

'Calm down,' Maria said through gritted teeth. 'The books say it will be hours yet.'

'Yes,' said James, 'but with the waters breaking, the chance of infection is higher, so we need to go now.' Both women looked at him, and he looked sheepish. 'I might have been reading a few books myself.' Maria hugged him tighter to her, and he dropped a kiss on her slightly sweaty head.

Lynn fawned over them for half a second, and Maria winced in pain.

'Get a blanket for the car seat, Lynn?' James urged.

Lynn ran and grabbed one, lying it on the van seat and helping James hoist Maria up the small step into the seat. She pulled the seatbelt around her and concentrated on her breathing. Lynn gave her a kiss and smoothed her hair back off her face.

Maria started to cry a little, overwhelmed.

'Thanks, Lynn, I love you.'

Lynn brushed a tear away from her own face. 'I love you too, my girl. Your mother would be so proud, you know, just as I am.'

Maria smiled through her tears. 'Will you be Grandma?' she asked, kicking herself for not asking sooner. Lynn burst into a sob.

'My darling girl, I would be honoured.' She looked over her head at James. 'Look after our girl. We'll meet you there.'

James nodded, getting ready to pull away. 'I will.'

They drew away from the kerb, and Maria saw Lynn run back into the shop, no doubt to close up and grab Cassie and Tucker. She wondered if she should call Mark and Annabel, but James was already passing her his phone.

'Ring Mark?' he asked, and she nodded. He answered on the first ring but Maria was already having a full-on contraction. She thrust the phone into James's hands-free cradle and bellowed like a bull through the pain.

'EEEOOOOOOOOO!'

There was a stunned silence for a moment, and then Mark's voice came over the line.

'James? What's wrong?'

James was driving as fast as he safely could through the streets of Westfield, heading towards Agatha's Mayweather Estate on the outskirts, beyond which lay Harrogate Hospital.

'Mark, the baby's coming. Meet you at the hospital?'

Mark spluttered down the line and Annabel came on.

'James, what's wrong?'

Maria grunted again, making a keening sound as she sweated through the pain.

'Anna! The baby's coming. I'm bringing Maria to the hospital. Meet you both there?'

'Oh my God,' she squealed. 'Yes, of course. Maria, you okay?'

'Yes, am okaaayyyyy!'

James grabbed her hand and she squeezed it tightly as he changed gears without letting go of her.

'She's okay, she's with me.'

'Finally,' she quipped. 'Drive safe, love you both.'

The line went dead and they were alone in the van again. The contraction went and Maria reached down, grappling with her underwear. James looked at her with concern as they neared Agatha's entrance gates.

'Mar, you okay?'

She shook her head. 'I need to take my pants off, I feel like the baby's coming.' She saw the blood drain from his face.

'Do it, I'm here.'

She wrestled them off and managed to get them into her hand. They were wet from the fluid, and she threw them out of the open window without even thinking as another contraction rode over her. The huge pants fluttered on the breeze for a moment before landing on one of the stone lions.

Maria groaned with embarrassment. 'Oh God,' she half-screamed, 'Agatha will kill me!'

James squeezed her hand, his face set with concentration as he raced to get to the hospital. She felt the sudden unmistakable urge to push.

'Oh God, James, I thought it would take longer! I think the baby's coming now!' The contractions were coming thick and fast, and she just concentrated on the pain, fighting the urge her body was screaming at her to push. She put her feet up on the dashboard, trying to ride the crescendo of pain. They were just driving along the road when James suddenly shouted, 'Hold on!' He swerved off the road, pulling into Westfield fire station. A man with a fire-department emblem on his T-shirt was cleaning equipment at the front and he took one look at them and ran over.

He stuck his head through the window as James slammed the handbrake on.

'You okay?' he asked. 'I'm Sam. Can I help?'

James jumped out of the van, running over to her side and standing next to Sam.

'Please, it's my girlfriend, she's having a baby right now!'

Sam opened the door and both men grabbed an arm and leg each and half-hoisted, half-carried her out of the cabin as Sam shouted for help from his colleagues. Two other men came out, one running back in and grabbing a blanket. They tried to carry her into the fire station, but Maria protested.

'I can't,' she said, crying with pain and fear. 'James, it's coming!'

Sam looked at James and they laid her down on the blanket on the tarmac. Two other men came and, turning away, held blankets up to protect her modesty.

'Okay,' Sam said. 'Well, er...'

'Maria,' James said. 'Maria... she's due today.'

Sam nodded, smiling. 'Well, I'm Sam, and you'll be happy to know I've delivered no fewer than ten babies in my job, and they're all healthy, bouncing little bundles of joy.'

His mate passed him some gloves and antibacterial gel, and he donned them after washing his hands.

'I just need to look, okay? James, is it?'

James nodded.

'Okay, James, you get behind Maria and support her back.'

James sat down on the driveway of the fire station on the blanket, and Maria sank down so she was lying between his legs. He supported her arms and kissed her head over and over.

'You've got this, Mar – I'm here.' They linked both hands together, their fingers tight around each other.

'I love you,' she murmured, half-delirious, and James kissed her cheek.

'I love you too. Now let's get Sparky here, safe and sound.'

Sam lifted up her dress, getting down to business.

'Okay, Maria, your waters have broken, yeah?'

They both nodded. 'About fifteen minutes ago. We got straight in the van. We thought she'd have longer.'

'First?' Sam checked.

'Yeah.'

'Ah, we have a little feisty one! Well, Fireman Sam will sort you out.'

'Fireman Sam?' Maria asked, thinking she must be more delirious than she thought. He winked at her.

'Yep, I know. Weird, eh?'

'Where's Norman?' she quipped, giddy with adrenaline. Another fireman appeared, holding a bowl of steaming water.

'Norman? It's his day off.'

James and Maria broke into laughter at the absurdity of the situation, and the firemen all grinned at each other. Another contraction started and Sam rolled up his sleeves.

'Right, Maria, this baby's coming, right now. Get ready, boys.'

'Ambulance responder is on route,' one of them said. Sam shook his head.

'We won't have that long. Ready, Maria? The head is ready to come out. When you get the urge to push, I want you to push. Hard. Go!'

Maria pushed with every part of her. She felt like her whole body was going to explode, and she could feel the bones of James's hand rubbing together with the force of her grip. James never moaned, just kept whispering to her, the warmth of him behind her spurring her on.

'Go on, baby, you can do this. Push!'

She pushed as hard as she could and Sam reached forward.

'Okay, okay, the head is here! Rest now, and on the next contraction your baby is going to be here! You know what you're having? It's a speedy one, that's for sure!'

Maria shook her head, laying her head back onto James's shoulder.

There was the sound of distant sirens in the background, and Cassie's car came flying past, driving up the road. Obviously on the way to the hospital. They would get there before them at this rate.

James held her tight as they waited for what seemed like for ever. Maria felt her muscles clench again, and put her head up. Sam looked at her and gave her an encouraging look. He was cute, his head shaved bald, big brown eyes looking out from his features. Strong eyebrows. The man looked like he had faced danger and punched it in the face.

'Ready?' he asked.

'Ready,' she said and, when the pain took hold, she pushed. Hard.

Chapter 21

One Year Later

The screams could be heard all the way down the corridor and Maria winced, remembering the day she had pushed her baby daughter into the world. Right there at the front of the fire station, with the burliest midwife she could ever have imagined in attendance, and James by her side. Just like he was now, sitting next to her in the waiting room of Harrogate Hospital.

Hope Elizabeth Chance was sitting on his knee, giggling at the faces he was pulling at her. Her blonde curls were fanned around her face, and Maria was once again struck by how much she looked like she did in her own baby photos, and how she had her own mother's eyes. She couldn't wait to tell her all about her mother when she grew up, and tell her how much her Grandma Mallory would have loved her, just like her Grandmother Lynn adored her now. She fingered the rings on her hand, recalling their perfect wedding just the month before. They had been married on the steps of the fire house, and Sam had been the one to walk her down the proverbial aisle, with Mark as James's best man. They had had a few awkward moments, but on the whole, their little family had found a groove with each other that got easier with each passing day. Hope had two daddies who loved her, two mummies who adored her, and plenty of spares. That was the best thing. They said it took a village to raise a child, and Hope had that. Right here in Westfield. Everyone adored her, and she was the happiest child in the world.

Another scream erupted, followed by a crash, and Mark and Annabel walked into the waiting room.

'Dada!' Hope shouted, and James put her down on the floor so she could toddle over. Mark smiled and, picking her up, snuggled her in close.

'Hello, sweetpea, is Auntie Cassie making a noise?'

Hope gurgled, playing with Mark's tie as he sat down with her. Annabel was looking anxiously at the door, looking a bit green. Maria looked at James questioningly, but he just shrugged.

'You okay, Anna?' she asked her, moving to sit next to her.

They could hear a commotion from outside in the corridor, and Annabel flinched.

'Do you think something's wrong?' she murmured. Mark put his hand over hers.

'No, love,' he said, putting Hope onto her knee. 'Here, say hi to Hopey.'

Annabel planted a big smacker on her tummy, making her laugh.

'Hey, baby!' she said, and Maria smiled, watching the two interact.

'You sure you're okay?' Maria pressed. Annabel had just opened her mouth to speak when the door opened and Tucker walked in, his black T-shirt torn and his left eye red and rapidly swelling shut.

Maria ran over to him.

'Oh my God, you okay?'

Tucker nodded, grinning from ear to ear.

'It's a girl!'

212

The whole room erupted into excited whoops and Maria picked Hope up and held her close.

'You hear that, little one? You have a new best friend, just like Mummy.' She hugged Tucker after James and Mark had finished congratulating him and slapping him on the back.

'Congratulations, Jesse! Are they both okay? What happened to your eye?'

He chuckled, his Australian twang filling the room.

'You know what she's like. I'm just glad she didn't manage to get a utensil. She kicked a midwife by accident and knocked her clean over the bed, catching me square in the face with her heel.'

Maria giggled, realising that must have been the crash they heard.

'What about the baby?' Tucker's smile widened, if that was possible.

'She's bloody gorgeous. Jet-black hair, just like her mother. Go and see her, she's just getting settled.'

Annabel appeared behind them, looking like a startled rabbit.

'How bad was it?' she asked earnestly. Tucker shrugged. 'It was amazing, to be honest, minus the injuries. I had to comp the midwives a meal at the restaurant, for their trauma.'

Annabel looked relieved, and Maria noticed her putting her hand over her stomach.

'Oh my God,' she said quietly, passing Hope to James and going over to her. 'You're pregnant, aren't you!'

Annabel's eyes bulged and she burst into tears. The men in the room suddenly became very interested in playing with Hope at the other end of the room.

'Yes,' she said, sobbing.

'That's a good thing, right?' Maria's heart sank. Was something wrong? Was it because Mark already had a child? Maria hoped it wouldn't cause problems, not when things were so good now.

'Yes, but…' Anna sobbed again. 'I'm terrified!'

Maria chuckled despite herself and pulled her friend to her.

'You and Mark are naturals. It'll be great and we're here for you, every step.'

Annabel sniffed and smiled weakly.

'You sure?'

'Of course! We're family!'

Later that night, after seeing Cassie and Jesse totally besotted with their new daughter, Catherine Alecia Tucker, and going out for dinner to celebrate Annabel and Mark's news about baby Smith to be, Maria and James bathed a very overexcited and sticky Hope and snuggled her in her cot in James's Harrogate home. Now their home. Maria still used the shop flat, of course, and it was handy for a break, or to change Hope, or put her down for a nap. A home from home. Happy Ever After was her home too. She had grieved her mother there, met the love of her life, met her family, and nurtured their daughter. She was so happy she would never have to let it go.

She was planning weddings again too, and she had rather a special one on the cards for next year. Her own best friend, marrying the hunky Australian she had picked up on a boozy night out and never quite shaken off. Bridezilla syndrome wasn't a problem for that wedding, though. Cassie would have got married at the side of KFC, dressed in her yoga pants. It would be a challenge, if nothing else.

They sat together on the sofa, watching Hope's chest rise and fall on the baby monitor screen, listening to her contented snuffles as James poured them both a glass of wine from a chilled bottle.

'Well, what a day,' James mused, holding the glass out to her. She reached for it and he pulled it back out of her reach, puckering up his full lips. She chuckled, leaning in to kiss him. He smelt of James: mints and aftershave. He smelt of their daughter too, and she kissed him again.

'What a day indeed,' she agreed, taking the wine from him and taking a long glug.

James sank back into the cushions, bringing her with him.

'I was thinking, maybe we should think about having another baby.'

Maria looked across at him, not quite believing her own ears.

'Another baby? You getting broody after today?'

He laughed, a low rumble that reverberated through his body to hers.

'Yeah, well, we have this big house, and a spare room. Maybe another Chance would be good. A playmate for Hope.'

Maria thought of baby Catherine, and Annabel's news.

'I don't think she'll be short of them somehow.'

James turned to her, sitting forward and taking her wine from her.

'Ah, Mrs Chance, but another baby in this house, made from you and I, that would be pretty great, eh?'

He started to unbutton her blouse slowly, flicking a look at the monitor and then waggling his eyebrows devilishly at her.

'Besides, we're newlyweds, so a bit of practice would be good, at the very least.'

She enjoyed the feeling of his warm, familiar hands on her body before she started to undo his shirt.

'Well, last time we took a chance it worked out well, didn't it?'

James smirked at her, pulling down her blouse and toying with her bra strap.

'Exactly,' he breathed as she ran her hands down his chest. 'Everyone needs a second Chance.'

She giggled at his quip. He bit his lip then, and she realised he was nervous.

'You're deadly serious, aren't you? You really want this?'

He looked deep into her eyes with the blue-green sparklers she loved so much. She would never get tired of looking at this man, of being the centre of his world. She imagined a baby, sleeping upstairs with Hope, those blue-green eyes, just like his daddy's.

'Yes,' he replied, dropping a kiss on her collarbone. 'I love you, Maria Chance. I want another baby with you, a sibling for our daughter. What do you say?' He kissed her again, this time on the lips, slowly.

She kissed him back and touched her forehead against his as they held each other.

'I say we're going to need a bigger village.'

Acknowledgements

As always, a big thanks to my editors, Anna Baggaley and Nia Beynon, who both worked on this book and made it so much better than I had hoped with their encouragement and hard work. Love to you both and the team at HQ Digital.

The writing community of authors, bloggers and readers is vast, and I thank each and every one of you from the bottom of my heart for your support, laughs and friendship. Here's to the next book, and the next exciting journey.

Turn the page for a sneak
peak at *The Long Walk Back*

PROLOGUE

That day. The day I learned an answer to one of mankind's big questions, what do you see when your body is at the point of death? Not your average day. An average day is going to work, coming home, parking your fat arse on the couch in front of the TV, a takeaway perched on your knee while you piss and moan to yourself about how skint you are, how the country is going to the dogs, how much you hate your job. That is an average day, one that blends into countless others through the years, till you wake up in your fifties, bored, bald and fat, wondering at what point the dreams of your younger self went down the toilet. That was never going to be me, and my choices in life led me to this day, what looked like my last day. Karma is a bitch, I hear you on that one.

An hour earlier, I was doing a routine sweep of the area with my unit. Of my thirty-one years on the earth, I had spent fifteen of them in the army. We were out in Iraq, pushing back the terrorists that threatened the small villages we were camped near to. Many of the villagers wanted us here, and the tensions were rising.

It's not like on the news. You think it all looks the same. Desert, broken buildings, busted vehicles, shattered people. There is no beauty on the news, but it exists here. We fear what we don't know, what we can't control, but here people live the same as us in many ways. I have seen photos on walls, gardens lovingly tended, children loved and cared for. The actions of few cause the outcome for many, and I saw it every day. I joined to serve, to have a purpose, but I also enlisted to find the family I never had. So now I fought for them too, with them by my side.

There had been a lot of unease the last few weeks, and you could feel the stress, the taut emotions of the people and the enemy, even through the hot, dry air. I had had a bad feeling in the pit of my gut for days, and when the shots had started firing, I knew why. They had been gearing up to take us down, and as prepared as we thought we were, we were still caught with our pants down that day.

'Pull back!' I boomed gruffly to my charges. 'Come on, go, go, go!' I started to run for the nearest building, the one we had just finished sweeping. It was abandoned, full of empty homes, food still rotting on tables that would never host a family meal again. I kept looking over my shoulder, watching my guys take shelter one by one. A hail of shots whizzed past my ear, and I threw myself against the side of the nearest car. Hunching down, I looked to where the shots were coming from. Two of my guys were still on the way to the shelter – one hunched over, not moving. The other, Travis, was dragging him to safety. Blood followed them like a trail of gunpowder as they desperately tried to escape. Another barrage of shots rang out, and Travis jerked. He had been hit, but he kept going, pulling Smithy along with him, hung over his shoulder. They weren't going to make it. I jumped up, firing a volley off at the top of the building, the source of the shots but they fired back. Hunching down again, I shouted at

Travis to get a move on, grabbing my radio and running towards them.

'Hightower, can you see him?' I screamed into the radio. My sniper on the roof, Bradley, was my ace in the hole.

'Nearly, the slippery bastard is hidden well. He has a child up there with him, using him as a human shield.'

I cursed under my breath. I reached Travis and grabbed Smithy from him. Travis was bleeding badly, but it looked like a shoulder wound.

We ran hell for leather towards the shelter, Hightower screaming into the radio.

'He's reloading Coop, get a move on!'

I was almost at the shelter, Travis was just ahead, racing to get ready to help Smithy, who was still out cold. My muscles burned from the effort of dragging him along with me, but I ignored the pain, pushing on.

'Almost there,' I shouted back into the receiver. 'Find a shot, and take him down!'

Hightower acknowledged and just as we reached the lip of the shelter, shots rang out again, this time with the 'phut phut' of the sniper rifle as Hightower followed orders. I was just wondering whether the poor child on the roof was okay, when a huge force pushed me straight off my feet, into the air. I reached out to tighten my grip on Smithy, but felt nothing but space. Hitting the ground, I struggled for breath, dust and debris raining down around me. Hightower was screaming down the air waves, mobilising the others.

I struggled to breathe, and my mouth was coated with a new layer of dust every time I managed to pull in a ragged breath. I could hear commotion around me, and moved my head to the side to look for Smithy. I could see him a few feet away, and I knew without a doubt he was dead. I turned away, already wanting to erase the memory of his crumpled form from my memory. I coughed, and felt a warm trickle run down my cheek.

Not good, I thought to myself. I could hear my friends, my comrades in arms, running towards me, firing shots off, barking orders at each other. There was no white light, no images of me running around in short trousers, nothing. I could see nothing but dust, flashes of weaponry, and the smell of panic and desperation in the air. I felt bone tired, and a little voice inside of me told me to sleep. I tried to shake my head, keep myself awake, but the warm feeling spread through me. My body wasn't responding. It was like slipping into a hot bath after a long, cold day. I could feel my muscles began to relax, and my throat filling up with liquid. I tried to spit, to turn my head, but my eyelids were already fluttering. I thought of the boy, no doubt dead now on the rooftop. I wondered if he had parents around to grieve for him, people who would mourn his death. And that's the last thing I remember.

CHAPTER ONE

Kate was pulling faces into the camera when the call came in to tell her casualties were en route. She turned around to face the opposite direction, shielding her son from the images of people who had been running behind her.

'Mummy has to go now, sweet pea, but I will call you back as soon as I can, yeah? Remind Dad to take you to football practice after school, okay?' Her son rolled his eyes.

'He never checks the calendar Mum, you know that. When are you coming home?' Trevor tapped her on the arm, waving to her son's image on the phone screen.

'Hey Jamie, good luck at practice! Kate, we have to go,' he said, frowning in apology. From the look on her colleague's face, it was bad. She blew a kiss at her son. Jamie rolled his eyes but blew one back.

'I am eight Mum, when I'm nine there are no more kisses, okay? It's well embarrassing!'

Kate laughed. 'No deal kiddo. I will be wanting kisses when you are all grown up. I have to go, see you soon. Love you.'

Jamie smiled weakly. She knew that this was hard for him too, but she couldn't miss the opportunity. 'Love you too Mummy,' he said, and his face disappeared from view as the call ended. She knew he would understand when he was older. She hoped that he would be proud that his mother went out there, did something with her life, that he would remember that instead of the times she worked late, went away, was an absent parent. Mothers were a different breed to fathers. Fathers could have it all, but mothers were judged no matter what they did. She loved Jamie, but when she stood there in a messy house, with leaking breasts and a screaming newborn, she knew it would never be enough. He was her world, but she still wanted the moon and the stars. Men could have that and no one batted an eyelid. I woman wanted to do the same? Judgement would follow. She wanted Jamie to grow up in a world where that particular glass ceiling was gone, replaced by open sky. If she could help smash it, all the better. She would make it up to him when she got back.

Kate threw the phone into her bag, grabbed her scrubs after throwing her clothes onto her cot bed and got herself ready in record time. Grabbing her kit, she raced to follow Trevor to the hospital tent nearby. She covered her eyes as best she could from the dust that the incoming helicopter kicked up in the sandy dirt that their medical camp was perched on.

Doing a three-month stint with the Red Cross as a trauma surgeon was not for the faint-hearted, but Kate Harper loved every bloody minute of it. She had two weeks left, and although she missed her boy dearly, she knew that going home to her usual hospital job would be an adjustment. Not as much as it would be going home to Neil, her husband of seven years. he had to admit to herself, the distance between them lately mounted up to more than miles, and she didn't quite know what to do about it. The thought of seeing him again filled her with anxiety. She knew that this trip had changed something between them, it had stretched the elastic of their relationship thin. She wasn't sure it could spring back this time. Did she even want it to?

Being here was a very different kind of working away. Their phone calls were always snatched seconds. When she did get time to call, the signal often dropped, leaving them to play frustrated phone tag with each other. When he was away for work at conferences, they could chat leisurely. Him from his safe snug hotel room at the side of some motorway. Her from their bed, with their son sleeping soundly nearby. Their conversations consisted of errands to run, Jamie's school day, their work days. The logistics of their married life together. Here, the calls were clipped, short. Checking in. Are you and Jamie okay? Is it bad there? She couldn't talk about her day. What would she tell him, about the lives she saved? The ones she lost? She didn't want to think about them, let alone try to form words, to explain them to a man who worked in a safe office all day, watching the clock for meeting times, not for giving time of death. It narrowed their conversations. She couldn't help but feel mad if he moaned about his day, about things that Kate had already realised didn't matter in the grand scheme. Neil got mad that she was so closed off and cagey about her life there. Other times she could feel the resentment in his voice, as though she were away on a girly holiday and he had been left holding the pre-teen. They could fill a book with everything they couldn't say. She couldn't remember the last time she had told him she loved him. She pushed it to the back of her mind, she had to work now. Some puzzles were easier to solve than others. Long distance relationships weren't easy. They both knew that, but it wasn't forever.

The chopper landed, the metal glinting in the early morning scorch of the sun. Kate grabbed her hair, pulling it tighter into her ponytail, and raced to meet the stretcher.

She snapped a pair of gloves on as she ran, though she wasn't sure how sterile they would be given the sand flying around. Her colleagues at home would balk at some of the makeshift operations set up in these tents. The medicine was the key though, patching people up, getting them home. The rest was done as best they could under the circumstances. It wasn't all pretty and clean here. In this environment, fighting death was bloody, messy and fast. Split second decisions were crucial.

'What do we have?' she asked the army medic pulling the patient out on the gurney, keeping his head dipped below the spinning chopper blades.

'One dead in the field, two injured. This one is Captain Thomas Cooper, his unit was ambushed. Multiple injuries, IED, left leg. Flatlined twice on the way here, his vitals are shot. He has shrapnel injuries to his leg and torso, he hasn't been conscious since impact.' The medic glanced across at her. 'We need to move fast.' Kate nodded, running alongside the trolley as they raced for the trauma tent.

'What meds has he had?'

'We started him on a course of strong antibiotics and 10mg of morphine. We had no time for anything else, we had to get him out of there.'

It didn't look good. Cooper's eyes fluttered, and Kate noticed what a beautiful shade of green they were, the contrast made all the starker against his deathly pale skin and blood splattered face. They raced into the tent, transferring him from the stretcher to one of the hospital treatment tables. He never made a murmur. Kate grabbed a pair of scissors from her kit and cut away the remnants of his trousers, showing torn black boxers underneath. His left leg was a bloody mess. They had to stop the bleeding, or he would lose his life too. Looking at his right leg, she saw shrapnel protruding from his bloody wounds. These were comparatively superficial wounds; had he not been running flat out, she surmised that both legs would have hit the homemade bomb and been in the same state.

The only reason this soldier had any leg at all was the position of his running body as the blast hit. She got to work, barking out orders to the staff running around the bed next to her. The whole tent was a hive of activity, and Kate blocked the noises out. On her first week here, she had been useless. She was no stranger to traumatic injuries, but the relative silence of the wards and operating rooms back home was a world apart from the sounds that surrounded her on a daily basis now. Strapping grown men, screaming, calling for their mothers, their wives, their gods, helicopters and booming sounds of bombs nearby, gunfire in the distance. All of these sounds had taken some adjustment, but now she tuned them out, was able to concentrate on what her colleagues were saying, the heart sounds she listened to in damaged chests, the gurgles and moans from the bodies she tended to. Kate ran over to Trevor.

'The Captain's not looking good. We need to stop the bleeders in his chest and right leg too. He's lost a lot of blood.' Trevor nodded, working on another patient as he listened to his colleague and one-time student.

'You have this Kate.' As she turned to run back, he shouted after her.

'Kate, save him if you can. He saved two others in the field, his troop only made it out because of his actions. Only one died, and he will be angry enough about that when he comes to. We owe it to him.'

Kate ignored the slab of thick tension that nestled in her throat.

'Roger that.'

'They used a kid as a human shield Kate, the sniper had to take them both out to save our men. An innocent kid. No one else gets to die today.' Kate ran back to Cooper. She thought of her earlier phone call with her son. Worrying about him missing football practice, whether he had eaten breakfast. A world away from being used as a weapon in a war he didn't cause or belong in. A mother had lost her child today.

Hours later, the tent was quieter, calmer. The gunfire in the far distance had abated somewhat, and the silence was almost eerie. Kate was exhausted, covered in dirt and grime that had mixed with the sweat of her frantic exertion to save lives in the middle of a warzone. They needed to be ready at a moment's notice, but the adrenaline of the last few hours had kicked in now and she knew if she went to bed, she would just lay awake looking at the ceiling of the tent, so she stayed. Sarah Fielding, a combat medic assigned to this unit, was at a nearby desk sorting through personal effects ready to bag and tag. They tried to save what they could, to either give back to the soldiers, or send back to their families. Kate went to the small kitchen area and grabbed a strong coffee, sitting down on a chair near the desk.

'Hi Sarah, you okay?' Kate asked tentatively, sipping at the strong hot drink. She felt the jolt of caffeine lick through her limbs.

'Yeah, I just hate this job,' Sarah replied, frowning. Kate noticed a familiar piece of clothing.

'That the Captain's trousers? Mind if I look?'

She shrugged. 'No, bag it up for me would you, when you're done? I still have a pile to get through and I need to get my head down.' Sarah looked across at her, smiling weakly. 'You should too.'

Kate nodded, taking the possessions from her colleague. 'I will, I can't settle yet. You go.'

Sarah placed a hand on her shoulder as she passed, squeezing it in appreciation. 'Night Kate.'

'Night Sarah,' Kate said over her shoulder. The Captain was still unconscious, whether from the sedation or his injuries remained to be seen. They had stopped the bleeding, and he was stable. For now. Glugging at her coffee, she set it down on the desk and started to go through her patient's belongings. He had the usual field stuff in his pockets, along with a wallet.

It had escaped the blast. His mobile phone was shattered, so she itemised it and put it into the bag. Opening the wallet, she looked through, feeling guilty for going through his personal possessions, but it needed to be done. Sometimes, all families got back were the contents of their loved one's pockets and bags, and even a half-eaten packet of mints was a comfort to a grieving mother. Photos and letters were the gold though. Looking through the wallet, she found amongst the cards and money a little stack of snaps. She frowned as she thumbed through them. They were all of him and his friends, in various barracks and war zones. No family pictures, no smiling mother and father, no rosy cheeked children cuddled by a proud wife. She noticed how handsome he was, smiling into the camera, laughing into another. His playful side showed, a man goofing around with his buddies in a rare peaceful moment. She wondered whether anyone would be trying to ring his phone. Worrying about why he didn't answer.

Trevor came into the room then, unnoticed by Kate till he took a sip of her now lukewarm coffee.

'Hey,' she said teasingly. 'Get your own!'

Trevor winked and drained the cup. 'You should be in bed. Want a fresh one?'

Kate nodded, already back to being absorbed in the images in her hands. 'Do you know the Captain?'

'Thomas Cooper, one of the good ones,' Trevor replied. How's he doing?'

Kate looked at Trevor, a frown on her tired face. 'Stable. For now. His leg doesn't look good. We're watching him for signs of sepsis.'

'He won't be happy if he can't go back into full service. Keep me updated. Has he woken up yet?'

Kate shook her head. Trevor's gaze dropped.

'Has he got any family?' Kate asked. 'There are only his army buddies in these photos.'

Trevor shook his head. 'Nope, Cooper is army born and bred. No family to speak of, as far as I know. He keeps his cards pretty close to his chest.'

Kate put the photos back, finishing her task and tying the bag up to go with the others. He was alone here then, like her. I suppose, really, they were all out here alone, which made it all the more important to have each other's backs. Except she had people, waiting for her, counting on her to return to them. She looked at the ward entrance, partitioned off by canvas doors.

Trevor went off to get more coffee, but when he came back, Kate was nowhere to be seen. He carried the cups through to the main ward tent, sure that a nurse would be grateful for the hot drink. Walking through, something made him slow his heavy step. At the end of the ward, next to Captain Cooper's bed, Kate lay in a chair, sleeping, one hand over Cooper's as they both slept. Trevor smiled to himself, going to find a tired nurse to caffeinate. That was Kate all over, all heart.

Dear Reader,

Thank you for taking the time to read my book. I hope you enjoyed it as much as I enjoyed writing it and, like me, fell in love just a little bit. I love to engage with readers, so feel free to contact me on Twitter and Facebook and let me know what you think, and to find out what else I might have written that tickles your fancy. I am already hard at work on the next book, so watch this space!

If you do get a moment, popping a review onto Amazon/iBooks/Kobo would be much appreciated. It not only brightens my day, but also helps other readers who might enjoy my stories to find me and take a chance on my books, and that's just brilliant all round!

🐦 @writerdove

f facebook.com/RachelDoveauthor

If you enjoyed *The Wedding Shop on Wexley Street*, why not try another delightfully uplifting romance from HQ Digital?

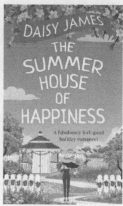